THE JADE EGG

THE CHAIN BREAKER BOOK 2

D.K. HOLMBERG

Copyright © 2020 by D.K. Holmberg

Cover by Damonza.com

All rights reserved.

No part of this book may be reproduced in any form or by any electronic or mechanical means, including information storage and retrieval systems, without written permission from the author, except for the use of brief quotations in a book review.

Want a **free book** and to be notified when D.K. Holmberg's next novel is released, along with other news and freebies? **Sign up for his mailing list by going here**. Your email address will never be shared and you can unsubscribe at any time.

www.dkholmberg.com

CHAPTER ONE

Gavin Lorren darted through the forest near the outskirts of the city of Yoran. It was supposed to be quiet here, and there was a certain sense of calm, but that wasn't the reason that he came. He came chasing someone.

Magic—he was certain of it—in a place that had long ago exiled it.

Trees arched high overhead, the branches sweeping far above him. Gavin hurried through the trees, ignoring the peacefulness, the shadows, and all of the stillness of the forest that was around him, trying to find the person he'd followed.

There *had* been magic. He was sure of it.

Why the forest, though?

As he ran between the trees, he was reminded of the last sorcerer he'd dealt with in the city. That had brought him to the forest as well. It couldn't be a coincidence.

He focused on the core energy within him while he jogged.

Ever since the El'aras attack and the knowledge that his friend Cyran had betrayed him, Gavin had begun to wonder whether the core reserves he'd learned to harness were more than just physical and mental conditioning. He'd been taught to reach into the depths of his own reserves, to draw upon hidden strength, but now he had to question whether it was something else. It *might* be magic.

He reached a small clearing in the forest. Gavin couldn't feel any sense of magic—or really anything at all. He'd lost sight of the blasted person he'd chased, which meant that now he was out in the forest alone, and didn't feel anything. The only thing he could feel was the power deep within him that he'd always called his core reserves. He didn't know if he was grasping for anything magical. It had never seemed magical before.

Training had taught him to harness that strength. Tristan had taught him to reach for that power so he could *be* something more. As he reached for it now, he couldn't help but feel as if there was some aspect to it he still didn't understand. If he had someone magical around to test him, it might be different. It was *part* of the reason he'd come running after the source of magic he'd detected with the dagger, but only partly.

Gavin pushed that thought away. He didn't really want anybody who had magic to test him. It was far better—safer—for him to continue what he'd been doing, to work and practice and train. The only problem was that the city of Yoran had changed.

Letting out a heavy sigh, he shook himself from his reverie. The forest was quiet around him. The smell of earth drifted up from the ground, which was damp from the recent rain. The wind also carried the bright fragrance of the trees' leaves and the scent of the flowers nearby—things that should be relaxing, but were not as much as he would hope. Not when he'd felt that magic only moments before.

And he was convinced it had come into the forest; away from the city.

Gavin pulled out the small silver sphere that Anna, one of the El'aras, had given him. He bounced it in his palm for a moment, tempted to use it—the same way he'd been for the last few days. Really, he'd been tempted by his curiosity in the weeks and months since the El'aras had left.

Could I uncover something more with it? Could I be something more? But how could I even think to ask that?

He shook his head.

"What are you doing?"

The voice intruded on the silence, and Gavin jerked his head around. It took him a moment to remember that Wrenlow was in his ear and not physically here with him. The magical enchantment Anna had given him was so much clearer than the old one they'd used before. The new enchantment fit into his ear, surrounded his lobe, and was attached by a silver chain to a band around his neck.

"Chasing some damn source of magic," Gavin said.

"Did you find it?"

"I lost it. I don't know where they went."

"Are you certain about what you detected?"

Gavin hesitated. "I thought I was."

"Well, Jessica wants you to return to the Dragon," Wrenlow said.

Gavin continued to look around the forest. There was an eerie sort of calm here that pressed on him. He didn't know if it was the strangeness of the forest or if it was him, but he could feel something odd about this place. It had been where the Apostle had attacked. Which was why it seemed too much of a coincidence that he'd ended up out here and drawn by magic.

He turned away from the trees. Staying here was doing nothing for him. In reality, even staying in Yoran was doing nothing for him. Ever since his employer had disappeared, his job offers had too—though technically Gavin had captured his employer and sent him off with a sorcerer.

Gavin had always been able to find some work, but it was a matter of doing the work he wanted to do. He wouldn't accept just any job—only the right kind.

With few jobs to choose from, he might be better off moving to a new city, especially now, knowing that his old mentor might still be alive. There were places beyond Yoran he could travel. Until he had a better sense of why Tristan would conceal his survival, Gavin needed to dig.

At this point, he felt he was biding time before the inevitable need to leave. Maybe it'd be easier for him to get moving now and head out of the city. He might even leave Wrenlow here.

His friend wouldn't be pleased. Wrenlow would want to come with him, especially after everything they'd been through together in their travels around the country. But for Gavin to investigate Tristan's survival, he would have to go someplace Wrenlow wouldn't be able to follow.

He hiked along a narrow path leading him through the trees and then out of the forest, and was greeted by the outskirts of Yoran. The massive, sprawling city rested on the northern aspect of the nation of Henethell. The buildings were all made of a gray stone harvested from several miles down the road, joined with a mortar that cast a thick green color to it. Thatched roofs covered most structures, though the roofs of some buildings toward the center of the city were made of slate—something rare in this part of the world.

The crowd of people moving through the street was not nearly as dense as the throngs farther into the city. Most people avoided this area and the nearby forest because of the rumors and myths that were spread about dangerous creatures within the trees. People who'd heard stories about what existed beyond the forest might be more afraid of it were they to learn those were more than rumors.

Gavin took in a deep breath. The edge of the city had a different energy and smell than the forest. He was a city boy at heart, having been raised and trained in one of the powerful Southern fortress cities. Though he hadn't spent much time within others during his training, he'd certainly spent plenty of time around them in the days since he'd left his mentor. Standing here now, he could feel the vibrancy like an energy that swirled around him.

"Are you coming?" Wrenlow asked.

"I'm on my way."

"Good. Jessica seems to think she has a job for us. She needs you here now, though."

Gavin frowned. "*Jessica* has a job for us? She knows the kind of work I do."

"I know she does, and I don't know if it's exactly the kind of job you'd normally take."

"Why don't you screen it for me."

"She doesn't want me to. Just get here as quickly as you can."

Gavin started to laugh, and the people passing by looked at him strangely. He couldn't blame them. A thin man wearing a strange brown cloak with a conspicuous dagger hanging from his belt was laughing to himself. If he saw someone like that, he would've viewed the person as a little bit mad as well.

He flashed a smile at the nearest person, and they darted away.

Gavin was taller and more muscular than most within the city. It was both a blessing and a curse. It was difficult to blend in, and he worked incredibly hard to master that ability. He hunched over, trying to hide his height. Even now, years after his training had essentially ended, Gavin still struggled to blend into a crowd.

Wrenlow's comment struck him as odd.

As quickly as I can?

That meant something was off.

He jogged forward, but the streets were packed, forcing him to take a detour. At another, he had to loop through an alley before seeing a way through.

What's going on here?

Something seemed determined to keep him from getting back the way he wanted. Gavin hurried through the crowd, elbowing past people, then paused.

Constables marched along the street. They wore gray cloaks that covered heavy mail, and they were out in more force these days. Most people in the city didn't have any idea why that would be, but he knew they were patrolling for the El'aras and any evidence of magic. Magic was outlawed in Yoran, and the constables must have some way of detecting its use, though Gavin didn't know how they managed that. Probably magic as well.

Gavin didn't think the El'aras would remain within the city, but he didn't really know. They could have lingered, and he wouldn't be any wiser to that. After all, he hadn't known that they were in the city in the first place until his last job. Before that, he thought Yoran would be one of the last places to house El'aras. Perhaps that was the point. By hiding here, they were protected by the unlikely nature of existing in a city where they were unwelcome and feared.

The constables stayed in pairs, their boots thumping across the cobbles. He followed them for a moment before veering off to another side street. He proceeded until he reached one of the main thoroughfares in the city. Another pair of constables was here. Strange. Though he'd seen more recently, there were even more out today.

Is there something taking place in the city that I don't know about?

The constables stopped every dozen feet or so before moving on. Even stranger still.

Gavin had been in Yoran long enough to be accustomed to seeing constables out on their patrols. Most of the time, they were harmless. They patrolled the streets not only to keep peace but also to search for signs of enchantments. It was one way that the people of Yoran prevented magic from being used around them.

Of course, the constables weren't necessarily good at their jobs.

"Have you heard any buzz about increased constable patrols?" Gavin whispered through the enchantment.

"What was that?" Wrenlow's voice pierced his ear, and he adjusted the volume slightly. The new El'aras enchantment gave him *far* more control than his older enchantment had.

"The constables. I've seen more in these few streets I've walked today than I have in several days. Something's going on."

"Something is always going on with them," Wrenlow said. "I don't think you can use what you're seeing now to make that determination. Just get back, will you?"

Gavin frowned. He'd been taught to look for patterns, and this was the kind that piqued his curiosity. Wrenlow might need him back, but he needed to see what was going on here.

He slipped along the street, watching for anything that might provide him with an answer, but nothing explained what they were doing. As he trailed behind them, he had to twist out of sight to avoid suspicion. He didn't want to draw too much attention.

Gavin waited as they made their way along the street. They stopped outside of a plain-looking building with no storefront, which suggested it was a home. He remained in the shadows, watching and frowning as the constables lingered outside.

What were they doing?

The crowd moved past them in between him and the constables, obscuring his view.

"Has there been a sudden influx of magic users?" he asked.

"I would have heard about it," Wrenlow said.

"Can you look into it?"

"I'll see what I can find. Maybe Gaspar will have heard something as well."

Gavin stared for a moment and shifted, moving along the street to get a better view of the two soldiers. When they started moving again, there was no evidence of what the constables had done. He clenched his teeth. He had no reason to rush in and evaluate the scene.

Why should I, when doing so would only draw notice to me?

"Check with Imogen too," he said to Wrenlow.

"Why her?"

"I think she knows more than she lets on."

"I think you're reaching."

Gavin smiled. There was one thing that he'd come to learn about himself—he needed to trust his instincts. There was something more to Imogen and the strangeness he detected around Gaspar's apprentice. He might not know what it was, but he was determined to find out. He supposed he could simply ask Gaspar, but that would take some of the fun out of it.

As he turned the corner, the constables stopped again. Like before, he could see no sign of what they were doing, especially with passersby blocking his line of sight. The constables simply stood there, and it didn't seem as if they were talking to each other.

"I don't like this," he said.

"What is it now?"

"The constables."

"Can you forget about them? I told you that Jessica wanted you to come back."

"I know she does, but I'm not entirely sure I need to be taking the job she has to offer."

"Can you at least come back so that she can hear it from you. She won't be thrilled if she has to hear it from me."

Gavin sighed. "Fine, but you're going to keep digging into this. I need to know what's taking place here."

He trailed after the constables as they continued, but then he stopped. A section of the street had been blocked off. All of the people around had been pushed back, leaving nothing but an empty street. That was strange.

As he stood there, a caravan of wagons moved through. All three were ornately decorated, made of gray and black lacquered wood. Dark metal ran along the length of each one, as if to prevent someone from breaking into them. Far more protection than what wagons in the city needed.

They were each guarded by several constables. Others moved in either direction along the street, preventing anyone from getting too close.

What is this?

Gavin stayed with the crowd that followed the procession. The wagons turned at the intersection up ahead.

An explosion rocketed through the street.

He hurried forward, but three figures dressed in dark robes arrived first. They raced toward one of the wagons with obviously enhanced speed—either naturally endowed or enchanted—and moving faster than he could even track. Gavin frowned at them. He had tried using speed enchantments before, but they disrupted his normal training. He found it easier to work without them. These people used enchantments with an incredible skill.

He'd never seen anyone use enchantments so openly in the city before. They must not have feared exposure, or they were completely unconcerned about the constables catching them. Given how quickly they moved, that was a real possibility.

They broke toward the wagon, knocking past the constables. Then they were gone.

The constables darted after them, also at incredible speed. Enchantments too? He hadn't known the constables used them. That made them far more dangerous. He would have to be more careful moving through the city.

The other constables pushed back on the crowd, keeping them at bay. Gavin had no interest in what was going on or in getting any closer to the constables, but he remained transfixed. Whatever he'd just observed was unusual, especially in Yoran.

In all this time, he hadn't seen anyone attempt to attack the constables before. The others were on edge, and a dozen of them moved away from the wagon, driving back the crowd.

An unfamiliar figure jumped from one of the other buildings. They landed on top of the central wagon and snuck inside. None of the constables seemed to have noticed.

Gavin waited, smiling to himself. Whatever this person was after had to be incredibly valuable. And the first attack had been a feint. *This* was the real attack. The person soon crawled back out of the wagon, jumped with incredible power, and landed on one of the nearby buildings. Their movement had to be enchanted as well.

The constables realized too late that they had been

targeted again. This time, they surged toward the wagons, which started rolling rapidly along the street before disappearing around a corner.

Gavin ignored the caravan. He wasn't concerned about that. What he *was* curious about was who had been daring enough to attack the constables and what they were after. He followed the figure, who raced along the rooftop and disappeared.

He was tempted to chase, though doing so along the rooftop would be difficult. Getting involved with the constables wasn't something he wanted anyway. Instead, he turned back toward the direction of the Dragon.

What am I missing?

Maybe it had to do with magic, but maybe it was something else.

As he neared the tavern, he started to have a sense that someone was following him. He slowed, pausing and scanning his surroundings. Dozens of storefronts lined the street. At this time of day, there weren't all that many people out. The crowd thinned, though there were still people who shopped in these stores and traveled through this section of the city. Gavin had spent considerable time in this area and knew his way around. He had wandered through here often enough that he recognized the feel of it, not only the sights and sounds.

This section was not nearly as populated as other parts the city, and the people that lived here weren't wealthy. Most of them worked in the various shops throughout Yoran. The residents didn't dress as formally as those who lived in the manor houses, but they also weren't as poor as those in the outer slums. Clothing here typically covered the wearer from head to toe and was drab, a sharp contrast to the bright colors preferred in some of the cities farther east.

Gavin leaned on one of the nearby buildings, trying to look as casual as he could without attracting any attention. He stared along the street, unable to shake the feeling that someone was watching him. There was no sign of movement, so he moved onward.

He meandered, making a point of not having any real direction to his course. He looked all around him as he did, searching for any sign of suspicious activity, but he didn't see or hear anything. Still, the feeling stayed with him.

He passed the Roasted Dragon, moving beyond it and along the street. He'd gone another dozen paces or so when the feeling started to fade. Gavin paused and veered off, circling around and coming back to the Dragon from a different approach. When he neared it, he hesitated and waited there for a moment, but the sense continued to fade. By the time he wound toward the rear entrance of the Dragon, the feeling was gone.

He slipped along the alley leading up to the front of the building. From there, he searched for any sign of someone watching the tavern. Gavin waited for a while, but the strange sensation never returned.

He ducked in through the kitchen of the Roasted Dragon and hurried inside the mostly empty tavern. Ever since the attack a few months back, Jessica hadn't done much to get it back up to full speed. She preferred to keep it running at a slower pace.

Jessica was a lovely woman with dark hair, a curvy figure, and full lips. He'd found the Dragon by chance, but he'd stayed because of her. Wrenlow sat near her, a notebook propped open on his lap the way that it often was. He was about ten years younger than Gavin, incredibly smart, and more of a planner than action oriented. Ink stained one cheek, and he rubbed at his temple, smearing it every so often.

The other person at the table was Gaspar, an older thief who used the Dragon as his home base. Gavin had come to know him during his time working in the city and found Gaspar to be skilled, if a little crotchety. Deep wrinkles creased his brow, and he ran one thumb along his prominent nose while looking at Gavin.

Jessica looked over to him. "Gavin. I'm glad you're finally here. This woman needs your help."

Gavin flicked his gaze around, settling on Wrenlow, who nodded toward a lovely young woman who sat across from them.

This was the person who wanted to hire me? She didn't look like my typical employers.

"Come on over," Jessica said, grinning at him.

Gavin couldn't shake the feeling of unease. Something wasn't quite right. It was a feeling he'd learned to trust and one that seemed to swallow him now as he approached the table.

CHAPTER TWO

"You're Gavin Lorren?"

Her voice was high as it trembled, and she fidgeted, twisting her fingers together. The woman had to be in her mid-twenties, with chestnut hair that hung in waves down to her shoulders. She had a deep blue traveling cloak around her, but Gavin's eyes were drawn to the full figure not quite hidden underneath. He forced his gaze back up to meet hers and nodded.

Jessica glanced over at him, grinning again. The owner of the Dragon was a beautiful, slightly older woman who'd welcomed Gavin to the tavern—and to her bed. "This is Gavin. I told you I would get him back here."

"I'm so glad that you returned. They weren't sure when you'd come back."

He shot a look over to Gaspar, but the old thief was staring at the hearth, almost making a point of ignoring him. He scrubbed a hand through his short gray hair in an expression of irritation. Gavin frowned. He'd missed something.

Imogen stood at the back of the tavern, quiet as usual while cleaning her sword. Gaspar's partner was a slight woman, whip thin, and had a dark air of mystery to her. Her narrow sword sheathed at her side was just within reach. Maybe she and Gaspar could do this job without Gavin. She traced a pattern along the blade, almost as if she were adding writing to it. Gavin studied her for longer than he should, trying to figure out *why* she worked so studiously at the blade.

"I'm Gavin Lorren," he said. "And you are?"

"I am Erica Delmonica."

"You're looking to hire me?" Gavin wouldn't expect someone like *her* to hire him. His normal employers were more the sort of men like Gaspar.

Erica nodded, looking from face to face nervously. "I heard you were incredibly skilled. I've been asking around to see who to hire, and everyone kept saying your name."

"I'm sure they weren't," Gavin said. The idea that somebody might be sharing his name throughout the city was almost as troubling as Jessica trying to drum up business for him.

She'd remarked on the fact that he hadn't been taking jobs, but he'd turned most down because he wasn't entirely sure what jobs he should be taking. Ever since the attack on the Dragon, ever since he'd been trying to better understand what he could do, Gavin hadn't been sure whether or not he *could* even take another job without drawing the wrong kind of attention here again.

"Only the people who know," she whispered. "It's not as if I was able to get your name from everyone. Most people don't seem to believe you exist. That tells me you're definitely the right person for the job."

"What job is it?"

"I need you to find someone for me," she said.

"Just find them?"

He looked over to Gaspar again, and this time the old thief watched him, something hiding in his gaze.

Maybe uncertainty? Or something else...

"Just find him," she said. "Why? Do you do other things?"

"Gavin is known as something of a skilled fighter," Jessica said.

"Well…" Erica said, then stopped.

Maybe she wanted an assassin, but she didn't have the typical appearance of someone looking to hire one. For that matter, Gavin rarely encountered anyone in the Dragon who had a job for him. Stranger still was Jessica's eagerness to help this woman.

"What is it?" Gavin asked.

"It might be dangerous. The person I need you to find has been taken from me. It's my son."

"Your son." He regarded her for a moment. "How old is he?"

"You're going to take the job?"

"I didn't say that, but I didn't say I wouldn't. I need more information before I decide."

"He's ten. He was taken from me."

Ten?

Gavin had a hard time believing that this woman had a son who was ten years old, but it wasn't impossible. "Where is he?"

"Isn't finding that out what you do?" she asked.

"If you want to hire me, you're going to have to give me a little more information."

"It's complicated."

"How?" Gavin asked.

"Because of where he went. I think… well, I might as well go on and say it. He's been taken by somebody with power. I don't really know where they took him, only that they left a marker behind. I don't think they meant to, but I suspect he kicked it free." She reached into her pocket, pulled a coin out, and slid it across the table to him. It was made of silver, and etched on the surface was a strange symbol, a series of triangles surrounded by a circle. "I found this. I don't really know what it means, but whoever is responsible left it behind."

"Why would somebody want to take your son?"

"I don't know," she said. "That's what I can't get over. There wouldn't be any reason for anyone to take him."

"Why do you think you need somebody like me? The constables could help you."

"I went to the constables, and as soon as they saw that marker, they wanted nothing to do with the job."

Gavin frowned. If she had gone to the constables, their refusal to help her said volumes about this job. It meant there was something there, whether Gavin wanted anything to do with it or not.

"We'll look into it," Gaspar said.

"You will?" She turned toward him, and smiled widely. "I knew it. I knew I'd come to the right place. Everybody had been pointing me toward Gavin Lorren, and they said his team could find my son. I'm so thankful that I was brought here. To you."

Gavin stared at her. His heart hammered, the strange sensation from heading through the street still troubling him. He pushed the feeling away but knew he needed to be careful, to trust his instinct. Right now, his instinct was telling him to pay attention to whatever he'd experienced before—and not so much to this woman.

"What can you tell us about him?" Jessica asked.

"He's going to be scared. He won't know what's going on, and he'll be afraid. Not that I could blame him. I'd be afraid too. I can't imagine what he's going through right now. I can't imagine that he…" Gavin trailed off as Erica leaned down, rubbing her eyes while tears streamed down her face.

Gaspar slid over and patted her on the shoulder. He whispered something in her ear that Gavin couldn't hear.

"Why did you bring me in on this?" Gavin whispered to Jessica.

"What would you have me do? She came in, talking about a son, and she said she needed you. Somehow, she'd heard your name somewhere. I thought you'd be willing to help."

"Why would I be willing to help? This isn't the kind of thing I do."

"You've not been *doing* anything. Other than sitting around here and sniping at Gaspar. I figured you needed to do something else."

Gavin sniffed. He hadn't been sniping at anyone, least of all the old thief. "Now you're trying to find jobs for me?"

"You aren't finding the jobs, so I thought perhaps—"

Gavin let out a frustrated sigh. It did no good. Jessica ignored him, turning her attention back to the woman.

"What are you willing to pay?" he asked.

Erica's eyes widened. "Pay?"

"If you want me to take the job. What will you pay?"

She looked from Gavin to Gaspar and then back to Jessica, a look of confusion on her face. "I didn't realize I was going to have to pay. I thought…" She forced a smile, then frowned as she rubbed a knuckle in her eye. "I suppose… well, I suppose I could pay. What is it that you normally charge for something like this?"

"I haven't taken a whole lot of jobs like this. Most of the jobs I take are a bit different."

"Different how?"

Jessica and Gaspar both shook their heads slightly. Gavin breathed out.

Am I really going to start taking jobs searching for missing children?

He looked from Gaspar to Jessica as he leaned forward. They both watched, though Gaspar seemed more concerned than he let on. "We can work out payment later."

"Oh, good," she said, breathing out heavily. "I just want to get him back."

"What else can you tell us about him that might be helpful?" Gavin asked.

"Or anything you can remember about the men who took him," Gaspar added.

"I didn't see them. It was dark. Late. They broke into our home and took him. I thought it was the constables at first, but they wouldn't do anything like that, would they?"

Gavin's recent experience with the constables suggested that maybe there was something to her hunch. Perhaps he should've paid more attention to what they were doing.

He frowned. "I don't think the constables would, but anything is possible."

Gaspar shot him an annoyed look. "I think what Gavin means to say is that we don't know the constables well enough to make that determination."

"That's what I figured," she said. "It's difficult to believe they would've done anything like that, but I don't even know. I thought their job was to protect us."

"It is," Gaspar said.

Gavin leaned back. He knew what Jessica wanted and understood why. She wanted him to have something to do, a sense of purpose. He thought he wanted the same thing, but would he really be able to find that sense of purpose while struggling with what he'd learned about himself—and about Tristan?

He didn't know.

"Gaspar will get the rest of the details." Gavin got up, pushed away from the table, and headed to the back of the room.

Gaspar shook his head slightly, annoyance flashing in his eyes. Jessica frowned but he ignored it.

Wrenlow was there, watching. "What is it?"

"I don't like this," Gavin said.

"I gathered that, but why?"

"I don't really know. It's just an instinct."

"Does that instinct have anything to do with the fact that Jessica found a job for you?"

"It's the *type* of job she found for me." And he thought it was it was more than that, though maybe it was about his hesitation in staying in Yoran.

"Finding this child is beneath you?"

Gavin arched a brow at him. "When have I ever thought anything was beneath me?"

"Well, that's true enough," Wrenlow said, chuckling.

"Think about one of the first jobs you and I ever did. When we took the job to protect Liesl Daemon from attack."

"We didn't know that was going to be as minor as it was."

Gavin snorted. "Seeing as how she was drunk when she came to us, we probably should have."

"Her husband was also drunk when you knocked him out."

"That's probably what saved his life," Gavin said.

"I doubt he would've attacked you had he not been drunk. Or me." A look of irritation flashed in Wrenlow's eyes that Gavin couldn't quite decipher.

"Maybe."

"They can't all be like the job in Kevlin."

"Oh, you mean the one that I failed?"

"You removed him from power. That's not a failure." Wrenlow grinned at him. "Sometimes, I think you have a different opinion about what you need to do than most people."

"That's not what I have. My issue is that my training has been of a particular kind. I know that training should be used for—"

"Helping people," Wrenlow said. "That's what you've always told me. And how you helped me."

Gavin shook his head. "I can only imagine what Tristan might think if he learned about my priorities."

"Does it matter?"

Gavin frowned. "I suppose it doesn't."

"It just strikes me as strange, that's all."

"That I'm objecting here?"

"That when it comes to something like this, something so objectively good, you're pushing back."

Gavin looked over to where Gaspar, Jessica, and Erica were talking quietly.

Could that be my issue?

Maybe his training had changed so much for him that he was unable to take a job that felt good. If so, that was a twisted fate.

"Maybe that's all it is," he whispered.

"I'm sure it is," Wrenlow said, nodding as if that had decided everything. "Anyway, now that you've got that taken care of, why don't you tell me why you went out to the forest again."

"For some quiet."

Wrenlow started to laugh. "I've never known you to go anywhere for quiet."

"Fine. I went out there to see if there was anything more I can uncover about the sorcerer."

"Why?"

"Because I've never faced anyone like him before."

He had encountered plenty of sorcerers, though none quite like this one. There was something different. Dangerous. He didn't really know what it was, only that he had never even heard of the man. Either the Sorcerers' Society had hidden his presence, or they didn't know of him. That might be even more dangerous.

"There are a lot of sorcerers you've never faced before," Wrenlow said.

"There are, but this one came looking for me. And he didn't have any trouble finding me either."

"That bothers you."

"It should bother you too."

"I don't know that it should. I'm not nearly as troubled by things as you are."

He leaned back and closed his eyes. Perhaps it really was nothing more than the nature of the job, but maybe it was that he had been beaten, trained, and taught that the kinds of jobs that he needed to take had to be a specific kind.

These days, most of his jobs had been smaller scale than what he had been trained for. As long as they paid, it didn't matter. Lingering in the city had bothered him for a while, but he hadn't revealed it to Wrenlow. Eventually, it would be time for them to think about moving on.

They had gotten comfortable within the city, but comfort meant complacency. Gavin knew far better than to become complacent. Those who did later ended up dead.

"I need to look for Tristan," Gavin whispered.

"What if he tries to find you?"

Gavin shook his head. "He wouldn't."

He remembered returning to the training compound, finding the trail of blood, the body trapped in the ravine. He had seen the clothing, the boots, even the ring, all pointing to Tristan.

Now, years later, Gavin knew that Tristan had faked his death.

Why would he do so? Had he known what Cyran intended?

"Why not?" Wrenlow asked. "Would he simply allow you to go away?"

"I think he'd view finding him as another test."

"Why would he test you in such a way?"

Gavin shrugged. "I don't know."

He looked around the tavern and watched as Jessica and Gaspar talked with Erica. He glanced at Imogen, who remained quiet as she watched the conversation from the far side of the room. Her fingers tapped in something like a pattern while she observed everything, but stopped when she caught sight of Gavin looking in her direction.

Eventually, he'd need to look for Tristan. But right now was the first time he didn't necessarily *want* to go venturing anywhere else. He was content. Maybe that was what troubled him the most. Any time he had a sense of contentment in his life, something always happened to disrupt it or strip it away from him.

Taking a deep breath, Gavin closed his eyes. "I'm going to rest a little while."

"Now?"

"Gaspar is going to get the details I need for this job, and I figure that between the two of you, you can look into anything she tells you. She has a marker that she says was left behind when her son was abducted. Why don't you look into that, see if there's anything you can find out about it?"

"What did it look like?"

"A series of triangles with a circle around it."

"What?" Wrenlow sat up and cocked his head, looking at Gavin for a long time before turning to watch Gaspar and Erica. "Are you sure about that?"

"Pretty sure. Why?"

"I need to know what exactly it looked like."

Gavin leaned over, and he traced the shape on the

table. He watched Wrenlow as he did, and the other man's eyes widened.

"What is it?" Gavin asked.

"I recognize that symbol. That's a marker for the Captain."

CHAPTER THREE

Gavin opened his eyes but couldn't see through the darkness all around him. A haze clouded his mind. Tristan knew how much he hated the darkness and how much he struggled with it.

Why would he do this to me now?

Tristan must have placed something over his eyes. Gavin tried to shift and throw the blindfold off of his face, but there wasn't any way for him to remove it.

A binding pinned his arms to his sides. Was it leather, or was it rope again this time? Each time Tristan had bound him, he'd wanted Gavin to focus on that core strength, that energy that filled him, to break free. Gavin understood that each one was a test, Tristan's way of challenging him, but he'd succeeded every time so far.

There would come a time when he wouldn't, but he hoped it would be quite some time before that happened. He didn't want to disappoint Tristan.

He tried again to look around, to see anything at all, but he couldn't. He moved his hands and feet, which were free, but the bindings around his torso, arms, and legs trapped him in such a way that he could do little else.

"Tristan?" Too much panic crept into his voice. That was a mistake. When it came to his training, revealing fear was considered a weakness. Gavin knew better than to show any vulnerability.

He gathered himself, holding onto his strength balled up inside, and tried to focus on the bindings around him. The last one had been made of leather, which meant that this one would be something stronger. So far, Gavin had been able to snap his way free of all the bindings Tristan used, but eventually...

No. He couldn't think about what would happen when he failed.

Tristan did not suffer failure well.

He tensed and strained, and something cut into his arms and legs. It took Gavin a moment to decide what it was.

Rope.

Tristan had bound him in rope.

The thickness of the rope suggested that it would be almost impossible for him to break free. He struggled against it but couldn't escape.

He thought about what Tristan had told him before, the way he'd wanted Gavin to find someplace deep inside of himself, to tap into a different sort of strength. But even as he focused on that, Gavin wasn't entirely sure there was anything for him to draw upon.

He strained again and again, and he failed again and again. His body grew sore and numb as he lost track of how long he was there, focusing on the energy within him and the power he strained against. Each time, he tried to push outward, holding pressure against the ropes.

There was movement near him, and he stopped struggling. Gavin turned his head in its direction and listened to the sounds coming toward him. It was soft; the steady footsteps of somebody approaching him.

Something struck him on the side of the face.

Gavin's head rolled with the force of the blow. It hurt, but he'd learned how to push that pain down, to suppress it so he didn't experience anything. The next blow came, sharper, from a different angle.

The wind guided him, the soft breeze of the blow telling him with just enough time how to anticipate it, and Gavin twisted his head so he could absorb most of it. At the same time, the blindfold came off. He could see.

Tristan stood in front of him. He was a muscular man, about the same height as Gavin, and brown of complexion and hair. There was a blazing intensity from him. Whenever they trained, he was always dressed in leathers that protected him. Gavin rarely managed to strike with enough force to injure him, though he had never really wanted to hurt Tristan. It was more the challenge of it and a desire to break through his protections.

"Better," Tristan said.

"I'm not going to be able to break these ropes," Gavin said.

"Are you so sure?"

"I can't tear through these."

"You can't because you choose not to."

"It's not a matter of choice. It's a matter of knowing the ropes are too thick to work through," he said, struggling against them while talking to Tristan.

"Then you will stay here," Tristan said.

"For how long?"

Gavin was accustomed to being forced to stay in one place for extended periods of time. He wasn't at all surprised that Tristan would hold him here.

"Until you break free of the bindings."

"And if I can't?"

"Then you can't."

Tristan slapped him, catching him on the left cheek with a sharp blow that overwhelmed his ability to ignore the pain. That pain sent Gavin wanting to pull away, tears streaming down his face. Because he'd allowed himself to cry, Tristan would be irritated enough to strike him again. He waited for the next blow, which would be just as sharp and just as painful, but it never came. He turned, bracing himself for the attack, but there was none.

Tristan backed away. "You have the strength within you, Gavin Lorren. You have always had that strength within you. You must find it."

"How?"

"If I were able to tell you, then you wouldn't be able to find it."

"That doesn't make sense."

"It makes perfect sense, especially if you understood the power you possess."

"I don't possess any power."

"Not with that attitude, you don't."

Gavin continued to strain against the ropes, but he could do nothing to escape from them. He tried pulling on them, struggling with the bindings. At least now that his blindfold had been removed, he could see what was holding him. The room was small, just enough to contain the chair he sat in, along with a basin near the wall. Tristan blocked his view of the door, though he could make out the faint outline of it. The thin light trailed into the room, barely enough for him to see. A faint glow surrounded Tristan. That was probably Gavin's imagination, or the effort he put into trying to break through the ropes.

The ropes were wrapped tightly all around him. His hands and feet were as free as he'd suspected, but he couldn't even move his fingers up to try to grasp for a section of the rope. He tried to shimmy his legs to loosen his bindings, but that didn't work either.

Gavin struggled again, and then he threw himself back.

Maybe I could break through the chair.

He strained, jerking against the straps and trying to pry his arms free, but every attempt failed. The bindings cut into his skin. Gavin pushed that pain away, ignoring the surge of agony that ripped through him.

His mentor had taught him how to do everything he knew. And now he wanted Gavin to learn how to break free of these ropes. Only, the chair was too stout for him to shatter. How was he supposed to break through ropes if he couldn't even break through the chair they were wrapped around?

He sat there and waited. Eventually, Tristan would have to return. He would come back and untie Gavin, or perhaps he would pose another challenge.

He never did.

Time passed. Gavin's throat began to dry. His bladder burst, and he soiled himself. Still Tristan didn't return.

Gavin waited. This had to be some sort of test. Eventually Tristan would return. But as time went on, he slowly realized that his mentor wasn't going to come. If he was going to get out, he'd to have to break free, much the way Tristan told him he'd have to.

Gavin had no idea what was required, but he didn't think he had the necessary strength. The bindings around him were too tight, and he didn't have any way to loosen them. If Tristan somehow believed he'd be able to rip through them with strength, then he was mistaken.

Frustration filled him. Gavin focused on his training, looking for some solution he had yet to see. Oftentimes, Tristan had already shown him the answer, and Gavin only had to find it. Too often, though, it was too difficult.

He focused on the energy within him, what Tristan

had called a core reserve of energy. A place of power. It was deep within him, and if he focused enough, if he dove within that power, Gavin might be able to call upon it and use that to get free. He steadied himself, breathing in and out, holding onto that sense of energy.

There.

Gavin pressed on the bindings wrapped around him, holding onto them as tightly as he could. The ropes strained, and he could feel the pressure around him, everything working into his flesh.

Still he pushed.

There was that core reserve of power.

But with as long as he had gone without food and water—time he'd lost track of—Gavin doubted whether he would even have enough strength or reserve to break free.

Even if I did, would Tristan know that I was free?

Maybe Tristan didn't care.

Gavin no longer knew whether any of this mattered to the man. It was possible that Tristan had only wanted him tested; to starve, to suffer. It wouldn't be the first time Tristan had tormented him in such a way, though it would be the first time he'd withheld food and water. Of course, Gavin was getting older. As he aged, the challenges posed to him became more difficult.

He reached for that power deep within him. He could feel that core energy simmering beneath the surface. Gavin drew upon it, and the power exploded outward.

The ropes resisted him, but then they snapped apart.

Gavin sagged back in the chair. He'd broken free of only the ropes around his arms, and he picked at the ones around his legs—a task that proved almost more difficult than he was capable of doing in this state.

He stood, wobbling slightly.

How long have I gone without food or water?

He staggered across the room. A basin of water rested there, and he picked it up, sipping at it. He knew better than to lap too hungrily at the water, especially after having gone as long as he must have without it. Gavin set the water down and breathed out, then leaned one hand on the door. He pulled it open and found Tristan sitting on the other side.

"Good," he said.

"That's all?"

"What more do you think I should say to you?"

"You left me there." He could barely get the words out. "Tormented me. You starved me."

"Good."

"You need to stop saying that."

"Because you feared death?"

Gavin took a step back, staring at Tristan.

Was that why?

He didn't think so. In his training with Tristan, he'd learned that death was a part of life. Fighting meant losing. Eventually, he would die. He had long ago come to terms with that.

The one key lesson Tristan had always tried to instill upon him was that when he fought, and when he eventually died, he should do so for the right reason. He should do so knowing that he'd fought the way he wanted to. If he trained well and was prepared, then any fight he entered would be one he could win.

Gavin leaned on the wall. "What now?"

"Now you prepare for—"

Tristan darted forward, driving his fist toward Gavin.

He was tired, but he knew this was another aspect of the testing. He dropped and spun his leg, trying to hook Tristan's, but he wasn't nearly as quick as he normally was. He tried to slam his leg into Tristan and trip him, but Tristan overpowered him.

Gavin stumbled forward, and he smashed his fist into Tristan's shoulder. Tristan grabbed his arm, twisting it behind his back, and then threw him forward.

Gavin stumbled again and then staggered away.

Tristan shook his head. "Better, but you still have work to do."

He jumped, spinning in the air, and Gavin recognized the technique. It was one they'd been working on recently. Gavin threw the appropriate block and then twisted, dropping down and punching the area where Tristan would land. He missed, everything half a step too slow.

Tristan flipped his leg around, catching Gavin in the back of the head with his heel. Gavin sprawled forward and didn't bother getting up. He didn't think he'd be able to.

Tristan stood over him, glaring down. "Get moving."

"No."

"If you don't get moving, you're going to take a knife to the back."

"What makes you think I'm not going to take that anyway?"

"Because you're going to get moving."

Gavin pulled himself up, moving slowly. Even as he did, he didn't know if it mattered. He could barely get himself going. Everything within him ached, a pained sense that left him with agony.

He got to his knees. When Tristan spun and twisted with a kick, Gavin reacted by throwing out his arm. He blocked, but barely so. Tristan smiled at him, a grim expression to it.

Gavin was prepared for the next strike. He deflected it and then went sprawling forward again. He rolled off to the side. It was a struggle to maintain movement. He attempted to get back up, but even as he did, he could feel Tristan barreling toward him again.

Gavin twisted, using everything in his ability to get back to his feet. There was another thing he could try. He somersaulted forward and crashed into Tristan's legs.

Tristan laughed as he stepped off to the side, and the sound of that laughter set him on edge. Gavin launched, driving forward with both fists, trying to catch Tristan in the belly. Still, the man laughed.

Gavin rolled again, kicking outward. Most of the time, he had to get lucky to catch Tristan off guard. He didn't know if he'd be lucky this time, but he was determined to throw himself at Tristan, even though his mentor didn't even seem to be fighting back.

He kicked and missed, and Tristan laughed again. He lunged toward Tristan, twisting and rolling, but his punch met nothing but air. He spun. Slowly his strength was returning. More than that, he could feel his core strength replenishing.

Maybe that was a mistake. Tristan had warned him that drawing upon core strength too often—and too powerfully—might drain his energy in such a way he wouldn't be able to recover. Gavin didn't know if it was true or not, but he was determined to defeat Tristan this time, which would involve using as much power as he could. He didn't care, and even if he did, that wouldn't have stopped him.

From a distance, he could see Tristan trying to reach the hallway. He was still laughing. At least, he was in Gavin's mind. Wrapped up as he was in his core strength, Gavin felt that energy roll through him as he held onto that power. He sprinted to catch up and then launched at Tristan, grabbing his shirt and throwing him. Tristan slammed into the wall and went ricocheting back.

Tristan got to his feet and grinned at him. It seemed as if Gavin could never hurt him, as if anything he did was little more than an irritant. Just once, Gavin wanted to do something that would actually hurt the other man.

"Better," Tristan said. "You learned to draw upon your strength."

"You told me I should be careful with it."

"You should be careful with it unless you are suffering. There are times when drawing upon your core strength is critical. Not only for your survival but for the survival of others who might be depending upon you."

"What happens if I overuse it?"

"Don't," Tristan said.

"I don't know if I have enough control over it to trust not to do that."

"I think the opposite is true. I think your experience with the others, even as weak as they are, is what makes you stronger."

Gavin took a step toward Tristan and nearly staggered. The strength within him started to fade again. As he tried to reach for Tristan, he fell, stumbling forward.

Tristan was at his side, and rather than trying to harm Gavin, he instead lifted his student. "Perhaps I was a bit too harsh," he whispered.

"What was too harsh?"

"The beating after you broke free."

"I thought you said that hardened me."

"It does, but you can't get so hardened that you don't have a core of compassion within you."

"Compassion?"

Tristan looked down at him, and Gavin had a hard time keeping his focus. More than that, he had a hard time thinking of his mentor as someone who had any compassion in him. Most of the time with Tristan, there was nothing but the edge. The violence. The desire to train. Gavin knew he would eventually need to be able to do what Tristan asked of him, to have the power he wanted for him. Gavin knew he would eventually need to be able to handle himself the way Tristan expected. He had no idea what Tristan was training him for, only that whatever it was had to be important.

"Just because I can be harsh doesn't mean I lack compassion," Tristan said. "And just because you've suffered doesn't mean that you should lose your ability to hold onto that compassion."

Gavin tried to stay awake, but he was tired—so tired. As he struggled, he started to drift, his mind starting to slip, and he drifted in and out, flashes of images coming to him before he passed out completely. When he came around, he was in his dormitory again. The dormitory where he trained and learned how to fight was a brutal place. In the considerable time he'd spent there, he'd come to think of the place as home, despite how sparse it was.

Tristan didn't believe in decorations within the training compound and certainly no decorations within the dormitory. The only thing Gavin had was the people. There were those he trained with and those he'd come to know quite well, including Cyran.

A wall of windows was high overhead, letting in a stream of light to the main part of the dormitory, the bright sunlight hot regardless of the time of day. Gavin had learned to hate the sunlight and the heat, much like all who came here.

The other students were there, but so too were the

ropes he'd broken free of. He rolled over and stared at the ropes.

Why would Tristan have brought them to me? Was it a reminder of his strength? Was it a reminder of my suffering?

Gavin never knew what the man intended.

He sat up and found the other students watching him. They looked at the ropes, and they seemed to understand. This was just another of the many times when Tristan set him apart from the rest. Gavin didn't understand what purpose Tristan had in driving a wedge between him and the other students, but every time he thought he was getting closer with them, Tristan would do something like this. Any sort of connection Gavin had with the other students would disappear.

It was difficult to make friends, mostly because many of the other students he worked with were also his competition. He had to fight and spar with them; had to defeat them. He spent more time with some of the others who were learning different techniques, working with medicines and herbs and healing balms. Perhaps that might be something he could learn, too.

He stood and took a step, but he stumbled and fell on the ground again. One of the other students turned away from him, and Gavin tried to reach for them but couldn't. He was tired and weak.

Why weren't they helping me?

Because no one helped him.

He was Gavin Lorren. The Chain Breaker.

They would leave him to suffer.

He lay on the ground for a long time until one of the other students helped him by propping him up and handing him something to drink. Gavin sipped the liquid, feeling the way it burned as it went down his throat. Gradually, his strength returned, giving him a little bit more power. When he finally climbed back into the bed, he didn't have to wait long before sleep claimed him.

CHAPTER FOUR

The inside of the Dragon was quiet. Several lanterns lit up the inside of the tavern, giving off a flickering, warm light. A crackling flame burned in the hearth, though unnecessary given the warmth of the day. The air still smelled of baking bread and roasting meats, the foods Jessica had made earlier in the day when she had more patrons. All of it felt like the Dragon.

"How sure are you that this is from the Captain?" Gavin asked, sitting at the table with Gaspar and Wrenlow.

Wrenlow held the marker in hand. He rubbed his thumb along the surface before setting it on the table and spinning it. "I'm sure. I've seen it a few times. With as much as he's involved in within the city…"

"How? You haven't left the Dragon all that often," Gaspar said.

"I might not have nearly as much as either of you, but

I've gone out. And I've seen this. I know I've seen it. And I do have contacts. That tells me enough about the Captain to know we need to be careful." Wrenlow looked up at Gavin. "He's dangerous, Gavin. Involved in all sorts of shady deals throughout the city. And he's connected. The constables won't even touch him."

"What does it mean that it's the Captain's mark?" Gavin asked, looking over at Gaspar. "You've lived in the city a long time. What do you think about it?"

"Surprises me the kid recognizes it. I sure as hell didn't," he said, nodding toward Wrenlow. "Damn man has been the bane of the city ever since the sorcerer's lost power."

"I have seen it," Wrenlow said, probably harder than he needed. "He gives them out to those who serve him."

Gavin grabbed the marker and set it on its edge, twisting it so that it spun in place in front of him. The marker had a distinct symbol on one side; a series of circles mixed with an image of a flame. Its design was too unique to be replicated unless it was by someone who truly knew the marker.

"I don't really want to go into the Captain's fortress," Gavin said.

"We couldn't," Gaspar said.

"Why do you say that?"

"It's dangerous."

"It's only dangerous if we go in ignorant," Wrenlow said.

"We?" Gaspar asked.

"Fine, you. Is that what you want me to say, that I'm not going to go? That I'm not nearly as critical a part of the team as you or Gavin or Imogen?" Gavin reached toward his arm, and Wrenlow shook his head. "Don't. If you're going to do anything, tell him off."

Gavin looked at Gaspar. "He works just as hard as we do. His role on the team is different."

"Because you don't let him have a more crucial role on the team."

"What would you have him do?" Gavin asked. "Sneak in alongside us? He's not a fighter. He's not a thief. He's the planner."

There were other titles he could give Wrenlow, and all of them would be equally true. He thought that "planner" would seem the most appropriate to Gaspar.

"You don't need him to plan. You just need him to be another voice in your ear."

"Maybe I do." Gavin turned and made a point of looking over at Wrenlow. "What do you propose? If we do have to go into the Captain's home, how would you suggest we go about it?"

"It's not possible," Wrenlow said.

"Good," Gaspar said. "I was afraid that you were going to offer some suggestion about how you thought we might be able to break into the one place in the city that's been off-limits to those of us who have lived here for the last few decades."

"I'm just saying that nobody knows what's in there.

Only a few people within the city have ever spent much time there," Wrenlow said.

A realization dawned on Gavin. "That doesn't mean nobody has. We can question them. Maybe we can find some of the information we need."

"Gavin," Wrenlow said, "no one is going to betray the Captain. Everybody is afraid of him. Hell, *I'm* afraid of him, and I don't even know him."

"You know him well enough."

"I know him by reputation. That's not the same as knowing him. Besides, I don't want to go in and risk getting the kid hurt."

"We're not going to be risking him. If the Captain has this kid, then all we have to do is be prepared. Watch. Be ready." Gavin wasn't sure it'd be that simple, but he kept that to himself. "Why don't you see what you can figure out. Piece together what's known about the layout of his home. Maybe we can find something that'll help us."

"That's not going to work," Gaspar said.

Gavin swiped the marker off the table. "You never know."

"What are you going to do?" Wrenlow asked.

"I'm going to go take a look at Erica's home. I've got to figure out why her son was kidnapped, maybe get a better sense of who she is."

"I can tell you who she is," Gaspar said. Gavin arched a brow and Gaspar grunted. "Not like that, boy. She was an easy mark. And her son would have been a target."

Gavin doubted it would be so simple. It never was. "I

still need to find it. I presume she gave you some idea of where it is."

"Some. Not enough for me to help you know where to find it."

"Oh, I'm sure that's not quite right." Gavin smiled at Gaspar. "If anyone knows how to find anything in the city, it's you, isn't it?"

"You aren't going to be able to use that on me."

"Use what?"

"Whatever you think that you're trying to do. I don't know if you think it's cute or what."

Gavin batted his eyelashes. "You don't think it's cute?" He was met with a glare, and he started to laugh. "Come on. I'm just going to take a look. If I go without you, you'll miss out on all the excitement."

"If I go with you, then I have to deal with whatever excitement you bring."

Gavin smiled and headed toward the door. He checked to make sure that he had his El'aras dagger and was comforted by its presence. He felt better after sleeping, despite not liking the dreams he was having.

Ever since coming to Yoran, he'd felt increasingly tied back to Tristan and his training. Partly that was because of the reason that he'd come to Yoran in the first place. Cyran had suggested that there might be jobs for him to take. The other part, he suspected, was because of his newfound knowledge that Tristan lived. Gavin now thought about his old mentor even more than he had before.

He sighed and pulled the door open. Out on the street, he blended into the crowd quickly. He rounded a corner, unsurprised when Gaspar joined him.

"I didn't think you were going to come with me."

"You don't even know where you're going," Gaspar said.

"No. I figured I would just wander my way around the city until I figured out where I needed to go." Gaspar frowned at him, and Gavin started to laugh. "I'm not serious."

"When it comes to you and some of the foolish things you do, I wouldn't be surprised."

They headed through the streets, and Gavin paused at one corner, raising his hand slightly. Gaspar didn't need for him to do it. He'd paused as well.

Three constables navigated in their direction.

"Something's going on with them," Gavin said. "I've been watching. It seems like more and more constables are moving in some sections of the city. I don't really know what's taking place, only that I don't care for it."

"It's probably nothing," Gaspar said.

"Probably?" Gavin glanced over to him, arching a brow. "You've lived in the city a long time. You know what's normal and what's not."

"I know what's normal, and…"

"That's not normal."

"No," Gaspar said.

The constables stopped while making their way along the street, much like when Gavin had been following them before. They paused, talking quietly, and it wasn't clear what they were doing.

Gavin shook his head. "I followed them the last time I saw them, but I didn't see anything."

"It's not a good idea for you to follow the constables."

"They aren't going to learn what we did with the El'aras."

Gaspar shot him a hard look. "You think I'm concerned about that? No, it's the enchantments we have." He tapped his ear. "They have ways of detecting them."

"How?"

"They have ways."

That confirmed his earlier suspicion that the constables had enchantments of their own. That would be the only way to detect others. "I'd like to get ahold of their technique."

"Why? Isn't your dagger enough?"

"It's a bit obvious. I'd like something that wasn't quite so deadly looking when I carried it."

"Don't worry about it. When you carry it, it doesn't look deadly."

Gaspar started off, and Gavin laughed to himself before following him. When he caught up, the thief was trailing after the constables—the very thing he'd told Gavin not to do. Gavin said as much.

Gaspar glanced over at him. "I don't have any reason not to follow them."

"You have the same thing I do," Gavin said, tapping his ear.

"Not on me."

Gavin frowned. "There's a reason she gave it to us."

"There's a reason she gave it to *you*. I didn't say I wanted it."

"You're ridiculous."

"And you've come in and disrupted everything I've been working for," Gaspar said. "Threw off my other jobs, too."

"I haven't disrupted anything. You've chosen to work with me."

Gaspar had taken all sorts of different jobs in the time that Gavin had spent in the Dragon, though rarely had the man taken one recently. It was almost as if he was avoiding them, possibly because of the El'aras attack on the tavern. There might also simply be a personal reason that was preventing him from taking on more jobs. Either way, it mattered very little to Gavin.

"I didn't have much choice in the matter."

"You had plenty of choice in the matter," Gavin said. "The only reason you started to do anything is because you wanted to offer Jessica your protection."

"Is that so different from you?"

"You know it's not. It's just that I don't think you can make the claim that you're doing anything I'm not doing."

Gaspar frowned. "Come on. If you want to check out this place and see where she and this boy live, then we need to get moving."

"Good. I was afraid you were going to run off and try to talk with the constables."

"Don't tempt me."

Gavin chuckled as they headed through the streets. Gaspar ignored him and followed some route he knew, though it brought them past large crowds of people. Every few streets, they encountered more constables. Each time they did, Gaspar paused, watching with a look in his eyes that suggested that whatever he was seeing troubled him.

For that matter, it troubled Gavin too. If what Gaspar suggested was right, then the constables were looking for sources of magic—something that involved danger to him and those who had enchantments like him.

"Come on," Gaspar said when Gavin stopped again. "They aren't here for you. Hell, I doubt they're even here for your old friend. More likely than not, they're just looking for signs of magic users. You think this is the first time the constables have come out in the city like this?"

"It is since I've been here."

"Well, it isn't anything new. And seeing as how I've been here longer than you, I guess I get to be the one to tell you when something is strange or not."

"If you say so, old-timer," Gavin said, grinning at him slightly.

Gaspar shot him a sharp glare before turning away.

They continued along the street. Gaspar guided them into an older section of the city. The buildings were more dilapidated, and not as much care had been put into maintaining them. The people here wore clothing that was tattered. Children ran wild in the street, rather than working jobs or apprenticing in some way.

Gavin was curious about where Gaspar was leading him, and as they neared the end of one street where it intersected with still another, he started to slow.

Gaspar paused at the crossroads, and he turned casually, motioning the other way. "Did you see it?"

Gavin scanned along the street, but he didn't see anything conspicuous. Whatever it was had to be somewhat obvious, at least given Gaspar's reaction. He continued to look, searching for whatever house it was that Gaspar was referring to, but he didn't see anything there.

"I'm not sure what you've seen," Gavin said.

Gaspar motioned, pointing at each of the five houses along the street. He stopped and nudged Gavin. "Look at that one there. What do you see?"

Gavin had been taught to observe with Tristan. With his training, he should be able to catch what Gaspar was trying to point out, but he didn't see what had triggered the thief. The house was no different than the others. It was a bit run-down, the paint on the door and the window frames faded. Some of the homes had plants in pots sitting outside, but not the fifth one. Unlike the others, a board was angled along one of the windows.

"It's boarded up," he said.

"Very good. Look at you, picking up on something I teach the youngest kids I work with."

"How many kids have you worked with?"

Gaspar snorted. "Everyone I worked with has been better than you."

"Well, I'm not a thief."

"You wouldn't be a good one. Now come on. Let's go take a look at this."

Gaspar led them down an alley, and he pointed at each of the homes before pausing at what Gavin thought was the fifth one. He motioned for Gavin to back up. "These two are connected," Gaspar said, gesturing toward two of the homes.

"How can you tell?"

"Look at them. Roofline stays the same. All the others here have some variation to them."

Gaspar tested the door and grabbed his lockpick set. He worked quickly, and then he stepped inside. The darkness swallowed him. Gavin hesitated before following.

"You see anything?" Gaspar whispered.

"I can't see much in the dark," Gavin said.

"You keep saying things that don't need to be said."

He could make out Gaspar, but he was only a few steps away. Otherwise, Gavin couldn't see much inside of the room. It was almost completely black. As he looked around, he searched for a lantern or anything he might use to illuminate the room.

He drew his El'aras dagger and was surprised that it was glowing softly.

"Where do you think the magic is coming from?" Gavin asked.

"With you here? Could be a lot of different places." Gaspar watched him. "Including you."

Gavin shook his head. "I know the El'aras were trying

to convince me that I have some sort of magic, but even if I do"—and Gavin had a hard time believing that he did—"I've never seen the El'aras dagger light up when it's just me."

There had to be magic somewhere. Which meant they had to be careful. He held the El'aras dagger away from him, using its light to see. It was enough for him to be able to make out some faint outlines in the room, but not much more than that. He continued to look around him, but he didn't see anything all that helpful.

Gaspar quickly moved through the house and peeked across counters, opening and closing cupboards quickly before moving on. He had a practiced style, and Gavin could only shake his head. He imagined that Gaspar had broken into countless other homes like this, doing this dozens upon dozens of times before.

"How often do you take jobs like this?" Gavin asked.

"Do we really need to have these conversations?"

"I was just curious."

"Save your curiosity for another time. Curiosity gets men killed while working."

Gavin chuckled. "The man I trained with said that curiosity made you stronger."

"Maybe in your line of work," Gaspar said. "The kind of work I do, curiosity can end with a knife in your back."

"The same thing can happen in my world."

"Right, but in your world, you *deserve* the knife in your back."

"You don't think thieves do too?"

"Not the kind of thieving I do," Gaspar whispered.

"And what thieving do you do exactly that makes it so you don't deserve such a fate?"

Gaspar ignored him, and he continued rummaging around the room. He disappeared through a doorway, and Gavin followed into what he realized was a bedroom. Gaspar had the wardrobe pulled open and finished sorting a stack of clothing, then pulled out a drawer and worked through that.

"There's nothing here," Gaspar said. "Some of Erica's clothing, some for a boy about the size she described, and nothing else. Not really."

"Did you expect anything else?" Gavin asked.

"You never know."

And here Gavin thought that he was the only one who'd been on edge and suspicious of Erica. Gaspar had been as well, which shouldn't have surprised him. You didn't get to be a skilled thief anywhere in the world, especially in a city like Yoran, without having some level of suspicion.

"I guess now we have to hope that Wrenlow can get information about the layout of the Captain's home for us to use," Gavin said.

Gaspar pushed past him, heading back out into the main part of the home. Once again, he traced his hand along the counter, working through it as if he might find something more. He turned and straightened. "I might be able to help with that."

"You might be able to help how?"

"I might know someone," Gaspar said.

"You told Wrenlow it was impossible. Who might you know?"

"It's complicated."

"Why?" Gavin asked.

"Well… because she used to be my wife."

Gaspar moved past him and stepped out onto the street, closing the door behind him. Gavin swept his gaze around the house one more time and noticed the glow still coming off of the dagger.

He walked outside and closed the door, then looked over at Gaspar. "You know you can't just leave it at that."

"I think that I can," Gaspar said. "Besides, I don't owe you an explanation."

"You don't owe me anything, but I sure would like it if you'd share."

"Yeah? Well you'd better get used to disappointment."

Gavin laughed and followed Gaspar along the street. His mind worked through the various types of people that Gaspar might have been married to, and he wondered if Gaspar would even allow him to meet her. Whatever else happened, Gavin was determined to follow the thief, if only so he could see who would have married him.

CHAPTER FIVE

The house Gaspar led him to was nothing like what Gavin would've expected. This section of the city consisted of enormous well-appointed homes, but this one was quite different than even the surrounding ones. There was something incredible about the massive stone structure that sat apart from the others and loomed high over the surrounding landscape.

The home was enormous and enclosed within a low outer wall. It could have been a manor home, but for the lack of a high surrounding wall and the bells trees that usually grew in the gardens within.

"This is where your wife lives?"

Gaspar shot him a glare. "Don't make me regret letting you come with me."

"I'm not going to make you do anything. I just thought—"

"There's your problem. Don't go digging into my past

unless you want me to do the same with yours. I'd wager you got more skeletons than I do."

Gavin laughed. "I'd take that wager. Besides, you aren't going to be able to deter me."

"I think I can try."

Gavin was unaccustomed to seeing Gaspar unsettled like this.

Maybe I should be kinder to the old man.

Gaspar was doing this to help, though Gavin hadn't even wanted to accept the job in the first place. He'd been drawn into this because both Gaspar and Jessica had wanted him to take it.

"What's her name?"

"There you go again, asking questions you don't need to know anything about." Gaspar stared at the wall, looking as if he were debating whether to head inside.

"If we're going to visit her, at least tell me her name."

"I said *I* was going to visit her, not you."

"If she might know something—"

"If she knows something, I'm going to be the one to ask those questions. Not you."

"Fine," Gavin said, raising his hand. "But I think I need to go with you because at your age you're probably deaf in one ear and someone has to catch the other half of it."

Gaspar's frown deepened. He let out a heavy sigh, opened the gate, and made his way toward the door of the home. Gavin followed him. He was going to have to ask Jessica about this later.

Did I even have to wait?

He tapped on the enchantment and waited a second for it to transmit, then said, "Can you ask Jessica about Gaspar's ex-wife?"

There was a pause, and then Wrenlow coughed. "Ex-wife?"

"Right. That's what I said. Gaspar claims she might know something about the Captain, so see if Jessica knows more."

"I can find out, but I don't know if she's going to say anything. You know how she feels about him." There was a pause. "How did Gaspar's ex-wife get brought up at all?"

"Well, we went to Erica's home and didn't find anything other than some clothing. I think Gaspar doubts you'll find out enough information about the layout of the Captain's home."

"That's not very nice."

"I'm just telling you what he said. Anyway, what does Jessica know?"

"Just a minute." There was silence on the other end, and Gavin hurried toward Gaspar. The man stood at the door, hesitating with his hand outstretched.

"Don't you bother him about this," Jessica said. Her voice came from a distance, and he could imagine her yelling at him through Wrenlow's side of the enchantment.

"I'm not doing anything," Gavin said.

"If he doesn't want to talk about it, then you don't talk about it."

"I think he owes us—"

"He doesn't owe you anything."

Gavin imagined Jessica looming over Wrenlow, his book spread open in front of him while trying to protect it from her.

Gavin shook his head. "Why don't you put Wrenlow back on?"

There was a moment of silence. "I don't think she's willing to talk about this," Wrenlow said. "Don't push him too hard. I guess that's the only advice I can give you."

"Thanks. I have that sense." Gavin tapped on the enchantment and joined Gaspar at the door. "Well?"

"Well what?"

"Are you going to knock or not?"

"I'm deciding whether it's worth it."

"Didn't you say we need to help Erica and that boy of hers?"

"Maybe," Gaspar said.

"Well, if you want me to do whatever I can to help him, then you need to do whatever *you* can in order to help him." Gavin resisted the urge to smile. He suspected that Gaspar knew though.

Gaspar's face was a dark thundercloud. It was almost enough to make Gavin laugh again. He reached past. Gaspar grabbed for his wrist, but not before Gavin got a good solid rap at the door.

"What do you think you're doing?" Gaspar hissed.

Gavin flashed a grin and shrugged. "I figured you weren't going to…"

He trailed off as the door opened. Gavin looked at the

woman on the other side of the door and frowned. This wasn't who he expected.

The person who answered was no more than fifteen, maybe sixteen.

"Is she..." he whispered out of the corner of his mouth.

Gaspar elbowed him, and Gavin jumped off to the side, wincing.

"Is your mother home?" Gaspar asked.

The girl looked at Gaspar and nodded. "I'll go get her. Who should I say is visiting?"

Gaspar frowned for a moment. "Just tell her it's an old friend from the Roasted Dragon."

The girl tipped her head, studying Gaspar with a quizzical expression on her face before nodding. When she left, she closed the door most of the way, but it remained open a crack.

"Is she yours?" Gavin whispered.

"I told you to be quiet."

"I think it's a reasonable question, at least in light of everything."

"In light of what?" Gaspar asked.

"Of the fact that she's here. She's in the home of your ex. And..." Gavin wasn't sure he should finish.

Gaspar watched him with a look of murder in his eyes. For a simple thief, he certainly gave off an air of danger in a way that surprised Gavin.

"We aren't going to talk about this," Gaspar said.

"I could just go and ask Jessica. You *did* say that you were a friend of hers from the Roasted Dragon."

"I'm warning you, boy. Don't push me."

Gavin started to chuckle but straightened at the look on Gaspar's face. He really should be careful. Seeing that expression, he decided not to say anything else. Instead, he took a step back, crossed his arms in front of him, and waited.

Gaspar shifted his weight, moving from foot to foot. Gavin didn't know the old thief to be nervous about anything, so it surprised him.

When the door finally opened again, the woman standing in the doorway had dark hair, much like the younger girl. She had a round face and was dressed in a colorful gown. She was lovely, but she was nothing like the kind of person Gavin would've expected—not that he had any idea about the kind of woman that Gaspar would've been with.

The woman's eyes widened when she saw Gaspar. "What are you doing here?" she whispered.

"I wouldn't have come if it wasn't a real issue."

"I thought you couldn't visit with me anymore."

"And I don't think I really can," Gaspar said. He glanced past her, his gaze looking into the home. "But someone needs my help."

"Someone always needs your help, Gaspar."

"Desarra—"

She shook her head. "Don't. You don't need to say anything. Much like I don't need you to say anything. After all, didn't we agree we both knew we couldn't be together anymore?"

"You know what happened."

Gaspar's back was tense, and Gaspar looked toward him, as if trying to indicate something to him. Maybe trying to tell Gavin he needed to turn away; to not listen.

How could he *not* listen though?

"Can we come in?" Gaspar asked.

Desarra looked over at Gavin, frowning. "I'm sorry. I should be more polite. I didn't know you had someone with you. An apprentice?"

Gaspar glanced over at him. "This one doesn't think he needs anyone's help."

"So he's more like you," Desarra said, smiling.

"Unfortunately," Gaspar muttered.

"I don't think you should come in. Not today."

"I understand. Can I ask you a question in confidence?"

"What is it?"

"It's about…" Gaspar trailed off as he looked past her again, and he seemed to notice the other girl. He waited for a moment before sighing. "Perhaps now isn't a good time."

"Now is fine," she said.

"I don't know that it is. Until we have more privacy, I…"

She stepped forward, giving the younger woman a pointed glance, and then pulled the door closed. Once outside, she stayed there with her hand on the door, looking at Gaspar. Gavin had seen an expression like that in other people's eyes before, and seeing somebody look at Gaspar like that was surprising.

It was affection, but it was a pained sort of affection.

"You really shouldn't have come," she whispered.

"And I wouldn't have, were it not necessary," Gaspar replied.

"I..." She looked over at Gavin, and she shook her head. "What is it you needed to know?"

"I need access to the Captain's fortress." Gaspar kept his voice low, and he sighed as he said it, looking all around him.

"You know I can't get that for you."

"You can't, but you know someone who can."

Her eyes widened. "Gaspar—"

"Another child has been abducted, and we believe the Captain has him held there."

Another?

There was more to what Gaspar knew than he let on.

"Are you sure?"

"This was left behind," Gaspar said, reaching into his pocket and flashing the marker Erica had found. "Everything we've been able to uncover suggests this is the Captain's."

Desarra took the coin, held it in her hand, then flipped it one way and then the other as if she'd practiced the motion. Gavin looked to Gaspar but he made a point of looking away from him. Desarra frowned as she studied it. "This is the Captain's marker. It's unusual, though."

"Why unusual?"

"It signifies someone from his household." She looked up at Gaspar. "Are you sure about what you're saying? The Captain is not known to abduct anyone. He works in…" She looked to Gavin a moment then back to Gaspar, who nodded. "Different matters. It's how he was able to move up in his position in the city."

What sort of different matters?

There was more going on here than Gavin knew.

"I'm not really sure at all. All I know is that this was left behind, and the person who found it is missing her son."

"How old is he?"

"Ten."

"So young," she whispered.

"So young," Gaspar said. There was a hint of sadness in his voice.

Gavin watched him and tried to understand just what it was, but he didn't dare say anything. Though he knew little about Gaspar, Gavin had a sense that his hearing this much of their conversation was more than what Gaspar wanted.

"I'll see what I can come up with," she whispered. "I don't know how long it's going to take me to figure it out, but I'll see what I can do."

"That's all I can ask," Gaspar said.

Desarra took a step toward him, holding her hand out. Gaspar didn't move toward her. She hesitated. It was only a moment, but it was a moment Gavin saw.

Letting out a pent-up breath, she nodded. "I can send word to the Dragon, I assume?"

"You can."

She smiled sadly at Gaspar before nodding at Gavin. "Nice to meet you. Be careful you don't follow too closely in his footsteps."

Gavin could only nod back.

When she stepped inside the house, Gaspar took a quick breath, turned, and motioned for Gavin to follow. "Let's get moving."

"Just like that?"

"What else do you think we need to be doing?"

"I guess I'm curious, that's all."

They reached the low wall and stepped through the gate, and Gavin paused to look back at the house. It might be his imagination, but he thought he saw someone looking out through the window.

"Don't push," Gaspar said. "I know what you're thinking."

"I doubt that."

"I can see it in your eyes, boy. You're thinking I'm going to tell you some grand tale about my ex-wife, but you'd be wrong."

"It seems to me that neither of you wants it to be ex anything," Gavin said.

"Is that right? What makes you such an expert on things like this? I thought you were an assassin."

Gavin looked around. The crowd of people that was out on the street was far enough away that they wouldn't have heard, but it was a measure of Gaspar's irritation that he'd even said that much as loud as he did.

"You might think otherwise, but I *was* trained to observe," Gavin said.

"You could have fooled me. In fact, you did fool me. From what I can tell, the only things you've been able to observe are jack and shit."

Gavin nearly smiled, but the irritation within Gaspar was enough to keep that at bay. He followed Gaspar. "What happened?"

"I told you that I'm not going to talk about it."

"Fine. Is she yours?"

Gaspar stopped and spun toward him with a knife out. Gavin's training kicked in, and he chopped down on Gaspar's arm, knocking the knife to the ground.

He stepped back, holding his hands up. "I'm sorry," Gavin said.

"No. At least you're competent in something." Gaspar quickly grabbed the knife off the ground and slipped it back into his sheath. "I shouldn't have done that."

"Is she yours?"

"Does it matter?"

"If it's going to complicate any of our jobs, it does."

Gaspar glared at him. "No, she's not mine. Is that what you need to hear?"

"How long ago were you and Desarra together?" Gavin asked.

"That's not the kind of crew we are."

"Then what kind are we?"

"I'm helping you so that you can get this boy," Gaspar said. "That's the only reason I'm doing this."

"It seems to me that you have more reason than that."

"And I'm telling you that you need to stop pushing."

Gavin needed to be careful. Gaspar had limits. He could be crotchety, but he was also useful, and Gavin needed to have him be a part of what they were doing. If he angered Gaspar too much, he ran the risk of him being unwilling to work with them when they made a run at the Captain's fortress.

"I'm sorry," Gavin said. "It's just that I was taught to push and ask questions in my training."

"Pushing only drives people away," Gaspar said.

"Maybe that's my problem," Gavin muttered. He'd certainly done enough of that when he was training with Tristan. It was part of the reason he had so few friends from that time. None, now that Cyran had betrayed him.

Gaspar looked over at him, and he shook his head. "Have you got it out of your system yet?"

"What?"

"All of your questions. Because that's all you'll get from me. You've seen what you seen, and you know more about me than damn near anyone. I'm not willing to bring you any closer unless you're apprenticed to me. Even then…"

"How many apprentices have you had?"

"There you go again, asking questions. Didn't I warn you about that?"

"You might've warned me, but I'm not always good at heeding them."

"Obviously."

They continued along the street, and Gavin watched for movement, anything that would raise his alarms. After having visited Erica's home, there was the possibility that they would come across something if it had been watched, but so far, there was nothing.

He waited, and he continued staring at Gaspar. "You still haven't told me if you've taken many apprentices."

"Not recently."

"What about Imogen?"

"You sure you want to talk about her?"

Gavin smiled, but Gaspar didn't follow suit. "Eventually, we're going to have to have a conversation about her."

"You can have that conversation. Not me." Gaspar grunted. "If you got to know Imogen the way I have, you'd understand what I have to fear."

"She has some talent," Gavin said.

"Which is more than I can say about you."

"What about the rest of your apprentices?"

Gaspar didn't say anything.

"What happened to them? Did they end up in jail?"

Gaspar studied him. "You really ask the wrong types of questions, don't you?"

"That's never really been my specialty," Gavin admitted. "Usually, I get a target, I go after them, and I remove them. That's sort of how my job works."

"Your job is terrible," Gaspar said.

"I didn't say it was any good. I just said I'm good at it."

"Have you ever given thought to doing something else?"

"All the time. That's why I'm in Yoran." Gavin sighed. But maybe not for much longer. It might actually be time for him to leave. Find the boy, then he could get on with things. Wrenlow would understand. "You know what happens when you get good at something?"

"I know," Gaspar said.

"You find you don't have much choice. You do what you can do, and you don't complain about it. How can you, when it's the only thing you know?"

"Just because you're good at killing doesn't mean you can't do anything else."

Gavin shrugged. "I'm saying that it's what I was trained to do. And there are people who need to die."

"I can't disagree with that."

"Which is why I do it. You've seen that I'm selective in the jobs I take."

"Selective, but you're still taking that kind of job." Gaspar looked over to him. "What if you decided to be something other than what you were trained to be?"

Gavin didn't have an answer to it, and Gaspar didn't push.

The Dragon was near, and Gavin moved more quickly as they headed toward it. The street around the Dragon was empty, the storefronts barely marked. Gavin's gaze drifted along them. He recognized the small signs, picking up on those for the seamstress, the lantern maker, the butcher, and the scribe. Gavin rarely spent much time in any of them. He had visited each, mostly to scout the dangers around the Dragon.

"I keep doing what I do because I have to," Gavin whispered.

"What makes you think you have to? Is it your training? Your mentor? Because if it's either of those, then you have a choice."

"Like you do?"

Gaspar glanced over at him as they slowed in front of the Dragon. "I made my choice."

"We all have choices. I'm telling you mine."

Gavin reached the door to the tavern and paused for a moment before pulling it open. It was time for him to get to work, see if he could figure out anything more, and create a plan to get into the Captain's building. Hopefully Wrenlow and Desarra would come through with the knowledge they'd need to get inside. If not, Gavin wasn't sure that he could even take the job. Jessica—and Gaspar, for that matter—wanted him to take the job, but without the necessary information, he wasn't willing to put those he was working with in danger.

Gaspar looked over at him as they stepped in the tavern, and the question in his eyes lingered. Gavin had his own questions for him, but he suspected that Gaspar would have no interest in answering them. Even more reason for him to ask.

Instead, he turned to Jessica, who was working her way through the tavern, which was much busier than it had been in quite some time. Gavin forced a smile.

"You aren't going to talk about what you saw," Gaspar said to him.

"If you say so."

"I do. And you aren't."

Gaspar peeled off, heading toward a table where Imogen sat, leaving Gavin at the entrance. She leaned forward, her dark hair hanging in front of her face, while she sharpened her sword by running a stone across the edge of the blade. As he had seen before, there was a pattern to her work, different than he used when sharpening blades, almost as if she knew something he didn't about the sword. Having seen her work, and knowing just how deadly she could be, he wondered if maybe that were the case. He still wanted to know more about her though. He walked over to the table.

"Well?" Imogen asked.

Her sudden comment took him aback. Imogen rarely spoke. "Well what?"

"Did you find out anything that might be useful in finding this boy?"

Gavin smiled. "Hopefully. We'll know soon enough."

She looked over to Gaspar. "Something's wrong."

"Yeah, he's probably going to be touchy for a while. We had to visit his ex-wife."

Her eyes narrowed a moment then she stood, sheathing her sword, and headed over to Gaspar. Another chance to get to know Imogen wasted.

CHAPTER SIX

Gavin stood in the small room he occupied at the Roasted Dragon, working with the El'aras dagger and practicing different fighting styles. He flowed from movement to movement, using one form, then another, each of them demonstrating various techniques that helped him stay fluid. He used the training style that Tristan had taught him all those years ago. It was one that forced him to work through each of the training techniques. With each one, he could develop his confidence, and it took very little time for him to gain the necessary skill so that he could fight anyone. Despite not using any enchantments, Gavin had never encountered anyone who posed much of a challenge to him. Even those with enchantments—and even sorcerers—had never been that much of a problem.

Until recently.

Coming to this city had created a new difficulty for

him. It was one he didn't care for and one that put him in danger, though he was trained for that. There was no point in fighting it. He needed to be ready for those dangers, which was the reason he trained.

Sweat glistened on his skin. He worked through the small space of his room, using the confines of the room to limit his movements, mimicking a fight. He didn't need to have an actual fight to practice like this. He could make it more difficult for himself, and as he fought through the various movements, he flowed from place to place. His mind went blank the way that it often did as he trained, though flickers of memories came to him—images of what he had learned from Tristan over the years and knowledge that he embraced.

A knock came at the door. Taking a deep breath, Gavin slipped the dagger into the sheath on his belt. He wiped the bead of sweat along his forehead and grabbed a towel from the chair. He dabbed it across his chest and pulled the door open.

Wrenlow blinked. "Am I interrupting?"

Gavin shook his head. "I was just training."

"You still do that?"

"Skills fade if they aren't practiced."

"But you've trained for so much of your life."

Gavin shrugged. That was part of the reason he continued to do it now. It made easier for him to maintain the habit. If he lost the practice of training, he didn't know if he'd be able to regain that. Already there were some skills that had faded somewhat because he didn't use them the way he once had. When he'd been training with Tristan, tested on a daily basis, his skills had been sharpened to an edge that had made him incredibly powerful.

"It's habit, more than anything else. Besides, it helps me clear my head."

"What are you trying to think through now?"

"I'm trying to get a handle on what we're going to have to do here."

"That's what I came for."

"Did you find something?"

Frustration washed across Wrenlow's face. "Not quite yet. Gaspar keeps looking, and my sources are digging into the details around the Captain, but so far we haven't been able to come up with anything."

"I have faith you will."

"I'm glad you do because I'm starting to question whether we're going to come up with what we need to know to get into his home. She didn't give us much of a timeline, but…"

"She didn't, which means we need to act quickly," Gavin said.

A child abduction could be dangerous. In some of the places that he'd visited over the years, children were taken into slavery.

"This still doesn't make a lot of sense to me. The Captain has lived in Yoran for decades. In that time, he's built up his fortress and created a position of power. Why would someone like that turn toward abducting children and sending them into slavery?" Wrenlow said.

"There has to be something more to it. That, more than anything else, is what we need to better understand," Gavin said.

"We've been looking," Wrenlow said. "I'm going to keep looking, and I remain optimistic that we're going to find the answer, but that's not why I'm here."

"Why are you here?"

He handed a folded slip of paper over to Gavin. "This."

Gavin frowned as he unfolded it. As he scanned it, his surprise deepened. "This is a request for a job."

"That's the way it looked to me. I'm sorry I opened it, but I wasn't sure whether or not it was something to interrupt you for. You've been up here for the better part of two hours."

Gavin shook his head. Two hours wasn't all that long to spend training, not compared to what he used to spend, but they went by quickly when he was focused. He wasn't as tired as he would've expected, though in the small room, there were limits to how much he could move around.

He skimmed the page, trying to figure out just what it was that he was asked to do.

First Erica had come looking for me, and now a letter?

This wasn't how he did jobs. At all. It was about concealment. Staying in the shadows. Avoiding detection. Now it seemed all of Yoran knew about him.

"Somebody wants to meet."

"I didn't know if you wanted to take another job or not."

"Well, it's been a few weeks since we've taken any."

"You took Erica's."

"I didn't really take that one by choice. That was more Jessica and Gaspar's urging. Anyway, I can go and look into this at least."

Wrenlow nodded. "I can go with you if you'd like."

"I think we can get back into the usual pattern we have for jobs, don't you?"

The relief that swept across Wrenlow's face almost made Gavin laugh. "I can keep looking into the details of the Captain's fortress while you're off on this job."

"I'm not going to do the job right now, Wrenlow. The letter is a request to meet."

He *had* been incredibly selective of late. Possibly he'd been *too* selective, but ever since the issue with Cyran, Gavin hadn't wanted to take too many jobs. If he were going to stay in Yoran, maybe it was time for that to change. He pulled on a shirt, and on a whim, he grabbed his cloak as well.

He felt to make sure that he had his dagger and knives. They were the only weapons he kept on him at any given time, though he was tempted to carry a sword. Travelers generally didn't have them in other places he'd been to, but many people carried swords in Yoran, so it wouldn't be out of place.

"You're going now?" Wrenlow asked.

"The request suggests they'll be waiting."

"I'll keep listening." Wrenlow tapped on the enchantment, and he flashed a smile at Gavin, who could only shake his head and chuckle. At least Wrenlow was getting back to his old self.

Gavin headed down the stairs and into the tavern. There was more activity than usual. He searched for Jessica, but he didn't see her anywhere. Gaspar sat at a table with Imogen, and the two of them were talking quietly. Her fingers tapped at the table as he'd seen her doing before, drumming a pattern. He looked over, curious as to what they were doing, but they didn't look in his direction. He considered saying something to Gaspar, possibly asking him to join, but he decided that he wanted to do the job on his own. It was past time he returned to jobs like that.

Gavin stepped out into the street and hunched down to stay low and blend into the crowd as much as he could. He weaved through the people, heading toward the meeting point. He stayed to the side of the street and moved past the seamstress shop, glancing through the window to see the arrangement of colorful dresses displayed. The proprietor, a woman named Marlowe who'd lived in this section of the city for decades, tottered around the shop, unmindful of him. He looked in the window of the next storefront and saw it empty. He kept his attention all around him, looking from storefront to storefront, before focusing on the crowd.

As he walked, there was a familiar sense that somebody was following him. He took a few side turns and twisted through the streets to see if there was anyone behind him, but he didn't see anyone. The crowd looked the way it should, and there was no sign he needed to be worried about. Perhaps there was nothing.

Typically, Gavin wasn't one to jump at shadows. He was trained too well for that. Maybe it was a matter of everything they'd been through and that he felt his time in Yoran was coming to an end. Or maybe it was more a matter of Cyran's betrayal. That had troubled him, more than he'd admitted to the others. Gavin was normally a much better judge of character, and having Cyran betray him in such a way made Gavin doubt who he could trust.

He turned another corner, and it seemed as if somebody trailed after him. This time, he caught sight of a flash of brightly colored fabric, which reminded him of Hamish. But Hamish had been Cyran wearing an illusion.

So if it wasn't him, who was it?

Rather than continuing to push onward and risking his meeting being interrupted by somebody following him, Gavin decided that he needed to investigate. The potential employer could wait. They would have to understand. And by taking his time, Gavin was protecting them. He switched directions, changing course to move back along the street but in a way that wouldn't be observed quite as easily.

The activity around here was sparse. There were other people out, but none of them seemed to pay him any mind. This wasn't uncommon, and Gavin had grown accustomed to people ignoring him. It was only to be expected, since he kept himself covered by his cloak and made a point of drawing himself down so that he didn't look nearly as large or threatening.

Besides, it was more than just his size, it was a matter of how much attention he paid. He knew better than to focus on too many of the people in the streets so that he didn't draw their notice. Gavin looked for trends instead, and as he scanned the street, he didn't see any patterns emerge.

Only... *there.*

One man kept making a loop. He looked as if he were trying to avoid glancing in Gavin's direction, but he wasn't doing a good a job of it. He was lean; dressed in gray pants and a jacket. Different than the bright fabric that he'd seen before. Which meant a second person was watching.

His hair was shorn, and there was a scar across his forehead. Gavin didn't see any sign of weapons. A soldier, but not one who was prepared to attack.

Gavin continued looking for other signs of movement. Where there was one, especially one who was unarmed, he suspected there would be another.

Why are they watching me, though? Did they know what I was doing here?

He didn't see how such a thing would be possible. He was only coming for information, not to take a job yet. There wasn't any reason for somebody to follow him.

Unless they knew he'd been summoned.

Could they be the ones who'd summoned me?

Gavin was more on edge than he'd been before Cyran

had used him. He made his way along the street, looking for any other signs of movement.

It was times like these where he thought that Gaspar would have been beneficial. Having the old thief with him provided another set of eyes, and he couldn't deny that Gaspar was incredibly skilled at searching for patterns. Not that he would ever tell Gaspar that.

He didn't see anything else and slipped back along the street. The other man made another circle and Gavin followed, taking up a path behind him. The man turned a corner, and Gavin darted forward and jammed his fist into his side. He pulled him toward an alley and set him on the ground.

Gavin crouched across from him, holding a knife in hand. "Why are you following me?"

The man blinked, wincing. "I'm not following you. I don't know—"

Gavin jabbed the knife toward him. "I've been watching you. You keep making passes behind me. You're following me. I want to know why."

"Like I said, I'm not following you."

He debated how aggressive to be. He didn't know anything about this man. He might have been following Gavin, but that wasn't reason to stab him. Besides, he still thought he might be able to get information out of him.

"What were you doing?" Gavin asked. "I observed you making three circuits around the block."

"You saw what?"

"I saw you. Now, if you want to keep denying you were

circling the block, go right ahead. I saw it. Unless you give me a good answer as to what you were doing and why you were there, I might have to…"

Gavin thrust the knife at him again and watched as his eyes widened. He let the man's imagination do the rest of the work, and he smiled to himself.

"I wasn't following you," the man said again.

"Who are you following?"

"I wasn't following anyone. I was looking at…"

Gavin leaned back, slipping the knife back into his sheath. "Who?"

"It doesn't matter."

"It matters. Who are you looking at?"

"She doesn't want anything to do with me."

"That's what this is about? A spurned lover?"

Gavin felt like an ass. Not because he had punched the man and dragged him off to the side of the street, but because he had misjudged the situation entirely. The man had indeed been looking at him, but maybe it was because he was trying to hide what he was doing.

Gavin shook his head. "If she doesn't want anything to do with you, then you need to leave her alone."

"I'm trying to leave her alone, but I just can't."

"Can't or won't?"

Not that it mattered to him. He didn't really care if this man stalked some woman he had a crush on, but there was something about all of this that troubled him.

The timing. What if he had been right all along? What if this man *had* been following him? He had the look of a soldier. The closely cropped hair. The scar above his brow. Even the build. All of it suggested he was trained—the kind of person that Gavin had fought before and that he would expect to follow him.

The man leaned against the building and breathed, as if he was trying to gather himself and control his breathing. Another sign of training.

"Who are you?" Gavin asked.

"I'm no one. I told you. I was just looking along the street because—"

"Because you have a crush on somebody. That's what you're telling me, and I'm telling you that I'm not sure I can believe you. So what I'm asking is for you to give me a good reason I should believe you."

"What more do you need me to say?"

"I think you need to show me who you were looking at."

"Please. Don't make me do it."

He shrugged. "I'm sorry. I'm just being cautious."

The man stared at him and frowned. Gavin simply waited.

After a moment, the man got up and dusted his hands on his pants. "If it's going to convince you to let me go, I'll show you. But don't make me take you inside her shop."

"Why not?"

"Because she's asked me not to go in."

Gavin almost chuckled. The story was completely believable. Were it a different time and were he not already on edge, he might have believed the man instead of pushing and pressuring him.

He forced the man forward and held onto the back of his jacket, keeping the fabric twisted in his fist. He walked close behind, ready for any suspicious movement.

What he wasn't ready for was someone to slam into his back.

The man in front of him spun and kicked, forcing Gavin to let go of his jacket and step back. He glanced over at another attacker, who was small, lithe, and compact with longer hair. She reminded him of Imogen.

He raised an eyebrow. "Not a spurned lover."

The man darted forward. Gavin blocked by lifting his leg and thrusting it so that he could throw off the attack. He twisted and spun his fist, driving it outward.

The woman blocked him. She was quick. Almost impossibly quick.

Could she have an enchantment?

Gavin hadn't fought against anybody who used them in quite some time. It was dangerous going against someone like that without enchantments of his own. Some of the ones he'd encountered in the past enabled people to be faster or stronger, while some helped with healing. But he didn't need an enchantment for fighting. That was one area where his training gave him the advantage.

He twisted around and kicked, connecting with the man's midsection. The attacker grunted and dropped to the ground. Gavin tried to dart forward, wanting to deal an incapacitating blow to the man's head, but the woman slid between them.

The people on the street had given them space. In fact, Gavin suspected that the crowd had disappeared altogether long before the fight broke out. Maybe they were all part of this.

Interesting.

The woman's hands darted rapidly in several quick thrusts. If Gavin hadn't trained the way that he had or experienced what it was like to fight somebody faster than him, he might not have been able to parry each blow. But he deflected one, then another, and each time he sent her attacks glancing off, he prepared himself to handle the next.

Gavin used her defense against her. She was backing away, and he summoned a hint of power from his core, nothing more than that. With that, he jumped, flipping in the air.

The suddenness of the movement surprised her. As he twisted, he brought his leg around and kicked toward her. He expected to catch her on the shoulder, but she maneuvered far more rapidly than he expected.

As he landed, she was already moving forward. She blocked his punch, and he swept his leg down. His kick connected, and she stumbled. Gavin kicked again, and she grunted as the blow landed on her side.

Something moved behind him, and he spun, driving out with his heel, and he connected again with the man's stomach.

Gavin cocked his head to the side. "You shouldn't lead like that," he muttered.

The man went stumbling down, and Gavin turned back to the woman.

She was gone.

He darted toward the man and unsheathed his dagger. He glanced at the blade. No glow. No magic.

Gavin jabbed the dagger toward the man. "Either answers, or you'll give me a reason to use it against you."

"No answers. We were just hired to trail you."

"Hired by whom?"

"I don't know. That's not how it works."

"Really?"

Gavin pushed the dagger into the man's side. He didn't press too hard or too deep, but just enough to draw blood. Just enough to make him believe that Gavin would push even harder.

And he would. He wasn't opposed to more violence if necessary. Gavin didn't know whether he'd been tasked to do anything more than give him a beating or if he would've left him bleeding out on the street. Neither of them had carried weapons, which was reason enough for Gavin to at least hesitate.

"I told you, I don't know," the man said.

"Where did you take the job?"

The man stared at him defiantly.

Gavin lingered, watching the man for a moment. "You aren't going to like the way this ends."

There was something about his movements during the

fight that disturbed Gavin. Maybe they were enchanted. Gavin pressed the knife deeper into his side.

The man's eyes widened in fear. "I can show you."

"Good. Why don't we start with that." Gavin shoved him. The man staggered forward. "Where did your friend go?"

"I don't know. She probably took off when you beat us."

"Who is she?"

Gavin couldn't shake how similar her fighting style had been to Imogen's. With her build, he could almost believe that they were related. He wanted answers, but with everything else that had been going on, he didn't have the time to get them. He wasn't even sure if Gaspar would provide answers to his questions.

"I don't know. We're paired up for the job," the man said.

"Don't think I'm going to believe that answer."

"It's true."

"You had to have had some conversation with her while working."

"Less than you'd think. She doesn't like to talk much."

Another similarity to Imogen. Gavin shook his head. "Tell me where we're going so there won't be any surprises."

"It's not far from here."

"How long have you been following me?"

"Since you left the tavern."

Great. Another person aware of the Roasted Dragon.

In the time he'd been in Yoran, Gavin had placed the Dragon in danger far more times than he preferred. At least this seemed to be a typical sort of attacker and not one of the El'aras.

Gavin could handle normal fighters; even several of them all at once. In fact, there was a part of him that wished he had the opportunity to go against more at a time.

"How long have you been waiting there?" he asked.

"Not long. They said you might be coming out."

"*They* said?"

"Right. They said it. We were supposed to follow you. If you came this way, we were supposed to slow you."

"Just slow me?"

The man nodded.

They reached the end of the street, and he pointed to a house that looked like any of the others around it. Most of the houses along the street were simple. They were all pressed together, one after another, an entire row of them. All were made of wood and with simple windows that looked out over the street. A few of them had obviously been painted at some point in the past, an attempt to give them more color that ultimately mattered very little.

The street itself was narrow and the buildings squeezed in, nothing like what was found in some of the more central parts of the city. Not much was different about this particular house. The windows were dirty, with no light shining through. No smoke drifted up from the chimney. People moved along the street, unmindful of the building.

Strange.

"Why just slow me?" he asked.

"I don't know. I didn't ask details."

Gavin grabbed the man's collar and threw him forward. "Well, let me tell you about the kind of jobs I take." They started toward the door. "You see this dagger?"

The man glanced back and nodded.

"I'm sure you're curious whether I'd be willing to use it," Gavin said.

The man looked up, holding Gavin's gaze for a moment. He nodded again.

"Don't tempt me, and you won't have to find out."

Gavin shoved him toward the door, and he stopped there for a moment. This wasn't all that far from where he'd been heading, but it wasn't the same house. He nodded at the door, and the man knocked. Gavin took a step back, holding onto the dagger.

He wasn't altogether surprised when it started to glow.

CHAPTER SEVEN

Gavin hadn't expected to see an older man answer the door. He had thick glasses, and he was dressed in a maroon gown. He flicked his gaze between the two of them, then waved his hand at Gavin's attacker, who shot Gavin a quick look before he walked away. There was something about this man that said he took care of himself. Sometimes older men let themselves go, but this man gave off the impression that he still was relatively fit. He was shorter, stocky almost, and had short black hair. His nose looked flattened to his face, and Gavin could almost imagine that it had been broken a time or two.

Gavin smiled. "I suppose I have you to thank for my greeting?"

"They were supposed to hinder you, nothing more than that."

"And you are?"

"Chan. Davel Chan."

"I suspect you know who I am?"

Davel stared at him for a moment and nodded. "You may come in, I suppose."

"Just like that? You aren't concerned about what I'm going to do?"

He eyed the El'aras dagger. "You might as well put that away. You aren't going to need it."

"I think I might keep it ready. Just in case," Gavin said, shrugging.

"It's your choice."

Davel headed into the home and Gavin paused, looking along the street. He didn't see the man he'd fought, but he did catch a glimpse of the woman. She was standing at the end of the street, watching him. The woman had a dangerous edge to her, and again he was struck by her resemblance to Imogen.

Was this woman enchanted?

Gavin didn't know if that was the case with Imogen or not. In Imogens' case, it might simply be a matter of almost impossible skill.

All of this was strange, though these days, Gavin wasn't sure if he was even able to take normal jobs. He had to believe that this was somehow tied to the reason that he'd been summoned.

But why?

When he stepped inside, the El'aras dagger started to glow more brightly. There was magic used here, and whatever was here would be considerable.

He looked around the home. It was cozy. A long

velvet-lined bench rested in front of one wall, and a similar one was on the other wall. A table with chairs surrounding it stood in the middle of the room. There was no hearth. Cupboards within the kitchen were closed, and a kettle rested on the stove. It was the only source of heat within the room.

"Close the door behind you," Davel instructed.

"Are you here alone?"

"Are you?"

Gavin smiled. He hadn't tapped the enchantment, though he was growing increasingly tempted to do so. It may be beneficial for Wrenlow to know what had taken place, but for now, he would keep the silence.

"Right now, I am," Gavin replied. "Others know where I'm going."

"The same could be said for me," Davel said.

"Why did you hire them to slow me?"

"They weren't supposed to attack you, though from the sight of the blood on your dagger, it seems as if that message wasn't conveyed quite as clearly as I would've hoped."

"You hired thugs to delay me, and you're surprised they attacked?"

"I didn't realize they were thugs." Davel turned toward him, and he held a mug out.

Gavin shook his head. "I'm sure you can understand why I won't take that."

"I suppose I can." Davel took a sip of the tea, and he watched Gavin. "Are you still taking jobs?"

Gavin started to laugh. "All of that to draw me here?"

"Well, if you are who I believe you to be—"

"Who you believe me to be?"

"The rumors of Gavin Lorren within Yoran have been too consistent and persistent for me to ignore."

"If you've heard rumors of me, then you know the kind of work I'm involved in."

"I'm well aware." He said it with a strange irritation in his eyes.

"Then who would you like me to target?"

"It's complicated."

"It always is," Gavin said.

"I feel conflicted about even asking this at all."

"As you should."

"Anyway," Davel said, ignoring the comment, "I thought that perhaps if anyone might be able to help with this task, it might be you."

"What task is that?"

"I need you to acquire something for me."

"Acquire?" Gavin frowned, arching a brow.

"You're a tracker, are you not?"

"Where did you hear that?"

"That's the rumor."

Gavin resisted the urge to groan. He had a strong suspicion about where that rumor originated from. More than that, he suddenly thought that he understood just why Davel Chan had believed that he could send thugs after him to slow him.

Balls.

"What do you need found?" Gavin asked.

"There's an item I need. As you can understand, in this city, it's not something I can openly pursue."

"An enchantment."

"It's not so much an enchantment as it is…" Davel sighed. "Well, perhaps it is an enchantment."

Gavin shook his head. It seemed that he was getting pushed to take very different jobs than what he typically did. By Jessica. And Gaspar. And even Wrenlow.

Were they trying to turn me into a different kind of person?

More than ever, he knew it was time for him to leave Yoran. After he found this boy. Until then, he wasn't sure he'd be able to leave.

And while I'm here, did I want to take jobs like this? Jobs that involved magic?

"I'm afraid you have the wrong person," Gavin said.

"I can pay. I have money." Davel set the tea down, and he raised his hands in a pleading fashion. "That's one thing I have in this city. I can't use my art openly, but I can pay."

Gavin wanted to sigh—to turn away, to refuse this man—but if he was going to leave Yoran, he needed money to do it. Not that he couldn't find enough paying jobs along the way, but having a few coins would make it easier for him.

"How much are we talking about?" he asked.

"Well, that partly depends upon you."

"What are you looking for?"

That might've been the better question. If it was something difficult or potentially dangerous, then he would need to ask for more. He didn't particularly want to go chasing after magical and enchanted items, but he could have Wrenlow look into it. It wouldn't be all that difficult for him to extend his resources to search for something like that.

"It's called the jade egg," Davel said. "It's an item of some power."

"And you believe it's in the city."

"I know it is."

"Why?"

"Because it was mine, and it was taken from me."

"If you know who took it, then go and get it."

"You don't understand. I can't just go and get it. I..." Davel looked down and avoided his eyes.

"You aren't as powerful as the person who took it," Gavin said. "That's what you're trying to say?"

Which meant that whoever took it had a considerable magical connection. From the way the El'aras dagger was glowing, Gavin suspected that Davel had considerable power too.

"Something like that."

"Who took it?"

Davel met Gavin's gaze. "An enchantress by the name of Zella."

Enchantress?

"What does she look like?" Gavin asked.

"Powerful. Older. She's been in the city for decades. And hides her presence."

"You know that magic is forbidden within Yoran."

"It might be forbidden, but there are people still practicing. Most of them are like me."

Gavin glanced toward the door briefly before turning his attention back to Davel. "You weren't trying to have them slow me at all. You were testing me." He frowned. "Did the man have an enchantment?"

"He did."

"What was it?"

"It gave him swiftness."

Gavin grunted. "He didn't seem all that swift to me."

"Which is why you're the right person for this job. I wasn't sure, and I didn't know whether I could even believe the rumors about you. I have to think that the way you were able to take them both down so easily…"

Gavin reached into his pocket, and Davel stiffened. He held out the scrap of paper. "This was you, I presume?"

He smiled. "I had to know you were coming this way."

"I see." At least Davel was prepared, if nothing else. "You need to tell me everything you can about this jade egg."

"It's small. It has a faint greenish glow to it. And you will find it within a metal box." He pulled out a piece of paper and handed it over to Gavin. On the paper was a drawing of the egg and the box.

"So you want me to find the box, and inside the box will be the egg."

Finding magic in Yoran wasn't necessarily an easy task, and this might be even more difficult than he thought.

Gavin had been involved with magic more often than he would've preferred since coming to Yoran, which was surprising given its status in the city.

After all, the punishment for using magic was so severe.

"I need some idea about how to find this Zella."

"I can't help you," Davel said.

"Because you don't know where to find her?"

"Zella, like so many of the other enchanters, has disappeared. Gone underground. There was a time when they worked more openly, but no one does these days. They can't risk it."

Gavin wasn't sure if there was going to be any way for him to find the information he wanted about Zella, but if nothing else, he suspected that completing this job would be worth a fair amount of money.

"What are you prepared to offer?" he asked.

"I thought I would see what you thought the job was worth."

Gavin smiled. "I'm sure you did. I'm curious what you were prepared to offer."

When it came to targets and hits, the kinds of jobs he'd fallen into lately, they paid because of the value of the target. Gavin had not hesitated to charge a premium for such tasks. Killing somebody was bloody work—and dangerous. In this case, he wasn't at all sure what he should be charging. He most definitely didn't want to undervalue his services.

"I could pay twenty gold crowns."

Gavin tried to keep his face neutral. Twenty gold was more than he would've proposed. Even more reason for him to have let Davel make the first offer.

But it also put him on edge.

If Davel was willing to offer twenty gold crowns, it suggested that whatever he wanted from Gavin was far more dangerous than what he was letting on.

"Thirty."

"Thirty? You do realize that twenty gold crowns is—"

"You're asking me to find a magical enchantress in a city where magic has been forbidden. You're asking me to find a magical item that's considerably powerful." He hesitated, unsure if that last part was true. "And it's going to take significant assets on my part to find it." Gavin forced a smile. "So, thirty gold crowns."

"I suppose I could come up with the difference," Davel said.

"I require half up front."

"Half? I can give you a third."

Which meant he had only ten gold crowns. And he'd banked on the idea of getting the rest. He must've known that Gavin was going to ask for half up front.

Gavin debated whether or not to push, but he wasn't sure if he should in this case. Even if he didn't complete the job, he would take the money. Not that he would tell Davel that.

"Fine, we'll start with ten. When I find Zella's location, I'll send word, and you'll provide an additional ten. When the job is completed, I'll require the final ten."

Davel took a deep breath, and then he nodded. "I can agree to those terms."

"Good. Now about that tea."

When he got back to the Dragon, Gavin took a seat across from Gaspar. The inside of the tavern was quiet. There were a few occupied tables, which was unusual these days. Several patrons had empty mugs of ale in front of them, and one had a tray of food. Maybe Jessica had decided to start serving others again. It was about time. Thankfully, she hadn't resumed hiring minstrels. Gavin didn't know if he'd be able to deal with that. She often chose the worst musicians, almost as if to taunt him.

He handed Gaspar the paper with the drawing of the egg. "Is this your doing?" Gavin asked.

"I think if you knew me better, you would know I'm not much of an artist."

"Not the drawing. The job."

Gaspar held his gaze. "What job? You already have a job."

"So you aren't responsible for putting out word on the street that I can find things for people?"

"Why would I do that?"

"Why *would* you?"

Gaspar glared at him. "We're busy enough as it is. I don't need to get into some debate with you about whether I'm trying to complicate things. Listen, boy, we need to figure out how to get into the Captain's fortress and rescue this kid. So what is it?"

"Some sort of magical egg. He called it a jade egg. Said it was stolen by a woman named Zella." Gavin watched Gaspar, looking for a spark of recognition in his eyes. Gaspar had been in Yoran for a long time. If such a person existed, he would have some idea who they were.

"Am I supposed to know who this Zella is?"

"I don't know. Do you?"

"Listen. If you're going to keep at this, I think we're going to have a difficult time."

"I'm just trying to figure out if you're playing a different game," Gavin said.

"None of this is a game, boy. We're talking about someone's life. I know that doesn't matter to you as much as it does to some of us, but it matters to me."

"Why is that?"

"Why is what? Why is life valuable? If I have to tell you that, then you had a greater failing when you were younger than I'd realized."

"No, not that. Why do you care so much about me taking this job?"

"It's not a matter of me caring whether you take this job at all. It's a matter of you finishing what you've agreed to."

"Seeing as how others decided on my behalf, I'm not so sure I agreed to anything."

Gaspar scowled at him, and Gavin resisted the urge to smile any more than he already was. Mostly, he was pushing Gaspar. He needed to know whether Gaspar was responsible for the rumors in the city, and from the way he was reacting, Gavin could tell Gaspar had nothing to do with it.

Which left either Wrenlow or Jessica. Gavin had a hard time thinking that Wrenlow would be responsible for that. He turned in place and saw Jessica working at one of the back tables, folding cloth napkins. He supposed he wouldn't put it past her to do that.

Maybe she wanted to keep him in the city more than she had let on. Now that he'd ruled out Gaspar and doubted it was Wrenlow, he had to question her. He started to get up from the table.

The door to the tavern opened, and Desarra walked in.

Gaspar's back was to the door. He shot a look at Gavin. "You're just going to get up and go away?"

"I need to talk to Jessica, and I figure you have your own issues to deal with."

"What sort of issues…"

Gaspar trailed off as he turned to see where Gavin was looking. He jumped up when he saw Desarra standing at the entrance.

"Who is that?" Wrenlow asked as Gavin walked past him.

"Gaspar's ex-wife."

"Oh," Wrenlow whispered.

Gavin took a seat by Jessica. He grabbed a stack of towels and began to fold them. "I had an interesting experience today."

"What was that?"

"A note was delivered about a job. I went out to find the meeting point, and I was attacked. It seemed as if the attackers were trying to test me."

"I suppose that in your line of work, they need to make sure you're everything they believe you to be."

"Maybe," Gavin said, looking over to Jessica. "But the man who ultimately wanted to hire me wanted me to find something."

"Find something?"

Gavin nodded. "It seems as if he heard rumors that I can be hired to find things in the city. I wonder where a rumor like that started."

"I don't know. Yoran can be a strange place. When rumors start, oftentimes they spread and—"

Gavin reach across the table and took Jessica's hand. "Did you spread that rumor?"

She looked over, meeting his eyes. "Why would I spread a rumor like that? You don't need my help finding jobs."

"I don't, but I wonder if you're trying to get me to take a *different* kind of job."

"Gavin—"

"I understand what you're trying to do."

"I'm not trying to do anything."

"You want me to stay here at the Dragon. With you." He smiled at her, and Jessica didn't return it.

She had stopped folding the towels. She rested her hands on the folded ones and looked at him. "I don't know what you think I might've done, but I'm not responsible. If there are rumors about you, then they came from a different source."

"If you say so," Gavin said.

"Gavin—"

"I took the job."

"You did?"

"It's not going to be easy, but seeing how well it pays, I thought I might need the money later on. Anyway, it involves me trying to dig for information about an enchantress. Zella."

There was a flicker on her face. Jessica recognized the name.

"Who is she?" he asked.

"I don't really know. I… I've heard the name before, though I don't know why."

"The man who hired me had some magical ability. I don't know if he was a minor sorcerer or if he was only an enchanter, but he made the El'aras dagger light up."

"You still use that thing?"

"It seems like I need to. Considering everything we've gone through, and especially considering everything *I've* gone through, having something that can reveal when magic is used around me is beneficial."

"So the dagger glowed around him."

"It did. Which tells me that not only does he have some magical ability, but he has enough to trigger the blade."

"And he wants you to find this Zella."

"No. The job wasn't to find Zella. The job was to find something called the jade egg."

"Do you think you can?"

Gavin shrugged. "I might be able to. I don't know. I'll have Wrenlow look into it, and even if we can't, it doesn't really matter."

"Why not?"

"Because he paid me part up front."

Jessica leaned forward. "Be careful, Gavin. If you took money from an enchanter or a sorcerer, you need to complete the job."

"I have plenty of experience with them," he said. "And I know what I need to do."

"I just want to make sure you aren't going to do something foolish."

Gavin held her gaze before glancing over at Gaspar sitting at the far table. "I don't think he's that thrilled that Desarra came here."

Jessica paused, resting her hands on the table. "I'm surprised she returned to the Dragon."

"Returned?" Gavin asked, watching Gaspar.

Jessica nodded slowly, tapping her hand on the table. "Back when they were together, she used to spend quite a bit of time here."

He still didn't know that much about Gaspar, but Desarra didn't strike him as the kind of person that would've been with the old thief. "What happened between them?"

Jessica shrugged. "I don't know all the details. All I

know is that something changed. He doesn't like to talk about it, and it was before I truly owned the tavern."

He frowned. "Who owned it before you?"

"My aunt."

"The tavern has been in your family?"

Jessica smiled. "I lost my parents back in the…" She squeezed her eyes shut, shaking her head. "It doesn't matter. My aunt owned the tavern, and when she died, she gave it to me. I've done my best to try to do right by her. In the time that I've owned it, I've known Gaspar in various roles."

"You've seen him change."

"I have. He started stealing."

Gavin laughed. "What do you mean that he started stealing?"

"He wasn't always a thief, Gavin."

"What was he before?" He couldn't imagine Gaspar as anything other than the thief that he was. It seemed fitting for him.

"You don't know?"

Gavin shook his head. "Gaspar and I don't have that kind of friendship, if it even is a friendship. He doesn't talk much about anything. Maybe that's because he's just old."

"He's always been that way."

"Old?"

She laughed softly. "You know what I mean."

"What was he before he became a thief?"

Given his skill, Gavin couldn't imagine him doing

anything else. Whatever he'd done would've been part of the underground—the same sort of thing that Gavin did, though he couldn't imagine Gaspar as an assassin or a killer of any sort. He'd seen Gaspar fight, but the old thief wasn't much of a fighter. Whatever he had done would be something different.

"He was one of the constables. He was a magic hunter."

"A *what?*"

"You didn't know."

Gavin shook his head and stared at Gaspar in stunned silence.

Desarra got up and reached toward Gaspar, almost as if she wanted to take his hands, but as had happened at the house, he didn't move toward her. After a moment, she turned and left the Dragon. Gaspar lingered at the table for a moment, his eyes closed, and he took a deep breath before getting up and heading over to them.

"Gaspar?" Jessica whispered.

"I have what we need," he said.

"What?" Gavin asked.

"She provided a layout of the Captain's fortress. Wrenlow can confirm it, but this should be enough."

Gavin looked at the stack of detailed pages in Gaspar's hand.

How would Desarra have been able to get that information?

Maybe it was best that he didn't know.

"As soon as we confirm this, we'll finish this job," Gaspar said.

Gavin wanted to say something and to ask a few more

questions, but seeing the look on Gaspar's face and the troubled expression in his eyes, he realized that would've been a terrible idea. It was better to leave him.

Instead, he reached for more towels and continued to fold them. That would help him focus his mind. It wouldn't be as effective as practicing or fighting, but maybe enough that he wouldn't have to stare at Gaspar and wonder about the old man. He wouldn't have to wonder why he left the constables. He wouldn't have to wonder why he got into thieving. And he wouldn't have to wonder about his relationship with Desarra—one it seemed that both still wished they had.

CHAPTER EIGHT

Gavin stalked along the street, moving under the shadows of night. He held one hand on the dagger, keeping it tucked away and off to his side. So far, there had been no additional movement, nothing that drew his attention, but he knew it was only a matter of time before someone appeared on the street. It was late enough that he'd been able to maneuver for this long without someone else appearing, but eventually, his luck would end.

"I can't tell that you're moving," Wrenlow whispered in his ear.

At least he was whispering. That was a new development for him. Since gaining the new enchantment from Anna, Wrenlow liked to yell in his ear. With the new El'aras enchantment, Gavin had the ability to adjust the volume and no longer had to listen to Wrenlow scream at him.

"I'm still moving," he replied.

He made the sound as little more than a soft breath of air, trying to call it out against the night. He didn't want anything or anyone to realize that he was here. Not yet. Eventually, it wouldn't matter. But for now, secrecy was key.

"If you're still moving, where are you?"

"Do you have to keep chattering?" Gaspar asked.

Gavin smiled to himself. The old thief was across the street, moving in another set of shadows. He did so far more easily than Gavin did, though every so often, Gavin was able to make out a shimmer of reflection, thanks to the moonlight. When he did, he made certain to let Gaspar know that he'd been seen. So far, Gaspar didn't seem to care.

"You're just jealous I'm not talking to you," Gavin said.

"There's no jealousy. You two need to stop bickering."

He grinned again, and he moved forward. At least Gaspar seemed back to his old crotchety self. Ever since Desarra had visited the Dragon, he'd been off. Now that they were making a run at the Captain's fortress, he needed Gaspar to be focused.

There was another shadow out in the night, though this one was far more difficult for him to see. Gavin had learned that Gaspar wasn't the most skilled thief in their makeshift crew. Imogen was.

She was deadly quiet. It was as if she practically floated above the ground, an enchantment carrying her forward. Gavin had yet to uncover her secret, but he was sure that there was one to be found. If it was simply that she was naturally that skilled, he didn't know if he would be disappointed or impressed.

"Is she ready?" Gavin asked.

"She's always ready," Gaspar said.

Gavin nodded, counting on Gaspar to have seen it. It would be beneficial if Imogen had an enchantment that they could use to talk to her as well, but the El'aras enchantment was made only for three-way communication. If only he'd taken the time to request something more.

He still could, he realized. Anna had given him a token as a means of reaching her and summoning her, but Gavin was loath to use it for something that was not an emergency. He had no idea how she would respond—or if she would. It seemed he should wait for a time when he actually had the need. There might be others who could help anyway. Given what Davel Chan had said about enchanters in the city, they could find one to help create an additional earpiece for them.

"Then we should go," Gavin said.

He darted across the street. The movement was as quick as he could make it without dipping into his core reserves of power. Gaspar was waiting for him. The old thief was swift, and he moved almost faster than Gavin did when he didn't tap into those reserves.

Imogen stood further along the street, though she wasn't going to break in quite yet. She would wait.

"Are you in position?" Gavin whispered to Wrenlow.

"I'm here."

"You always wanted to come out on a job."

"I wanted to be a part of a job, but I'm not sure that I wanted to be a part of *this* job."

Gavin smiled to himself again, imagining Wrenlow sitting on the rooftop two streets away. Not that Gavin would blame him. There was something to be said about spending time out in the middle of the night with nothing but the darkness as a companion, uncertain of what might happen.

He glanced over toward the building. He knew that Wrenlow wouldn't be able to see much from there, but his focus would be watching the street, not seeing beyond the wall. Still, for *this* job, they needed as many eyes as possible.

Gavin glanced over at Gaspar. "Are you ready?"

"I'm ready as I will be."

"If you want to stay behind, I'm sure Imogen would be more than capable."

"She most definitely would be, but I'm not letting you drag her into this."

"You don't even know what's going to happen," Gavin said.

"I have a fairly good idea about what will take place. Knowing you, whatever plan we have will fall apart, forcing us to fight our way out."

"If that's the case, then I might prefer to have her with me. Especially since the only reason I'm here is because of you."

Gaspar glared at him. "If there's a fight, you'd definitely want to have her with you. I'm here to make sure the plan stays on target."

Gavin started to laugh but stopped when he realized Gaspar wasn't joking. Of course, he wouldn't be. In Gavin's experience, Gaspar rarely joked, and certainly never about anything like this.

They reached the wall surrounding the fortress. Desarra had given them the plans they needed, Wrenlow had confirmed it through his sources, and now...

Now it was Gavin's turn.

"Are you ready?" he asked Gaspar again.

"You don't need to ask a thief if he's ready. I'm always ready."

"I never know. Given your age, I thought maybe you fell asleep."

Gaspar scowled at him. Gavin chuckled, scrambled up the wall, and dropped over to the other side. He immediately rolled, kicking and twisting so that he didn't land in the bells trees.

When he got to his feet, he hissed into the enchantment, "Careful. The trees are dangerous."

Gaspar rolled off the top of the wall and landed next to Gavin, completely avoiding the bells trees. "I noticed. I was impressed you were able to twist out of the way. I thought maybe I'd need to inoculate you after you carved yourself up on those bells trees."

"When did you notice them?"

"I saw the trees out there when we were scouting. Figured you caught sight of them, but these days, I don't even know how much you see. For a man as skilled as you claim you are, I have a hard time thinking that you're really as dangerous as you want me to believe."

Gavin just laughed softly. These days, he didn't feel that dangerous either. "You could've warned me."

"Warning you takes the fun out of it. Besides, I still like to test just how skilled you are."

Gavin shook his head. "You were testing me."

"Everything's a test, boy."

It sounded like something Tristan would say.

Gaspar nodded toward the fortress. "Keep moving. Now that we're inside, we don't want to linger. Your friend will be able to tell us if there's anyone coming, but we have to act quickly."

"Are you still able to hear us?" Gavin whispered to Wrenlow.

"I still can hear you. It sounds a little bit off, but that might just be the way you're talking."

Gavin hesitated. Something sounding off usually meant that there was magical interference. He didn't like it, but there wasn't anything to do about it now.

He started forward through the beautiful garden. There were many different flower beds, all adorned with blooms of different colors—roses, tulips, daisies, among others. The fragrances filled the air, giving a beautiful vibrancy to this place. Bells trees dotted the inside of the wall, a prized possession of many upscale homes in Yoran. Gavin suspected that most of the homeowners grew them for their supposed luck or for their beauty, and that very few of them used them defensively because of their razor-sharp leaves. In a place like the fortress, however, the trees very well could've been part of a defensive plan.

When they reached the outer edge of the fortress, he paused to look over at Gaspar, who stood on the other side of the doorway. Gavin nodded. Gaspar slid over and twisted the lock, which didn't budge, and then began to pick at it. He worked quickly, his nimble fingers activating the lock, throwing the door open far more rapidly than Gavin would've been able to do. He would've used brute force if he was doing this job on his own.

Of course, Gavin knew better than to do this job solo. Though he had worked alone for a long time, there was something about a job like this—going into a massive fortress and taking this kind of gamble—that called for support.

Gaspar stepped inside. Gavin unsheathed his El'aras dagger and followed. It didn't glow—a good sign. Once inside, he quickly scanned their surroundings.

They were in a massive entry hall. Swords lined the walls, all of them exhibited in a way that looked decorative but also deadly. They were made of steel, and they gleamed with the faint light of the single lantern still lit in the entryway. The marble floor displayed an image that seemed to be an incomplete map of the region, which emphasized Yoran's position in all of it.

"Nothing subtle about this," Gaspar whispered. "Given what we've figured out about the layout of this place, your target is likely to be on the third floor. Get moving."

"Not my target. *Our* target. Remember why I took the job."

"I remember. Let's get the boy."

"What about you?"

"I'm your support, and that's it. Helping you find your way through this. Not fighting, if that's what you're asking about. I'm the thief, remember?"

"I'm heading toward the rooms that look like they could hold this boy. You notify me if you see anything," he said, tapping the enchantment, "and maybe intervene if there's something coming my way."

"I'll consider it," Gaspar said. "Get moving. Don't want to be here longer than we have to be."

Gavin shook his head but started up the stairs. They had as much of a floor plan as they were able to obtain. It had taken time on Wrenlow's part to confirm the details of the floor plan, and that had been cobbled together from people who had been here before. Desarra had done it in a day, which left Gavin with questions that Gaspar preferred not to answer.

Despite the double-checking they did ahead of time, there were aspects to the plan that weren't quite right. The door they came across was a few paces away from where they believed it would be, and the landing was slightly larger than they had anticipated. Much of their intel came from someone else's recollection, and building a map on that was difficult.

"How does it look?" Wrenlow asked.

"I wish you could see what I can see," Gavin whispered.

"You could've asked her for a better enchantment."

"I can only imagine what she would've said if I'd suggested she needed to improve the type of enchantment she was willing to give us. It's a wonder that—"

"You two need to be quiet," Gaspar hissed.

"There's no one here," Gavin said.

"You have no idea who might be listening. Do you think you're the only two who have an enchanted way of speaking?"

Gavin froze. He hadn't given much thought to that possibility before, though he probably should have. Knowing what he did of Yoran and the way that people presumably hated magic, he'd found a surprising amount of it throughout the city. Some of it was obvious, but not all. There were aspects to some of the enchantments he'd seen here that had caught him off guard.

"Let's just say you and Desarra did a great job," Gavin said into the enchantment.

Gaspar shot him a look of irritation at the mention of Desarra's name.

"Thanks," Wrenlow said.

Gavin hurried up the stairs and turned the corner, then paused on the third level. He wasn't far from where he needed to end up. He looked all around him and counted the doors. He worked his way along and marked them off.

The sound of footsteps came toward him.

"Gaspar?" he whispered into the earpiece.

"Not me," Gaspar responded.

Gavin spun and found himself face-to-face with what he assumed to be a soldier from his silence and fighting stance. He guessed that this man was skilled with a blade, but there was a difference between skill and *skill*.

Gavin had *skill*.

He twisted, turning the dagger upward and forcing it away. He jammed the attacker on the side of the head with the hilt of his dagger, which knocked him toward the ground. The man didn't pass out from the blow. Instead, he spun his leg. Gavin jumped over it, flipping in the air and landing a kick. His boot connected with the side of the soldier's head, knocking him unconscious.

Gavin glanced down. He couldn't leave him here. An unconscious body would raise questions if another patrol came out, it would rouse the entire guard.

He hoisted the soldier. "Which rooms are empty?" he whispered.

"How am I supposed to know?" Wrenlow said. "The reports we had didn't give us that information. Desarra gave me the layout, and I confirmed it. That's it. We weren't able to determine which rooms were empty and which were not."

"I need to know which ones you *think* might be empty."

"What did you do?"

"Nothing," he said.

"Gavin—"

"You need to just tell me which one you think is empty."

"Maybe the third one," Wrenlow said. "The others should all be bedrooms."

Gavin dragged the soldier down to the third room and leaned his head against the door, listening for a moment. There was no sound from the other side, so he tested the door and gently pushed it open.

A closet.

At least there was that. He could leave the guard here. If the man awakened, then he would raise an alarm, but Gavin hoped he would be gone by that time. Gavin wondered if he might be able to jam the door closed, but there wasn't time.

He closed the door and leaned on it as he looked along the hallway.

Which room do I need?

If only Desarra had said more, though Gavin had a nagging suspicion that she knew more than she was letting on. It was too bad Gaspar had never let him question her.

Once he chose a room, Gavin and Gaspar had to be ready. They were bound to raise an alarm. He scanned the doors and picked one.

He darted forward along the hall to the door. He paused, resting his hand on it and listening, but he heard nothing. He didn't even feel anything on the other side. Gavin twisted the handle and pushed it open.

Two guards stood stationed at another door. They were dressed simply in gray mail and leathers with a short sword sheathed at their sides. One of them carried a crossbow, which would be beneficial if they were able to get to it in time. One of the men had a long, hooked nose, and the other had a scar on his neck. They looked rugged, as if they had been through a scuffle or two. Still, Gavin didn't fear going through them. He'd been around men much rougher than that before.

This was nothing but an antechamber. Gavin slipped in and closed the door as the guards turned their attention to him. He flashed a smile.

Their speed surprised him. Not El'aras quick, but still quick. Enchanted quick.

He twisted and spun in a Sudo move before dropping. He drove his fist toward one soldier's stomach, and the man wrenched out of the way, avoiding his blow. Gavin jumped and tried to land a kick, but their enchantments allowed them to back up more rapidly than he could move.

Both men carried short swords. Gavin wasn't interested in killing them. Not unless he found they'd done something to the boy. Still, if it came down to him or them, he'd have to choose himself. It was the choice he'd make every time.

He focused on his core reserves and called upon that power. As it bubbled up within him, he exploded toward the nearest of the men. When the soldier swung his blade, Gavin struck it down using the El'aras dagger.

The blade bounced harmlessly away from Gavin, clattering to the stone floor. Gavin twisted, punching up and catching the man underneath the chin, sending his head ricocheting back. As he slowed to the next movement in this pattern, he swept his leg around toward the other soldier.

He was gone.

Gavin spun and found the man standing behind him. *That was quick.*

Wrenlow chirped in his ear, though his voice was muted. Gavin ignored it as best as he could, and if there'd been time, he would have silenced him altogether.

He jumped and kicked off a wall, landing with the man across from him.

The small size of this room gave Gavin—and his dagger—somewhat of an advantage. He didn't have to deal with the overall length and difficulty of a sword. Within this space, a dagger was much more useful.

He ducked low and drove his fist forward. The swordsman was quick and cut him off. Gavin rolled to the side, popping up to feign an attack before dipping back down. As he rolled again, the other soldier caught his ankle.

Shit.

Gavin kicked away, but his rhythm had been thrown off. The first attacker was waiting and swung, and his sword cut into Gavin's back. He pushed the pain away, though his mind processed it. It was a fairly deep wound, and if the sword had struck him in the right way, it was possible that it had punctured his lungs.

He tried not to think about what had happened. Even

if it were a punctured lung, Gavin had to keep fighting through it. Thankfully, he healed quickly. If he survived.

When he spun again, he twisted his foot. Pain surged in his back from the movement. Fighting through the pain was an exercise of mental strength. Gavin's training had helped him learn how to ignore such pain, and even now he recognized how to push it to the back of his mind, but he had to be careful. One of the detriments to that kind of training was that he often didn't know just how seriously he'd been hurt.

The swordsman watched him, as if he knew what Gavin was going through. Gavin focused on the core strength within him again and then burst forward. The sudden violent nature of that attack was enough to throw his attacker off guard. He darted forward, weaving through movements, and he stabbed the dagger into the man's shoulder. His sword dropped to the ground. Gavin finished the movement by bringing his knee around and slamming it into the man's face. The soldier crumpled.

Gavin panted for a moment and had to gather himself. When he was ready, he turned toward the door. There was no sound on the other side. He'd made plenty of noise, and anyone outside the room would have heard him, but it didn't seem as if there was anyone there. He tested the door and then pushed it open.

The sleeping chamber was enormous and looked nearly as large as the dormitory where he had first trained with Tristan. That had housed two dozen boys and girls of his age. This was a single room, with a single bed that was massive enough to fit three to four people in it. A silky canopy curved down above it. This room was much nicer than anything he had ever seen.

Who slept in a place like this?

It was quite formal—fancy even. It didn't fit into the rest of the fortress's decor.

Gavin moved inside. There was an emptiness to the room that felt hollow, as if he had missed something. He had no idea why he felt that way, only that he believed it to be true.

He headed back toward the antechamber for a lantern, and the El'aras dagger started to glow.

"Balls."

"What is it?" Gaspar whispered through the enchantment.

"Magic. And a lot of it."

CHAPTER NINE

Gavin backed toward the door and quickly tried to survey everything around him. There had been a guard in the hallway, two in the antechamber, and now there was another one here in this room.

He just hadn't seen them.

The dagger had detected them though. He supposed he should be thankful for the dagger and what it could pick up on, especially its ability to find magic. Gavin held the dagger out from him and used its light to see. He reached the back wall and looked around, but he didn't sense anything moving.

"Have you found anything yet?" Gaspar asked.

"Nothing of much use," he whispered.

He swept the dagger around in an arc, and then he started using a different technique. It was one that he'd found effective when he'd faced others with power, but it was one he hadn't had the opportunity to use in quite some time.

He searched for any feelings of resistance as he moved the dagger around him. Gavin swept the dagger from side to side, but there was nothing. The dagger continued glowing brightly, though the El'aras dagger seemed to glow more brightly around people who had more power.

Gavin remained where he stood. The boy was in the room. He was certain of it.

Why all this protection for a child they'd abducted?

His gaze settled on the bed, and he saw something he hadn't noticed before. The child was sleeping there.

"What's happening in there? Have you found the kid?" Gaspar whispered in his ear.

"I might have," Gavin said.

"Might?"

He took a deep breath and slipped forward, and something struck him. Gavin was knocked back. There *was* a magic user here.

Power struck him in a flurry of movements, but he ignored it. It reminded him of some of the beatings he'd taken when he was still learning. Magical energy attacked him, almost as if it were trying to pummel him. He couldn't tell the source, though there seemed to be *some* direction to it.

Gavin stepped forward again. He braced himself with every step and dove into his core reserves with each one, despite the danger in doing so. There were limits to that power.

He held out the El'aras dagger. Somehow, it seemed as if doing that buffered some of the blows. They didn't strike him quite as hard. He started to sweep it away from him, carving as he took each step. That softened the blows even more. The El'aras dagger cut through whatever magical attack was striking him.

Gavin fought his way forward with the dagger. The attack on him started to ease. Another step, and he reached the bed.

There was no sign of the sorcerer responsible for the attack, though Gavin was certain it *was* a sorcerer. It had to be, given the strength of that attack. It was far more powerful than any enchantment would be capable of.

The child lay there, sleeping soundly. Gavin held onto the El'aras dagger, then he scooped the child up.

What were they thinking, hiring an assassin to kidnap a child?

He should have left it to Gaspar and Imogen. This kind of job seemed more up their alley. Of course, this wasn't so much kidnapping as it was rescue.

He didn't see anything else in the room. The pressure continued to batter him, but Gavin ignored it and tried to fight through it. This proved more difficult now that he'd picked up the child, but he still swept the El'aras dagger out in front of him with his free hand. The power that blasted into him eased with each motion, though not quite as much as it had. Holding onto the child seemed to dull the dagger's effect.

He started toward the door. There was movement beyond.

Had the guards gotten back up?

Gavin had been careful not to kill them.

He took a deep breath and stepped out into the antechamber, bracing for an attack. The magical pummeling persisted, a physical battering with an unseen power, but something else was there too. The two guards were still down, but there was another person here: thin and tall, with a sense of power that came off of him.

The man didn't strike him as a sorcerer, though Gavin admittedly didn't have enough experience with sorcerers to be able to pick one out at first glance. He could feel the magical effect and knew there was a danger to what he detected now.

Is there more that I'm missing?

This newcomer had a balding head, a prominent forehead, and dark eyes that swept around the inside of the chamber. A bright gold ring adorned one hand and a massive earring hung from his left ear.

The man cocked his head, studying him. "What do you think you're doing, taking my child?"

Gavin looked down at the boy he was carrying. He seemed to be sleeping, but Gavin couldn't be quite sure. "Is this your child? I thought it was—"

He didn't have a chance to finish. The man darted forward, sweeping his hand around in a quick flick. The technique was familiar, but he hadn't expected to see a Noru pattern here. Gavin blocked it, twisting around, but as he did, the other man followed suit, changing styles. He frowned at Gavin, but there was something else in his eyes: hunger.

Crap.

Gavin had seen that look on opponents before; the kind that suggested they wanted to fight. They *longed* for the fight. It seemed that this mission was about more than simply recovering the child. This man wanted to use this as an opportunity to challenge Gavin, to test himself. But he wasn't going to get that chance. Gavin wasn't about to be someone else's sparring partner.

"The Captain, I presume?"

The Captain smiled tightly and tipped his head in a slight nod.

He flicked his wrist and held onto the dagger, using it as an extension of himself. The other man was forced to dance back. The Captain turned and dove out of the way, driving his foot upward as he did. It was an effective move, especially with Gavin holding onto the child. He wasn't going to be able to react on that side as quickly as he normally would.

This man seemed to know.

Gavin took a step back. He wasn't going to have much room to maneuver in the small space of the antechamber, especially now that he was holding onto the child and expected to engage in hand-to-hand combat.

He regarded the Captain, trying to take stock of him and get a sense of who the man might be. He was more capable than Gavin had expected.

Gavin rotated to put himself between the child and the Captain, and he sprinted forward, turning the movement so that he could catch the brunt of the attack. He pushed the sudden surge of pain down, forcing his mind to shut it out. He'd known so much pain during his life, and he could ignore it now.

Gavin would be ready for the Captain to make a mistake.

Everyone made mistakes.

The Captain surged forward, driving a twisting hand down. Gavin blocked by turning his hand against it, and he brought his knee up. The Captain parried Gavin with his own knee and twisted it off to the side. It was almost enough to force Gavin to stumble. He mixed in a hint of the drunken sailor technique by teetering forward and catching himself before whipping out with his leg, which he wrapped around the Captain. He kicked, and the Captain went flailing ahead.

Gavin used that opportunity to dart forward, and he drove with a chopping motion, catching the Captain on the back of his shoulder. The man started to fall but spun again.

Gavin was forced to jump back as the magical attack struck him, punching him on the side of the head. He was dazed and shook his head to push that pain away.

It didn't seem fair that he was under both magical and physical attack, but he found that things often weren't fair.

He decided to focus on the magical attack. He had an

idea but didn't know if it would work. If he *had* magic, it would, but otherwise... He embraced the core power and then exploded it outward like he had when he'd been trapped by Tristan and needed to break free of his chains.

The relentless pummeling stopped.

The child gasped.

The Captain glared at Gavin. "What did you do to him?"

"What did *I* do to him?"

The magical assault suddenly made sense.

Had it been the boy? Did I have it wrong?

The woman, the request for help, even her home had all fit.

The only thing that hadn't was the Captain's response.

The Captain kicked, and Gavin brought his leg up to block. He rotated and followed through with the movement, stepping outward and lashing forward with his other foot.

It was a dance.

He twisted and turned, kicked and spun, drove one foot and one fist, using all of the various fighting techniques he'd mastered. It took everything in his power to combat the Captain's moves.

Had he more space, and if he weren't under this kind of attack while trying to hold onto a child, he might've had an easier time. Even that wasn't a guarantee. The Captain was skilled.

"Where did you train?" Gavin asked.

"What?" The Captain was almost breathless.

"Your fighting style is familiar. You're obviously well-trained. I'm just curious where."

He was genuinely curious, but at the same time, he wanted to throw the Captain off to disrupt the flow of his attack. The man took a step back, regarding Gavin for a moment.

"I trained with Santos on the Isle of Isaw."

"Interesting. I haven't heard of—"

The Captain darted forward, using Gavin's distraction against him.

Balls. He *was* skilled.

Gavin was tempted to set the child down, but if he did, then he gave up one advantage that he had. So far, the Captain hadn't been willing to attack Gavin on the side where he held the child.

If the child could be used as a shield...

He hated the idea of using a child to protect himself, but he didn't know if he had much choice in the matter. Not if the Captain was going to keep striking at him like this.

Gavin pushed the child forward, forcing the Captain to turn his attack. He relented, releasing the blow he would have lunged at Gavin with. Instead, he dipped down.

That was the opening Gavin needed. He twisted and kicked his foot out, connecting with the side of the Captain's head. The blow would have been devastating and knocked most people unconscious. Instead, the Captain flowed with the movement, his maneuver making it so he absorbed even more of the attack than Gavin would've expected him to do. He shook his head and then rolled off to the side.

Gavin anticipated the roll. He stepped forward, simultaneously bringing his hand down in a hammering motion and his other foot up. One of the two would strike, but he had no idea which one it would be.

The Captain might jump up, and if he did...

His hand slammed into the back of the Captain's neck. It hurt, like driving in iron. The Captain was thin but also wiry, filled with muscle, and the attack hurt Gavin almost as much as it seemed to be hurting the Captain.

Enchantments.

Gavin smiled to himself. That had to be what it was.

He'd fought many people over the years. Few had considerable magical power but many possessed magical enchantments. In his experience, those with enchantments were quick to use them. Against somebody with considerable training like Gavin, an enchantment might be the difference between surviving a fight and failing.

He darted back and reached for his core energy again. When the Captain turned toward him and started a new attack, Gavin twisted, pushing the child closer to the Captain.

Surprisingly, the child had not come around during the fight. If what Gavin now suspected was true, the child was the sorcerer who'd been attacking him, and Gavin had knocked him out by blasting through his assault.

The Captain ignored the next kick and turned toward him, swinging upward. His attack was off though.

With the way Gavin was fighting and how he held onto the child, the Captain didn't have the same safe ability to continue striking him. He had to be cognizant of where the child was. Gavin started to shift his attack, changing how he faced the Captain, using the child.

Gavin landed another blow to the side of his opponent's head. As before, the pain made it feel like he was striking iron. In any other time, he might've marveled at the enchantment and wanted it for himself. Having a way to withstand a fight would be incredibly valuable.

He was going to have to use some other strategy. He wasn't going to be able to kick through the Captain; not without shattering his own leg. Gavin healed quickly and didn't doubt he would recover, but he might not make it out of the fortress.

A different technique was needed, but it was going to involve something a bit more dangerous.

"Be ready," he whispered to Gaspar.

"Be ready for what?"

"To run."

He turned and shifted the boy from one arm to the other, the suddenness of the movement surprising the Captain. Gavin whipped his leg around and swung it up and over, connecting with the Captain's head. A painful crunch rolled through Gavin. He didn't know if anything was broken, but pain coursed through him.

The Captain cried out.

Gavin landed on his uninjured leg and tested the other.

Maybe broken. Hurt and throbbing, at the very least. He didn't know. He pushed the pain away.

He dove and collided with the Captain, slamming the man's head against the stone. The Captain shook off the blow. Gavin turned, and his leg tried to give out. He focused on his core strength.

He'd done that too often during this attack. He needed to be more careful. Calling upon that core energy always seemed to weaken him, and at this rate, he might fail entirely before he managed to escape.

He spun, using the child's legs as a weapon. The Captain darted out of the way and Gavin kicked, catching him in the groin. It was a cheap technique, but when fighting, cheap was often effective. The Captain grunted, crumpling to the ground.

Gavin started toward the door, and the Captain reached for him. "You aren't going to get away."

"I already have."

He reached the hallway and detected movement. He pushed away the pain but struggled. There was too much agony. The Captain had hurt him, and that was *after* he'd been stabbed. That pain was nothing right now.

Gavin limped toward the stairs.

A guard appeared.

"A little warning would've been nice," he whispered to Gaspar.

"A warning about what?"

"How many guards have you let past?"

"There haven't been any."

Which meant they were somewhere else.

Gavin shook his head. He focused on the guard and kicked. At least he had enough strength remaining to drive the guard back. The man bent over, and Gavin twisted, dropping his elbow down. It caught the guard on the back of his head, and he collapsed.

Gavin stepped forward, but the pain in his leg became too intense.

He called upon the core strength again, using the energy within him, and he took another step. He whipped his leg around and kicked the guard in the side of the head. It was much more rewarding to kick someone who didn't have enchantments of stone protection.

He headed down the stairs, pausing at the landing to see if there was any sign of any movement. Gaspar hadn't been able to give him any word of guards coming. They probably should have had him wait on one of the upper levels rather than on the lower levels. They'd made the mistake of being more concerned about somebody coming through the main level of the fortress.

There was no one around. Gavin staggered down the stairs. The pain still throbbed, but he held it at bay, keeping it at the back of his mind. When he reached the bottom level, Gaspar was waiting for him.

"You got him?"

"I got him," Gavin said.

"What happened to you? You're bleeding."

Gavin looked down. He hadn't noticed. "The Captain. Or the guard. Don't know."

"We were supposed to do this without stirring the Captain."

"I didn't stir him." Gavin nodded toward the door. "Can we do this outside? I don't want to stay here any longer than I need to. Besides, I'm hurting a little bit."

"I didn't think the great Gavin Lorren got hurt."

"He does when he kicks people enchanted with stone."

Gaspar frowned. They reached the door, and noise behind them picked up. Gaspar waved Gavin ahead. He didn't argue.

He limped into the garden and reached the wall. Gaspar grabbed the boy and carried him over. Climbing took all of Gavin's strength and concentration, and he landed on his good leg as he dropped to the other side. He bore the weight of it, but it hurt.

"What happened to you?" Gaspar said. "It's more than just the bleeding."

"I got attacked by a sorcerer," he said, taking the boy back from Gaspar.

Gaspar frowned. "A sorcerer?" He looked back at the Captain's fortress. "In Yoran? What happened to him?"

"I'm carrying him."

CHAPTER TEN

The tavern was quiet, and Gavin stared straight ahead, trying to ignore the irritation within him. Pain lingered, but it wasn't the kind of pain he would have a hard time pushing away. Rather, it was everything else that was difficult for him to ignore. He hadn't been nearly as injured as he'd thought. The knife in his back had hurt, but even that had started to heal. Maybe not normal, but functional. That was enough.

He looked over at Gaspar. He was talking quietly to Imogen at a table nearby and had muted the enchantment. Gavin couldn't hear much of what he said, but Gaspar stood and waved his hands in an animated way, suggesting he was irritated.

This was supposed to have been a straightforward job. Go in, grab the boy, and then return him to Erica. But a sorcerer? That added a wrinkle none of them wanted.

Wrenlow returned from the back room. His eyes were

red, and he had a look of uncertainty. He shook his head, frowning at Gavin as he took a seat across from him. "You sure about this?" Wrenlow asked.

"At this point, I'm not really sure about anything."

"But are you sure the boy is the sorcerer?"

Gaspar paused in his conversation and turned, looking over at Gavin.

Gavin ignored him and watched Wrenlow. "I know what I felt."

"Magic takes time to manifest. It's what I've always read," Wrenlow said. "It requires training. Concentration. It requires somebody to have the time to perfect the necessary skills."

"Sorcerers use spells and other natural items to accentuate power they draw from themselves." That was how Tristan had explained it for him, at least. "Their power is different than enchanters who have a similar power."

"The magic not *quite* the same. They have to place power into something."

Gavin touched the enchantment he wore. "Either way, it's more than I understand."

Wrenlow watched him, saying nothing, though the brightness in his gaze said more than enough. If Gavin were part El'aras, what kind of magic might he have? Their power was different than that of sorcerers *and* enchanters.

"So the boy?" Wrenlow asked.

"I know what I felt."

"How? I mean, *how?*" Wrenlow leaned back, rubbing

his eyes again. It was late, and they were all tired, but probably Wrenlow most of all. He wasn't accustomed to staying up as late as the rest of them. Gavin didn't need much sleep, so staying awake like this wasn't all that difficult for him. He suspected Gaspar had an easy time as well. The old thief struck him as a consummate professional, and they never really needed much sleep. He didn't know about Imogen though. Gavin looked over toward her and the deep frown on her face.

He returned his gaze to Wrenlow. "I don't know how. When I was in the room with them, I was under attack. I could feel the blows striking me." Gaspar turned and watched him. "I thought there was a sorcerer in the room with me. I ignored the pain."

"If he was responsible, there couldn't have been all that much pain," Gaspar said.

"You'd be surprised," Gavin said. "It's not the size of the sorcerer but the source of their power that's the key to their strength. I've faced sorcerers who were massive men who were not nearly as powerful as some much smaller. Think about Cyran. When we faced him, he wasn't the largest of men, but he was incredibly skilled."

Gaspar's mouth twisted into a sour expression at the mention of Cyran's name. "If he was so powerful, then how were you able to ignore the blows?"

"My training has taught me to ignore that sort of thing," Gavin said.

"That's right. Your fabled training. Your master. Ever since *she* left, you've been looking into him."

"I haven't been looking into him since Anna left."

Gaspar stood from the table and hesitated. "Don't think I'm not aware of what you've been doing, boy. I know what you had him"—he nodded to Wrenlow—"looking for. You think he has resources in Yoran I don't have access to? What you're looking into is dangerous." He looked around the Dragon.

Gavin flicked his gaze over to Wrenlow, who shrugged. "If he's alive, I'd like to know more about him."

"If he's alive, then you're not likely to find anything in Yoran."

A creak at the stairs behind him caught his attention, and Gavin swiveled to see Jessica coming down. She smiled, but her expression soon shifted. The tension in the room was palpable. "What did I miss?"

"Nothing," Gavin said.

"Right. Nothing. When it's the two of you trying to figure out who is bigger than who, there always seems to be something," she said. Wrenlow laughed. Jessica shot him a withering look, and he fell silent.

"How's the boy?" Gaspar said.

"He seems to be fine. He's sleeping. We need to get word to Erica that we have him."

"I don't think it's safe for us to leave him upstairs," Gavin said. He still didn't know if Erica knew her son was a sorcerer, but feared she did—and why she'd kept it from them.

"Because he's a sorcerer," Gaspar said.

Gavin turned to him, nodding once. "Yes. That's

exactly the reason. What happens when he awakens and starts to draw upon his power?"

"Well, then I suppose that you go and do whatever it was that you did to incapacitate him the last time," Gaspar said.

"Enough," Jessica said.

She was the only one who had the ability to silence them all. There was something in her tone—a command and a sense of urgency—that none of them wanted to trifle with.

Gaspar nodded, then he headed toward the kitchen and disappeared. Imogen took a seat on the far wall, leaning back and appearing bored.

Jessica came and joined Gavin at the table, perching on the edge of a chair. She had a stack of towels and laid them out on the table. "You're sure about him?" She lifted one of the towels and started folding it.

"As sure as I can be," Gavin said.

"I don't need any more trouble at the Dragon. The last time was more than I could handle."

"It wasn't more than you could handle. You survived."

"Survived. Barely recovered." There was a haunted expression in her eyes. "I don't need that back here again, Gavin. Promise me you'll do everything in your power to ensure that doesn't come back here."

There was a pleading note in her voice, and Gavin wanted to do anything he could to make that promise, but he didn't know. She'd been the reason he'd taken the job. He could see in her eyes that Jessica knew she was at fault.

Still, she was asking for his help.

"I'll do what I can," he said. He took one of the white towels and folded it the same way she did. Jessica watched him, as if doubting he could do it without making a mess of things.

"I know you will." She took a deep breath and let it out slowly, then turned to Wrenlow. "Why don't you go and see if Gaspar needs any help in the kitchen?"

Wrenlow opened his mouth as if to object, but Jessica shot him a hard look. He shook his head and darted off.

"Did you really need to scare him away like that?" Gavin asked.

"We need to talk," she said. "If this boy is a sorcerer, we need to talk about what that means."

"I don't know if you want to get involved in that," he said.

"He's sitting in one of my rooms in my tavern. I think I very much want to know what that means. He's too young, Gavin."

Gavin sighed. "What do you know about sorcery?"

"More than most here."

"That wouldn't be all that difficult."

"You view Yoran as this place where magic is impossible, but it's only because most people are afraid of it. We have our experience with magic, and we recognize the dangers of it."

"Most places in the North are like that," he said.

"Yes, but out of necessity. Haven't you seen that?"

"I haven't stayed in any place long enough to look into

it." It was more than that though—he hadn't really cared to look. Magic was a part of the world, and when there were enchantments or other aspects of the world that involved magic, Gavin didn't run from it. He'd been trained to deal with it. "He's too young to be a sorcerer, but somehow, he is. I don't know what it means."

"Were there others?"

"What do you mean?"

"Others like him."

"He was the one Erica hired me to find." Gavin set the next folded towel down, and grabbed another.

Jessica didn't look up as she took another towel. "I know, but what if there are others within the fortress?" she asked.

It was something Gavin had considered, though he'd discarded the idea. "I don't think so. The Captain was there too quickly."

"Maybe he placed an enchantment to know whether somebody was coming to rescue him."

"It's possible," he said.

"Gavin, there's something you should know."

"What is it? You're hiring another terrible singer?"

She ignored the jab. "I have an enchantment around the Dragon."

Gavin looked around the tavern, though he wouldn't have known if she had.

"I have for quite some time," she admitted.

"I haven't noticed anything."

"It's subtle. It cost me a considerable amount of money to have it placed, and for a long time, it wasn't necessary."

"What sort of enchantment is it?" he asked.

"One designed to ward off those with magical energy."

"I would say you were scammed."

"Why is that?"

"Considering what we recently went through and the way the El'aras marched in, I don't think it really works. That's not even getting into what Cyran did."

"The enchantment needs to be activated."

"Why wouldn't you have activated it?"

An embarrassed flush washed through her face. "I didn't say I was smart about enchantments, only that I knew I should have something placed. It was to protect me. Protect my people. I was young. It was early on in my time owning the tavern, and I was barely twelve when I took it over. Not long after the last sorcerer had been expelled from Yoran."

"How long ago was that?"

"Twenty years," she said.

"Considering everything I've experienced here, I would've expected that the city hated magic for much longer than that."

Twenty years wasn't long enough for people to forget about the power. It wasn't long enough for people to have abandoned magic. Of course there would still be people who embraced that power. It would explain many things.

"Anyway, I had paid for an enchantment to be placed on the tavern. It was a time of great difficulty in the city.

We were all trying to do what we could to remove any magical influence."

"So you reacted by having magic placed on your tavern."

"I reacted by trying to protect the tavern and preparing for the possibility that the people who had magic wouldn't leave." She smiled slightly. "I didn't say it was the best plan."

"Considering how you didn't enable the enchantments, I don't know if it was."

"I didn't leave them completely inactive either," she said.

"What happened to them?"

"It's a complicated story," she said.

Gavin glanced back toward the staircase. It was quiet. He hadn't heard the child move, though he didn't know if he even would. Hopefully, the child would sleep for a long time. Gaspar, Wrenlow and Imogen remained in the kitchen.

"I think we have time," Gavin said.

"There was a time when magic in the city was dangerous. The last sorcerer in Yoran was a violent man, Gavin. You can't imagine what that was like."

"I've been in plenty of places where sorcerers have operated openly."

"Dark sorcerers?"

"It's been my experience that all sorcerers have the potential for darkness," he said.

"Why?"

"I don't know. We saw what Cyran was willing to do. I think the power corrupts them."

Gavin had never met a sorcerer he could trust. Even the one who'd come for Cyran had been untrustworthy. Gavin still waited for him to return for revenge, though he suspected that he and his companions were too insignificant to him. The man had no reason to do so.

"We were scared," Jessica said. "It was the reason I was willing to hire an enchantress, and I paid considerable money to have those wards placed on the Dragon."

Enchantress. That reminded him of what Davel Chan was looking for.

"If you were willing to do that then, why not activate them when the Dragon was under attack by the El'aras?"

"I didn't know anything about the El'aras at the time," she said. "If I had, then maybe I would have, though..." She shook her head. "I don't know. Maybe I wouldn't have. It wasn't the first thing that came to mind."

"I think you should activate them."

"I have."

"And?"

"I'm don't detect anything," she said.

"What makes you think that you would?"

"That's part of what the enchantment is. It's bound to me in a way that's supposed to give me the ability to detect the magic user." She glanced toward the stairs. "And it's *supposed* to separate magical users from their power. All I wanted was..."

"Safety," Gavin said.

"I suppose," she said, taking a deep breath. "I don't detect anything, which makes me wonder whether this boy is what you claim."

Gavin looked toward the stairs. "He is, Jessica. I felt it."

"I know you felt a sorcerer attack," she said. At least she didn't deny it the same way that Gaspar did. "But what if it isn't exactly the way you thought it was?"

"What other way would it be?"

"I don't know. All I'm saying is that maybe there was somebody else there. Sorcerers have a way of concealing themselves. It's possible that a sorcerer might've been able to hide from you."

Gavin shook his head. He didn't think so. But then, at the time, he had been so fixed on trying to get out of that room and away from the blows raining down on him that he hadn't been as focused on whether there was anybody else in the room.

Could there have been another *sorcerer in there?*

"There might be a way for me to tell," he said.

"How?"

"We ask him."

"He's a child," she said.

"Even a child would understand what he was doing."

"Are you sure you want to do this?"

"What do you think I'm going to do?" he asked.

Jessica frowned at him, setting down the last of the folded towels. She'd managed to fold about twice as many as him. "I can see that look in your eye, Gavin Lorren. I know you well enough to recognize that expression. You intend to torture him."

"He's a child. I don't have to torture him. Before we give him back to Erica, we should know. We *need* to know."

"I hope you don't do anything to him," she whispered.

She followed Gavin up the stairs to a room on the second landing. He paused at the door, resting his hand on it. There was nothing from the other side, but he waited for a moment. When he was convinced that there was truly nothing, he pushed open the door.

The boy was resting. Then again, Gavin had thought that the boy had been resting when he found him in the fortress. He unsheathed the El'aras dagger and glanced down at the darkened blade. There was no magic here.

Jessica looked over at him, a troubled expression on her face.

"I'm not going to use it on him," he whispered. "It's my way of determining whether there's any magic."

Gavin headed over to the bed, sat in a nearby chair, and examined the child. Erica had said he was ten, and the boy's thin face reflected his youth. He had long wispy hair and a sharp nose. Freckles on his cheeks made him look even younger. When Gavin had first scooped him up, he had thought that the boy was underfed, but maybe that was just his body. He was sleeping soundly—or seemingly so.

"You can open your eyes," Gavin said.

"He's sleeping," Jessica said.

"He's not sleeping. He wants us to think he is. Look at the breathing pattern. It's too irregular. When someone's asleep, they breathe regularly."

He watched the boy, holding the dagger out.

"I'm sleeping," came a murmured reply.

Gavin smiled. "People don't often answer questions in their sleep either."

There came a soft curse. The boy opened his eyes and looked at him. Dark pupils stared up, reflecting the faint lantern light in the hallway. "Are you going to stab me?"

There was less fear in the boy's voice than what Gavin had expected.

"I didn't plan on it, but you never know. It depends on what you do. If you give me a reason to, perhaps I will."

"Why would I give you a reason to stab me?"

"I don't know. Why *would* you?"

"Gavin—" Jessica started.

He glanced over at her and shook his head.

"Who are you?" Gavin asked, leaning forward and holding the dagger pointed at the boy. He tried to look casual with it, not wanting to appear overly threatening, but at the same time he wanted it to appear somewhat so. He needed the boy to know that he was someone not to be trifled with. He realized he hadn't asked Erica the boy's name. That might have been a mistake. How would they know they had the right person?

"My name is Alex."

"Alex?" Gavin leaned back, frowning. "How did you end up at the fortress?"

"What?"

"The Captain's home. How did you end up there?"

Gavin was convinced the Captain wasn't related to Alex, but he wanted confirmation. He wanted to hear it from Alex that the Captain wasn't his father.

Only then would he be willing to send word to Erica.

"I was taken when training."

"Training?" Jessica asked, stepping forward. "What sort of training?"

"Training," Alex said.

Gavin smiled. It was almost an admission of sorcery, but the boy seemed to recognize that admitting such a thing was dangerous.

"How did you learn to attack me?" Gavin asked.

The control and skill used to pummel him when he was leaving the Captain's fortress had been considerable. If Alex had that level of control, then Gavin wanted to know more about that type of sorcery to make sure he was prepared for it.

"I don't know what you're talking about," the boy said.

"See, I think you do." Gavin leaned forward again with the dagger. Gavin tried to keep from looking too terrifying but wasn't sure if he managed. At the same time, given how dark it was in the room, it was possible that Alex wasn't able to see anything.

He sat back, still holding the El'aras dagger in place. Alex's gaze lingered on it, staring at it almost as if he recognized it.

"I don't know what you're talking about," Alex said again.

Gavin needed him to know his mother had sent them after him, but he still didn't know for sure. Something felt off. Gavin trusted that instinct.

Now wasn't the time to tell Alex that his mother had sent them.

Not until he knew more about Alex and his magic.

"If that's the way you want to play this out, then that's fine. But you're here, and I'm the one who broke you out." Gavin waited to see if there was going to be another attack, but he didn't feel anything. "And if you try to use magic on me, I'll know. And you should also know that I was able to withstand the last attack."

Alex watched him. "I don't know what you're talking about."

Gavin could only smile. At least he was consistent. "I hope not. If there's any evidence of magic while we're here, we're going to have trouble."

"I don't know what you're talking about," he said.

"Go to sleep, Alex. We'll talk more when you wake up."

Gavin stood and headed toward the door, and he pulled Jessica with him. He waited outside the room for a moment, lingering with his hand on the door. He felt no sense of magic, and the El'aras dagger didn't start to glow. If Alex attempted to draw upon power, he couldn't feel it. It was possible he wouldn't even be able to detect it.

"I don't know much about that boy, but he's hiding something," Gavin said, turning to Jessica.

She watched him, frowning deeply.

"What is it?"

"You're right," Jessica said.

"Right about what?"

"They're hiding something."

Gavin nodded. "That's what I just said."

"But you're not right about what they're hiding."

"What do you mean?"

"That's not a boy. That's a girl."

CHAPTER ELEVEN

The street was dark, and Gavin paced slowly with his hand on the hilt of the El'aras dagger. He was prepared, should anyone appear, though mostly he was concerned about Erica. She had deceived them, though Gavin should've expected it. It happened often enough that he was accustomed to it.

Besides, why hire someone like me for a task like rescuing a child?

Gavin wanted answers. Until he had them, he wasn't going to release the boy—the girl, he had to remind himself—back to her.

There were shadows along the street, but he didn't see anything. He hated the darkness, and his eyesight had never been good at night. He didn't want magic around him, but he was actually thankful when the El'aras dagger glowed because it gave him some light in situations where he wouldn't otherwise have it.

Gavin searched for signs of movement, but there wasn't anything. He continued pacing back and forth along the street. At one end, a small group of people made their way up the street. He could smell the ale drifting off of them, and from the way they staggered and stumbled, he suspected that they had just come from one of the five taverns that lined the area. None of them were quite as nice as the Roasted Dragon, though Gavin might be a little bit biased.

He stayed in the shadows, watching until they passed. It was as easy for him to wait in the alley as it was for him to pace along the street, but on the street at least he was moving. At least he was doing something.

Attacking the Captain had been a dangerous plan from the beginning. Gavin should've known better than to have rushed in there without more intel. But the information that Desarra had provided and that Wrenlow had corroborated suggested it was reasonable.

He leaned back, watching the street. She was to meet him soon.

It was a dark night. No moon. No stars. Hints of clouds drifted across the sky. The only light came from the few street lanterns. In this section of the city, there wasn't generally a need for more.

The crowd of people was the only grouping that he had seen since coming out here. Every so often, there would be a single person making their way, usually stumbling. Never anything more. Even the constables didn't patrol at this time of night.

He lost track of how long he'd been waiting. His attention peaked when he finally saw a shadowed cloak moving along the street. Erica.

She'd promised she would come alone, but then again, she had also claimed she was looking for a boy. And had said nothing about him—or her—being a sorcerer. As she moved along the street, Gavin stepped out of the alley and joined her.

She jumped but calmed herself quickly. "I wasn't sure if you were going to come. I didn't know if I had given you enough time."

Erica looked just as lovely as she had when he'd first seen her. Her green eyes were a little darker in the night, and the cloak hid the figure Jessica had teased him about.

"I'm here," he said.

"Did you find him?"

Gavin studied her for a few moments. "I found him."

"He was there? Was he… was he hurt?"

"No. But you should know that extricating him from the fortress was harder than we had anticipated."

"I told you I was willing to pay. You were the one who named the price."

Gavin grunted. "I did. And you were also aware that it wasn't the kind of job I normally take."

Was that why she had hired me? Could it have been that she wanted the assassin, not that she wanted me to rescue the boy —girl?

"What do you mean?" she asked.

"You knew what kind of work I normally do." They

paused at a street intersection, and he turned to face her. "I'm starting to wonder if you hired me for that specific purpose."

"I wanted my son back."

"Really? Describe him to me."

"What do you mean?"

"Describe your son to me. I want to make sure I brought the right person out of the fortress."

"He's about ten. Wispy brown hair. He has delicate features, sharp cheekbones, a pointed nose. A little rosiness to his cheeks. You can't miss him. There's even a single mole right here." She pointed to her left cheek.

That could have described Alex. Of course, it could have described many people in Yoran. Many of them had the same wispy brown hair, along with the fine, almost delicate features that Alex had.

"Any other distinguishing characteristics?"

"What is this about? I thought you'd found him. That's why I came to meet you."

"I just want to make sure that I did the job you hired me to do," Gavin said. He placed his hand on the hilt of the El'aras dagger. "I think I told you when we first met that I'm typically hired for different purposes." He watched her. "At the time, you said you didn't know what those were, but I wonder if you know more than you're letting on."

"Gavin?"

"What were you really after?"

"Where is my son?" She raised her voice, and there was something almost panicked about it.

He was tempted to believe her. Part of him *wanted* to believe her, but he didn't know if he should. Perhaps that was his mistake in the first place. He had believed that she was a mother searching for a lost son, and he hadn't even given as much thought as he should've to the possibility of who she might be and what she might be after.

"You came to the Dragon looking for a specific person," he said.

If she'd come to the Dragon for Gaspar, it might have been different. Even a thief might've been better for the job than an assassin. At the time, Gavin had thought it was simply a case of a rumor of a name, but it had to be something different. Perhaps something more. He should have thought more about it before now.

Gavin had been used by others over the years, and for the most part, it had worked out for him. He hadn't killed anybody going to the fortress. Nothing had been done that couldn't be undone. Only, he *had* attacked the Captain. If the Captain learned who he was and decided to come after him, he'd have to deal with a different set of consequences. With him connected to power within the city, he had the potential to be dangerous.

"I came because I heard you were skilled. All I wanted was somebody capable of getting my son. I figured it needed to be somebody with enough talent for that."

The panicked sound in her voice picked up, and yet

this time there was something else within it that troubled Gavin even more—almost as if she were acting.

Now he was suspicious.

He held onto the El'aras dagger, but he didn't withdraw it.

"There are probably stories about me within the city," Gavin said. "And if you leave Yoran, there are definitely stories about me and about the person I've been in those places." He leaned forward and held her gaze. "You hired an assassin to find your son."

He looked for some sign of shock. Concern. Worry. Nothing on her face changed.

"You said you found him," she said.

"What were you expecting me to do?"

"Did you find him?" There was a harder edge to her voice.

Gavin smiled. "Who is he?"

"You found him, though?"

"If you don't answer my question, I'm not going to answer yours," Gavin said.

"You will answer."

A strange streamer of green swirled around him, attempting to trap him. It matched the color of her eyes.

Magic.

Of course it would be. Why would he have expected anything else? She'd been willing to come into a place like the Dragon and had fearlessly approached him—a man she claimed to have heard of, one who had a reputation in

Yoran and elsewhere of being a dangerous assassin. Yet she had been unfazed in asking for his help. People simply didn't approach assassins if they didn't have some sort of power of their own.

"You're going to regret that," Gavin said.

"Where is he?" she asked again, her tone harder than before.

Gavin started to focus, paying attention to the core energy inside him. Out in the darkness of the street, it was easier to embrace that energy deep within him. He didn't know if it was magic like Anna claimed, but if it was, then it was a part of him that he'd been trained to reach. As he attempted to access that power, to dive deep to grab hold of it, he could feel it surging up within him.

It gave him the strength to find a way to reach for the bindings around him that came from her green swirl of power. He focused on them.

The Chain Breaker.

That was his nickname, earned through the games he'd played with Tristan.

The leathers and the ropes had been the easiest. The chains had been more difficult. It wasn't until he had learned to tap into that core energy that he'd been able to find a way to escape from the chains, when he was no more than thirteen or fourteen. They had given him his nickname.

Over time, Tristan had used heavier and heavier chains as a test meant to see whether Gavin could escape. He had required more and more strength to progressively break free from them.

Now he had to wonder if Tristan had been training him for something else.

Gavin pushed out, exploding out of the bindings around him. He withdrew the El'aras dagger and was not surprised to find it glowing. He darted forward, jabbing the tip of the dagger toward the woman. In the past when he'd broken free of magical bindings, he hadn't thought he was using magic at the time, but he probably had been.

"Try that again, and you will find this blade buried in your neck," he said.

She watched him. There was no fear in her eyes, only determination mixed with something surprising. Hatred. "Did you find him?"

"No," Gavin said.

"What?" She jerked free, using a hint of her green magic to blast at him and stagger away. He didn't fight her at this point. He simply stood, watching. "I thought you said that you found him."

"You hired me to find a boy. I didn't find a boy."

"A girl," she whispered, shaking her head. "Of course. He was masking the presence. Clever."

"What was that?"

Erica twisted her hand, and another swirl of green began to work its way around Gavin, thickening and becoming substantial. This time, it started to spiral up from the ground, working more and more rapidly as it weaved up and around him. It started to trace around his thighs, winding up like vines growing around him. He focused on his core energy and tried to break free, but the way that she was holding it made it difficult for him to blast out of.

Instead of trying to fight his way out, Gavin used the El'aras dagger. He carved through the green vine. It peeled away, dropping to the ground before disappearing.

He darted forward, and this time he jabbed the dagger into her shoulder. She cried out.

Gavin withdrew and stood across from her. "I warned you."

"You really are everything I expected," she said.

"Who told you to expect it?"

"The Maker of Chains."

Gavin took a step back, staring at her. The choice of words couldn't be coincidental.

What did she know?

"Who is the Maker of Chains?"

Could it be Tristan?

He'd trained Gavin to be the Chain Breaker, so it would make sense, but Tristan wouldn't come after him like this.

She smiled. "Where is she?" she asked.

Gavin shook his head. "I need to know who sent you."

Somebody knew about him and what he was capable of doing.

Was it one of the El'aras?

He didn't think that Anna or any of the people with her would have betrayed him. He stared at Erica, uncertainty filling him in a way it hadn't in a while.

It wasn't that he was afraid of this sorceress—or enchantress, he had to acknowledge. The bindings of power around him were different than what he'd seen from sorcerers, although he suspected that they were all on the same spectrum of power. She could have some strange enchantment that allowed her to use her magic in this way. If he could find it, he could disarm it and keep her from using it on him.

"You will bring me to her."

"I don't think so," Gavin said.

"You will. She is far too dangerous for you. If you don't, everyone you care about in that filthy tavern will suffer."

Magic started to swirl away from her hand again, and Gavin darted forward, anger surging up within him. He jabbed the dagger into her other shoulder and then spun, kicking behind her knees. She dropped to the ground.

When she was down, he brought the dagger up and slipped it underneath her neck. "You aren't the first person to make a threat to my friends, but I warn you it will be the last time that you make one."

She watched him, unconcerned. The lack of concern in her eyes was the most troubling thing about her. He'd expected some response, and Gavin didn't even know how to react.

He had to have answers. If she hadn't mentioned the name, he might have been willing to kill her and leave it at that.

The Maker of Chains.

Had he not believed that Tristan lived, none of this would've been an issue. But he *did* believe it. Anna wouldn't have said that to him were it not true. She wouldn't have come to him and shared with him that there was something he needed to know were it not true.

Gavin grabbed Erica. He pulled her along with him. She had injuries to both shoulders, but it was possible she could heal herself with magic.

He needed someplace to hold her. Bringing her to the Dragon, close to where he now had the girl, wasn't the right strategy. There was another place he *might* be able to bring her.

As they moved through the streets, she didn't fight. She said nothing to him. They passed a few other people, but Gavin didn't look in their direction, and they didn't look in his. He was mostly concerned about running into one of the constables. They might question why he was dragging a woman with him, and he'd have to either reveal she was an enchantress or knock them down.

He didn't have any trouble though. The forest rose in the background as he reached the street, and he was getting tired. He'd been forced to draw upon his core reserves as he pulled her along, worried about her using some of her power on him. There was a limit to how much he could hold, and he feared he drew close to that limit.

When he reached Cyran's home, the windows were dark like they had been in the days since Gavin had sent him off with the El'aras. He quickly unlocked the door, tossing her in front of him, where she sprawled out on the floor. He stepped inside and closed the door behind him.

"What are you going to do with me?" she asked. It was curiosity, not concern, that filled her voice. There was still the edge of hatred there.

"You and I are going to talk."

"Here?"

"Did you have a better place in mind?" he said.

A layer of dust hung over everything in the home, and Cyran had emptied almost everything he'd kept here. There were no furnishings other than a table and pair of chairs. The cabinets had been cleaned out. The air had a stale, harsh stink to it.

"There's something off about this place."

"I'm sure there is. It was once a sorcerer's lair."

He didn't know if that would intimidate her or not, but if it did, then good. Maybe she could detect something magical about it and could pick up on some element of the residual energy that remained following Cyran's departure. Even if she couldn't, he didn't care. All he cared about now was holding her somewhere, although he didn't know if he'd be able to keep her here either.

He lifted her again and threw her into one of the chairs. "Tell me about the Maker of Chains."

"You're concerned."

"No. Simply curious."

She glared at him. "I can tell when a man is concerned. When I came to you at the Roasted Dragon, you were not worried, which surprised me. Most men would have been concerned about the job I hired you for."

"I'm not most men."

"No, you are the great Gavin Lorren." She said his name with a flourish and with a hint of an accent, a familiar sound that suggested that she knew something more about him than even he did, along with something of a sneer to it.

The only other person who had said it in a similar way had been Anna—though without the sneer—and the sorcerer. Maybe the Maker of Chains was not Tristan at all. It could be the sorcerer who'd trained Cyran.

Gavin would have no reason to believe the sorcerer would have left him alone—no reason other than the fact that he'd sent the sorcerer away. He'd completed the job, and that alone should've been enough reason for the sorcerer to move on, but Gavin had enough experience with sorcerers to know that they didn't simply leave someone they found valuable. Given what he had done on behalf of the sorcerer, Gavin had proven he was valuable to him. That could have been a mistake.

He let out a heavy sigh and pulled the chair out, sitting across from the enchantress. He watched her for a reaction. The panic and the pleading notes that had been in her voice were gone. Now there was nothing more than a sense of amused confidence. It was so different than the woman he'd seen before.

"What else do you know about me?"

"You are Gavin Lorren. An assassin for hire. A man widely known as one of the most skilled in this part of the world." She leaned forward. "And perhaps somebody with more talent than the rumors would suggest." That was a hint about magic, though he wouldn't acknowledge that. Her smile faded into a slight pout. "Is that not enough? I thought having a reputation like that would be all a man like you would need."

"Perhaps," he said.

"Perhaps you are wondering whether I know you are known as the Breaker of Chains." She glared at him. "Intriguing that there is a Maker of Chains and a Breaker of Chains. Don't you think?"

"Who is he?"

She continued to glare at him. "I will keep that to myself."

"Fine. Keep it to yourself all you want. I'll hold you here until you decide to talk."

"How can you hold me here when you're trying to protect her?"

Gavin got up and glanced down at her shoulders. The bleeding had stopped. It dried around her robes, though it wasn't nearly as bloody as what he expected. He ripped the fabric and wasn't surprised to see that the wounds had completely recovered.

He hurriedly jabbed the El'aras dagger into her shoulders again. She winced and clenched her jaw without crying out, but by limiting her ability to move her hands, he minimized the type of magic she could use. He realized that there was something else he could do: eliminate her magic altogether.

Cyran had used a poison on him that had taken away his magic, even though he wasn't aware of it at the time. That was what he needed now.

Could Cyran have suspected that I had some magical tendencies?

He left her sitting in the chair and kept an eye on her as he headed toward Cyran's cabinets. He hadn't spent much time searching through them. They were empty, but he doubted that Cyran would've left them completely barren. He wouldn't have had the time. Gavin searched through the cabinets for anything useful.

If only he had paid more attention during Tristan's training when it came to poisons. He'd been so much more focused on honing his fighting techniques. There wasn't anything in the cabinets he could use.

He dragged her to the back room. Cyran's home was small and compact, but it *was* a sorcerer's lair. There had to be something more here. He searched the home, looking all around him for a reason that Cyran would have wanted to have *this* place.

When he reached the rug along the floor, he paused.

He'd looked everywhere else. Why not *beneath* it?

He rolled up the rug, and a small trapdoor caught his attention.

Gavin smiled. He flipped the door open, and stairs led down into the darkness. There weren't any lanterns here, and he suspected that was because Cyran wouldn't have needed them. As a sorcerer, he would've had some way of casting his own light.

Gavin lifted her over his shoulder and started down the ladder. When he reached the bottom, complete darkness enveloped him. He wasn't able to see anything other than the faint light overhead.

He continued forward, feeling his way slowly. When he took a few steps, the floor started to glow. The tension within him faded. That was useful magic.

A narrow hallway led to a small corridor. When he reached the door at the end, he paused. The door was made of iron, and there were symbols all across it. Gavin tested the handle, finding it locked.

He set the woman down. "How do you open this?"

"I'm not going behind a sorcerer's door."

Gavin tested the door again, resting his hand on the handle. Gaspar might have known. If only he were here.

Maybe he could be.

Gavin tapped on his enchantment. "Gaspar, if you can hear me, I need you to come to the edge of the city to Cyran's home. There's a trapdoor in the back room. Go down into it, and you'll find me."

There was silence. It was possible Gaspar didn't have

the enchantment on him at the time. Finally, there came a crackling.

"Why?" Gaspar asked.

"Because Erica is an enchantress. Or a sorcerer. I don't really know."

There was a brief moment of hesitation, and then Gaspar said, "I'm coming."

CHAPTER TWELVE

Gavin looked at Erica and held out the El'aras dagger. The home was dusty and old; long since abandoned. He had not spent much time here ever since chasing Cyran from the city, though perhaps he should have investigated it.

"That's an interesting blade you carry," she said.

"It is, isn't it?"

"I heard there was an El'aras infestation within Yoran."

"Infestation? I think you might need to be a bit more careful using terms like that. If you know anything about the El'aras, you would know that they would be a little touchy about such an insult."

"I know more than you can ever imagine about the El'aras."

Gavin frowned at her. "Do you?" He knew almost nothing about her. He needed to use this time and this opportunity to find out more. There was something more about her than what he had seen so far. He suspected she was not a mere enchantress. If she were, she'd be much more uncomfortable with everything that had gone on. It suggested to him that she truly was a sorcerer, though he had never met a sorcerer quite like her. She had magic and enough skill to heal herself, which suggested immense talent.

"What do you want with this girl?" he asked.

"It's not what I want with her. It's what someone else wants."

"The Maker of Chains."

"Yes," she said.

"Why?"

Gavin had so far chosen not to reveal that the girl had magical ability. He didn't want to release that information quite yet. That had to be held back until Erica proved she knew something. She might already know the girl was magically gifted.

"Who do you think she is?" she asked.

"It doesn't matter who I think she is. It matters who your Maker of Chains thinks she is."

"As you can already tell, he feels that she is somebody important. By providing her to him, you will have done a great service. Would you not want to do a great service on behalf of the Maker of Chains?"

Gavin leaned back against the wall. "Should I want to?"

"Yes. You should very much want to."

"I'm done working for mysterious employers," he said. "And sorcerers."

"We had a deal. I might not be who you thought me to be, but you agreed to the terms."

"I agreed to the terms when you were a mother looking for a missing son. And if you heard anything about the El'aras infestation, as you call it, then you would know that there was a sorcerer acting within Yoran at the same time." He watched her face, and she showed no expression. "You are in his chamber."

"This is the lair of an *active* sorcerer?"

He shook his head. "Not any longer."

"Interesting," she said softly, some of the edge in her tone shifting.

"I defeated him. He's gone from Yoran."

"I'm well aware that there are no sorcerers currently active here."

"Why?"

"Because otherwise I wouldn't be here," she said.

He furrowed his brow. "What do you mean?"

She shook her head. "With all of your potential and all of your talent, you still don't know?"

Gavin stared at her. "Consider me uninformed."

"It's more than just being uninformed. I would say you're ignorant."

"Careful. This ignorant person was the one who managed to incapacitate you."

"Even the dumbest can get lucky at times."

"Is it luck, or is it skill? Do you think I was so poorly trained?" he said.

She glared at him.

Gavin smiled, and he started to laugh. "You really are an interesting woman."

"Why?"

"Here you are, trapped, and yet you remain defiant. I find that intriguing."

"I'm sure you would." She moved, reaching for her robe and pulling it around her.

Gavin realized that her wounds had already begun to heal. He darted forward and prepared to stab again, and she held her hand up, trying to block him. There was no attempt at magic in it.

"There's no need to do that again," she said.

"I don't need you attempting to escape."

"Have I looked as if I'm trying to escape?"

"Only because you can't. Not right now," he said.

"You might be surprised at what I can do."

Gavin glanced over to the door. "What do you know about a sorcerer's lair?"

"More than you."

"Obviously. I don't have any magic."

"Are you sure about that?"

"I don't have *your* kind of magic," he said.

She arched a brow. "Are you sure about that?"

Gavin let out a heavy sigh, and he held onto the El'aras dagger. He watched the blade out of his peripheral vision, waiting to see if she might use a hint of magic. He wanted to be prepared for the possibility that she might draw upon something.

Of course, he didn't know if her magic was going to be too potent for him. He watched for something in her eyes, some expression that would suggest that he needed to be more careful, but he didn't see anything.

"Just tell me why he wants her," Gavin said.

"You obviously have uncovered the secret about her," Erica said. Her voice had softened, but given the way that it had changed during their interaction, he didn't know which one was really her.

Is she the hard-edged woman who was confident and strong? Is she the one who was panicked and scared at the idea of her son being taken from her? Or is she this person, the one who seems thoughtful, almost pensive?

He didn't know. Maybe it didn't matter.

He smiled. "I've discovered a little bit about her."

"A little bit. You wouldn't have been quite so on edge had you not discovered more."

Someone with the power Alex had demonstrated would be a threat to someone like her. *That* was the reason she'd hired Gavin, hoping that he'd be the man his reputation said he was.

"You wanted her dead," Gavin said.

"I wanted her removed."

The choice of words struck him. They were the same words that had been used when he'd been instructed to find the Apostle.

"Removed. Does that mean dead? You *did* hire an assassin, after all."

"An assassin who makes choices." She looked up at him, holding his gaze. "Did you think I was so poorly prepared?"

"No," Gavin said.

"Good. I was well aware of your predilections. You make choices. You decide who lives and who dies. An interesting choice for an assassin, wouldn't you say?"

"I would say I can be picky with my jobs," he replied.

"Interesting. Picky with your jobs when you're an assassin for hire."

"Doesn't mean I don't get to make a choice about which jobs I take."

She smiled at him. "I suppose not. Is that something your master taught you?" She sneered as she said the word "master."

"So you didn't want the girl dead," he said.

"It wouldn't have been the worst outcome," she replied.

Gavin had saved Alex, so what would she think of *that* outcome? "What do you want with her now?"

"We want the same as we wanted before."

"Which is?" he asked.

"The danger controlled."

Gavin chuckled. "I would suggest that you're the danger that needs to be controlled."

"Only because you don't quite see the truth. I'm not sure you're *capable* of seeing the truth, but you will. In time, I suspect that you will."

He frowned and shook his head. "Anyway. What were you going to do with her?"

"I was going to take her from the city. Yoran is not a place for someone like that."

Gavin could only shake his head again. "I want to know what you planned for her."

"Will it change that much for you?"

"No," he said, "but it might change something for you. If you give me a reason to let you live, then…" He smiled, spreading his hands. He held the El'aras dagger out at her, watching it. It was glowing a little bit, just a faint light now, but enough that he recognized that she was pulling on some power. "The more you do that," he said, nodding to the dagger, "the more you give me reason to make certain you don't walk out of here. As we've determined, I choose my jobs. In this case, I could choose to make *you* my job."

She started laughing softly. "You are everything I was hoping that you would be." She got to her feet, and she took a step toward him.

Gavin pointed the dagger at her, waiting for her to try to move closer to him. She made another attempt, but he jabbed toward her with the dagger. "You've already seen that you aren't going to be able to use your magic on me," he said.

"You might disrupt some of what I can do, but I doubt you can disrupt *everything* I can do."

She spread her hands off to the side.

Gavin didn't expect her to hold him any better than she had the last time. She had already tried to wrap him with some sort of vine magic that had crawled up his legs. Were it not for the El'aras dagger, he would have already succumbed to it.

The blade started to glow even more. She was intensifying her magic.

The ground started to tremble.

Balls.

"I don't know where you are, but I need you to get here soon," he said into the enchantment.

"I'm trying, but I hit a bit of a snag," Gaspar said.

"What sort of snag are we talking about?"

"The sort that involves the constables."

Gavin looked across at the woman. Whatever she was doing was building rapidly. If he waited, she was going to be able to complete it. He had no idea whether this magic would be something he would be able to withstand. He needed to act—and quickly.

Using the El'aras dagger, he darted forward…

And slammed into what seemed to be a wall.

She watched him from the other side of whatever magical enchantment she was building. Gavin pressed on it, but the invisible barrier was too much for him. He tried to jab through it with the El'aras dagger, but that didn't accomplish anything. He stabbed again and again, but with each attempt, he met the ongoing resistance.

He took a step back.

The ground continued to tremble. The stone overhead started to shake, debris raining down around him. If he remained here for too much longer, he was going to be caught by whatever this attack was.

Gavin had no idea what was taking place, only that it had considerable power to it. He threw up his hands and protected his head.

He ducked down and backed away. If he knew what was on the other side of the door, he might head there, but there wasn't any way for him to open it. He turned, moving toward the other end of the hall and toward the ladder.

A section of the ceiling dropped, crashing in front of him. The sound was terrible inside of the confines of the tunnel. Gavin darted back, trying to stay free of the raining debris. The enchantress—or sorceress, given the strength she demonstrated—was gone.

Everything still trembled around him. He could feel the effort of it as everything started to shake. The lair was going to collapse on him.

"If you're still up there, you need to keep moving," Gavin said. "She's gotten away from me."

"She's what?"

"She collapsed the tunnel. I can't get out the way I came in. Get back to the Dragon. Make sure Alex is safe."

"First you abduct her, and now you want to ensure she's safe?" Gaspar asked incredulously.

"I think the sorceress wanted her dead."

"She's a sorceress now and not an enchantress?"

"Which is why we have to try to understand what's going on," Gavin said.

The shaking persisted. He looked all around him to see if there was anywhere he could go, but the ceiling started to crack. Already it was falling, and he could feel the energy in here starting to build, the pressure of it was almost more than he could endure. He backed up, looking toward the wall, and the only place he could go would be toward the locked door.

Gavin reached the door. The stone continued to tremble and collapse all around him. He didn't have much time. He reached for the handle and pulled.

Nothing happened.

"Dammit, Cyran, let me in," he whispered.

He called upon the energy within him, the remaining reserves he had, and he jerked on the handle. This time, there was more shaking, and Gavin didn't know if it was coming from all around him or if it was something he was doing. It seemed as if it was the ceiling, the floor, even the walls.

Gavin focused on his hand, thinking about what he did when pushing out through his core reserves. If he could do something similar now, he hoped he could break the door open. All he had to do was force that out of him…

He pulled.

The energy within him exploded.

He'd never felt anything quite like that before, but as it burst free of him, he could feel something shifting. The change was dramatic, almost overwhelming, and within that change, he could feel some part of him shifting as well.

He pulled on the door again, and it came open. Gavin darted into the room beyond and pulled the door closed, listening as it clicked and sealing himself inside. He breathed heavily, trying to slow the panic that had set in. The tunnel collapsed on the other side of the door. Thunderous explosion rumbled as the entirety of the tunnel was destroyed.

He didn't even need to open the door to know what had happened. Gavin held his hand on the door, feeling the trembling on the other side. He remained there for a long moment and took another deep breath, then turned and saw the room on the other side of him. A pale glowing light radiated from the stones. Sorcery. It was subtle—and impressive.

It was enormous—far larger than he would've ever expected—and filled with strange artifacts. Out of everything in the room, what drew his attention was a table with a brightly glowing blade resting on it.

He tapped on the enchantment. "Gaspar?"

There wasn't any response.

He still needed to reach the old thief, but the contents of the room intrigued him.

Gavin headed to the table and paused in front of it, studying the blade. It was similar to the El'aras dagger in the way it was constructed. The deep gray appearance reminded him of the El'aras, but the styling was something altogether different. The blade itself had a slight curve to it, and symbols along its length obviously had meaning, but he had no idea what they were. He studied them and felt like he should recognize them, but he didn't. Not El'aras, at least not that he thought. The kinds of weapons they forged were more decorative, with intricate carvings along the hilt and the blade guard. This one had a simple leather-wrapped hilt and a forked blade guard on either side.

Gavin reached for it, and an invisible barrier surrounded the blade, preventing him from touching it. He pressed his hand forward again, and again he felt resistance from a barrier that kept him from being able to reach it.

Poking it with the El'aras dagger didn't help. It was glowing just as brightly as the other blade.

Strange.

It must have been some sort of protection that Cyran had placed to ensure that only he was the one to reach the sword.

But why? What about this sword was so important to Cyran that he would want to protect it so?

Gavin grabbed the El'aras dagger with both hands and jabbed it down with a firm grip, stabbing into the barrier. It bounced off, and he went flying. A jarring sensation rolled through him. He dusted himself off and stood back up, and he cursed under his breath.

"Gavin?"

The voice came in his ear. It was faint, as if the magical

enchantment was muted, but he could hear Wrenlow's voice.

"Wrenlow, can you hear me?"

"Not very well."

"Gaspar needs to head back. If you can reach him, call him back. The woman who hired me is a sorcerer, and she escaped from me."

"What do you mean she escaped from you?"

"Only that. She attacked me with magic, and I realized she was a sorcerer. She got free of me. As I told Gaspar, we need to make sure Alex is safe. Erica's going after her because she wants her dead."

Even that might not have been completely accurate. It could be that she only wanted Alex removed, whatever that meant. He had to get out of here. Then he had to go and protect the Dragon.

Again.

Because of me.

Again.

Shit.

Gavin stabbed at the barrier once more, but his dagger bounced off the protection.

He didn't have time to mess with this. Now that he knew where to find Cyran's lair and that there were interesting things here, he could come back, assuming he could somehow escape it in the first place.

He pulled on the door. He hadn't expected it to close and lock, but something sealed him inside. He jerked on it with all his strength and tried to pry the door open. Still, nothing changed. Taking hold of the handle, Gavin squeezed and focused on the reserves of energy within him.

He hated that he kept going toward that power, and at the same time, he could no longer deny that it *was* some sort of power. The more he accessed it, the more certain he was that it was tied to something within him.

It had to be related to magic. Magic he controlled.

Gavin yanked on the door while pulling on the reserves of energy within him. The energy built, and then it exploded out from him. The door came open. He stood there for a long moment, trying to understand just what he was seeing.

Debris was piled so high that he couldn't possibly dig his way out. There wasn't anywhere for him to go. He was trapped.

"Gavin?" Wrenlow whispered through the enchantment.

"What is it?"

"I think the sorcerer is here."

There was a shout and a scream, and then everything from his side went silent.

"Wrenlow?" Gavin said.

There was complete silence.

"Wrenlow?"

He was gone.

Gavin looked out at the heaping pile of stone. Somehow, he was going to have to get out of here. The enchantment crackled again. Another scream came echoing through it. He couldn't identify *who* had screamed.

Anger built within Gavin.

He stared at the obstacles before him.

He was the breaker of chains. Could he be the breaker of stone?

CHAPTER THIRTEEN

The pile of stones seemed impossible for Gavin to find any way through. He thought about how he had been taught to break through chains and the way he had been taught to hold onto that core energy within him to do so. The only problem was that this was something entirely different.

He leaned on the stones, pushing his shoulder against it. He used contact to break through bindings before, so he hoped it would work now. If he could use that, he could break free of the stone, then get out of here.

As he pressed his shoulder up against the stone and focused, he couldn't feel anything change. Even as he attempted to dig into the core reserves that he knew he had, there wasn't anything.

What about using the dagger?

Gavin had no idea if he could even push power out

that way, but the El'aras dagger *was* magic. If *he* had it as well, he had to think it would work for him.

Gavin took a deep breath and focused on the core energy within him. In order to embrace that power, he was going to have to recognize that it was more than just energy.

He stabbed at the stone. The El'aras dagger was powerful, but as he slammed it into the stone, it sent some of the rock flying off to the side and raining down. It wasn't going to be enough. He tried again, calling upon the core reserves of power within him, and he jabbed at the stone.

As before, it didn't do enough—not nearly enough. It was possible it would work, but even if it did, it was going to take far too long for Gavin to get through. The silence from the enchantment left him unsettled. He *had* to get to his friends.

He needed a better way to focus this power.

The sword.

Looking behind him, he found the sword lying on the table.

What better focus of power would there be than that?

He darted over to the table and tried to pierce through the invisible barrier. Knowing Cyran, he would have prepared for someone to try using brute force. If that wasn't going to work, then it'd have to be another type of magic.

Gavin pressed his hands on the barrier and pushed. At first, nothing changed. He continued to push and press down, bearing his weight on it. It seemed that the more he pushed, the more the barrier resisted.

Maybe he had to move more slowly. He held his hand above it. The barrier pushed back, but not nearly as firmly as it had before. He moved gradually, easing his hands down. The barrier started to shift. He simply rested his hands, not shoving them with the same force as before.

Then he was through the barrier. Gavin felt for the hilt of the sword and started to lift it, but he remembered how he had needed to ease through the barrier. He drew it upward gently, and it moved as if he were pulling it out through mud.

Finally, the sword was free.

He darted toward the stone and focused on the blade. It glowed with the same energy that suggested magic was all around, similar to the El'aras dagger. Gavin shoved the dagger into his belt and then leveraged the sword into the stone, and put everything he could into it.

They trembled.

It might work.

He shoved harder.

A little more trembling.

Not enough, though.

What if I carved at the stone with *the sword? If there was magic in it, I might be able to use that against the stone and break free.*

He swung.

The stone shattered.

Gavin swung the sword again and slammed through

the stone, carving through it within a few strokes. The debris cleared, giving him an open pathway to the tunnel, and he saw the ladder—and the way out.

He sprinted to the ladder and climbed back into Cyran's home, and he paused just long enough to look around once. He hurried outside and closed the door behind him, then he raced along the street.

It seemed as if it took an impossibly long time for him to get to the Roasted Dragon, but when he reached it, there was movement outside of the tavern. He had no idea who was there, but given the time of night, anyone there was not supposed to be.

Gavin darted forward, holding onto the sword. A dark-cloaked figure turned toward him, and a burst of power struck him. He ignored the blast, focusing instead on the figure itself. There was something unusual about them. The power that struck him was incredible, almost more than he could withstand, though he'd faced magical attacks before. This was just one more—only that this was another attack on the Dragon.

He was responsible for bringing this attack here. Once again, he had brought magic to a place that did not deserve it. Once again, he was responsible for bringing that power to bear in a place that had long ago exiled power. No one had said anything to him, though they didn't need to. He felt the blame regardless.

He could feel energy around him, though he didn't know why. It was possible the core reserves of power within him somehow alerted him to the power that existed in the world.

The figure wore a black cloak, and colors swirled around them that reminded him of the vines the sorceress had used against him, so different than other sorcerers he had faced. Others had power, but they were forced to use spells and incantations, not just throwing power out like this.

Whoever faced him was powerful.

Swinging the blade, Gavin carved through the magic, and then he swiped across the sorcerer's chest. They fell in a spray of blood.

Another attack started toward him, beginning to sweep power around him. Again it reminded him of the same lines of energy that Erica had used on him, but this sorcerer didn't seem as capable as she had been. Gavin cut through them, and the magical vines dropped harmlessly away from him.

He spun and slammed the flat of the blade against the sorcerer's forehead, and then he dropped, kicking and driving his heel into their back. Something cracked, and they went staggering forward. He hesitated as he watched the cloaked figure move toward the entrance to the Dragon.

Gavin raced toward the door and opened it, revealing the chaos inside. Strange vines of energy spread out all over, almost as if trying to crawl along the walls. He couldn't see the sorceress.

Gaspar was backed against the wall. He looked over at Gavin and nodded. "Took you long enough."

"I had to carve through some stone."

"New sword? Didn't think you would've had time to pick one up."

"Cyran left it behind for me."

Gaspar chuckled, and he nodded toward the staircase. "I don't know what they're doing, but they're using magic to hold us at bay."

"Alex?"

"Upstairs, but Jessica is there."

"She should have known better," Gavin said.

"Imogen is with them," Gaspar said. That meant something more to Gaspar than it did to Gavin.

He carved through the green vines and raced toward the stairs. He headed up and detected a sense of ongoing energy at the top. He could feel the strangeness of it, and he focused his power into the sword.

He used it to attack the energy here. The sorceress wasn't anywhere to be found, but he could feel her effect, and the occasional streaking line of power along the walls suggested she was still here, even if he couldn't see her.

At the end of the hall, near the room where they had placed Alex, he felt resistance. Gavin swiped through it with the new sword and found that he was able to carve through it far more easily than he had been able to do before. He pulled the room door open and found the sorceress inside.

She stood near the door with power creeping away

from her, heading toward Alex, Jessica, and Imogen. Imogen swept that narrow blade of hers toward everything that the sorceress did and somehow managed to keep the magic at bay.

Maybe she had an El'aras blade.

It was a different style than the one Gavin had, but it seemed to withstand the attack fairly well. She worked quickly, swinging the narrow blade at each of the vines the sorceress sent at her, holding them off. She had positioned herself in front of Jessica and Alex, but it wouldn't be long before those vines overwhelmed her. Gavin darted forward, rolling in front of Imogen, and he swept the sword through the vines.

The sorceress smiled at him. "You escaped. You really are quite capable, Gavin Lorren."

"You would've been better off killing me."

"I'm not sure I can kill you. I thought I might be able to delay you longer than I did, but perhaps you're far more skilled than I had been warned." She glared at him. "Regardless, you *are* troublesome." She shifted her attack, and the ground seemed to flow up, magic manifesting as something physical as if earth and plants and everything swallowed him.

Gavin acted quickly. He swung the sword, but there was nothing to cut. Other than the vines she'd been using, this new magic seemed to flow up from the ground right below his feet. He didn't have anything to target. He tried to kick, but the power confined him, holding him tightly.

The sorceress took a step forward, smiling at him.

"You really should have stayed behind. You won't want to see this."

She took another step, and she began to swirl power away from her. It darted outward toward the others, forcing Imogen to move quickly to block that magic. The end of her blade moved in a blur, faster than Gavin was even able to keep up with. For a moment, he could only watch, his training immediately making him judge her skill and question how he might fare matched up against someone like Imogen.

He'd mastered many different fighting styles and was an incredibly skilled sword fighter, but seeing Imogen swinging the blade like she did suggested that she was not just a skilled sword fighter but something even more than that. She was a master.

He focused on the way the sorceress tried to trap him. The energy around him swept up from the ground. Gavin kicked, but his feet didn't move. There had to be another way that he could get free, another technique he could try. His mind tore through the various strategies he knew. He might be able to uncurl his body to find the necessary energy to loosen the hold on him. He twisted in place, trying to free his feet, but wasn't able to.

Jessica gasped.

Gavin took a deep breath, focusing on what was holding him, and then kicked. It was the only thing that he could think of doing. He thought he might be able to loosen the barrier around him, but it was going to take a different approach.

He tried again, twisting once more. As he did, he could feel energy within him. He pointed the sword down at the ground and traced it around. Whatever the sorceress was doing to him seemed to be emanating from the ground itself. If he could somehow find a way to pull free of that, then he could get out of this. He continued to turn, bringing the sword around him in a steady circle. When he pushed power out from him, he felt the resistance around him change. He kicked again. The resistance eased.

Gavin twisted to the side, and he brought the sword through. On a whim, he pulled it between his legs, bracing himself for the possibility that he might cut through his own flesh, but he didn't. He was free.

He rolled toward the sorceress and swept the sword, carving through the vines of green energy she sent away from her. The first attack sliced through them. She tried to fight him, but Gavin held out, using everything in his power to resist the way her vines attempted to entangle him.

Imogen darted forward, and whipped her narrow blade around in a series of arcs. The sorceress turned to her, moving her hand in a pattern.

Imogen was thrown back.

Gavin continued carving through the magic she held, and then it faded. The sorceress stumbled before turning her attention to him in full. The power coming from her was an enormous surge of energy. He braced himself, gripping the hilt in both hands. The curved blade absorbed most the power, sending it off on either side.

She glared at him.

When the power was gone, Gavin rolled forward, swinging his feet in a twisting motion in the Hoshon style of fighting.

The sudden shift was enough. He caught her, sending her flying backward. Gavin shifted through the movements. He turned to the side, bringing the sword up and swinging it down, but the strange winding vines of power wrapped around his wrists and arms, holding him in place.

She got up and reached for his sword, but Imogen ran forward and jammed her narrow blade into the woman's belly. The vines withdrew, retreating backward and disappearing.

Gavin brought the sword back around, preparing to attack, but there was no need. She'd released him. He positioned himself to the side, ready for her power to unleash at him again, but it didn't. Instead, the ground shifted once more.

"You're going to regret angering the Maker of Chains," she said.

Gavin braced himself, prepared for whatever energy she might draw out of the ground. If she used that against him again, he wasn't sure if he'd have enough strength to carve through it quickly enough. So far, he'd gotten lucky.

A wave of darkness swept up from the ground,

consuming her. It collapsed, and nothing remained. She'd disappeared.

He breathed out slowly, looking at the spot where she'd been. He glanced over at Jessica, her eyes wide, panic within them. Alex had a calmness about her, an emptiness.

What else had she seen?

"Come on," he said, motioning to the others. "It's time for us to get out of here."

"What did she do?" Jessica whispered.

"I don't know. She's a sorcerer, and one of considerable power."

"I thought the Dragon was protected."

"There's only so much that can be done to protect against a truly powerful sorcerer," Gavin said.

He grabbed Alex, and it was a wonder the young girl didn't resist. She went along with Gavin, and Imogen helped lead Jessica out of the room, down the stairs, and into the main part of the tavern.

Gaspar stood and stared, saying nothing.

The tavern was empty. Everything was in disarray. Tables were turned on their sides, and Jessica worked quickly through the tavern, tipping them back up and placing the benches and stools where they belonged. A few bloodstains pooled on the ground, though not so many that they couldn't be scrubbed up. The air hung with a strange odor, a mixture of sweat, blood, and something he couldn't quite place.

"What was that?" Jessica asked, taking a seat at a table. "*Who* was that?"

Imogen went to the kitchen and brought back a mug of ale, which she placed in front of Jessica.

Gavin shook his head. "As far as I know, she was the one who hired us, but I thought she wanted us to find him—her," he said, nodding to Alex. "Now, I'm not so sure. It seems to me like she's more interested in killing Alex."

"Why? Who is she?"

Alex raised her head and haunted eyes met Gavin's for the first time. "She is the Mistress of Vines," Alex said. "She is life. And she is death."

CHAPTER FOURTEEN

The inside of the Dragon was still in complete disarray, though Jessica had gone to work trying to get the tavern back together, organizing chairs and tables, letting Gavin and Gaspar move bodies far enough away from the Dragon that the constables wouldn't come here to question them. It still didn't feel like enough.

It was empty, which was not altogether surprising at this time of night. There was just the small grouping of them at one table. Gaspar sat off to one side near Imogen, Wrenlow sorted through his stack of pages, and Alex sat next to Jessica, who seemed to be trying to console the young girl.

"We need to know more about the Mistress of Vines," Gavin said. He looked over at Alex and tried to hold her attention, but she looked away.

"I've heard of the Mistress of Vines," Gaspar said.

"When?"

"Before," he said.

The tension between them lingered. Gavin knew Gaspar didn't care for the idea that he'd learned Gaspar had once been a constable, but why would that even be an issue? It didn't matter now. Gaspar was something else. He had *become* something else. He'd continued to grow and change and evolve. Like all men had to.

"Who is she?" Gavin asked.

"Someone who shouldn't be in Yoran," Gaspar said. "Back when the war was going on, the Sorcerers' Society called to her for help. She didn't answer."

"Because she's powerful." Gavin looked over at Alex. "What I want to know is what she wants to do with you."

"They're trying to take me," Alex whispered.

"Who is?"

"*They* are. I just want to go back with my family. That's all."

Something about this didn't feel right to Gavin. The steady blows he'd felt when Alex had attacked had been significant, but there was something off. It *hadn't* been a sorcerer's magic. "You're an enchanter, aren't you?"

She nodded slowly. "I don't have much skill. What I have isn't that useful."

Gavin chuckled. "I think you're wrong there. And your family?" She shook her head, as if to say they were gone. "You were taken from them by the Captain?"

"I was taken, but…"

"But what?"

"I don't really know what happened to them," she said.

A part of him went out to her. As strange as it was, he understood what she had gone through. When he was younger, there had been many who'd been brought in by Tristan, presumably to be safer, and he had trained them. Gavin wasn't the only one.

All of them had come from some place of sorrow. All of them had been freed from the life that they had known. And all of them had been introduced to something far more dangerous.

"Did the Captain tell you what he expected of you?" Gavin asked.

"He didn't expect anything."

"He would've expected something. They all do."

Gaspar looked over, frowning at Gavin for a long moment.

"What now?" Jessica said.

"Now… now I don't know," Gavin said. "We now have an enchantress—or sorceress—angry at us. We now have to deal with the danger of the Captain. And somehow we have to figure out what to do with her." He tilted his head toward Alex.

"You don't have to do anything with me," she said.

"We have to do something. We can't let you leave until I've neutralized the Mistress of Vines," Gavin said.

"I don't need you to protect me."

The El'aras dagger rested on Gavin's lap, and it started to glow again. He looked over, smiling at her. "You've just proven my point."

"What did I prove?"

"You can't go using your magic around the city like that."

"Why? Are you afraid they're going to catch me?"

"The constables *will* catch you," Gaspar said softly. "They're trained to find those who use magic. The constables are skilled at it. They have enchantments that allow them to pursue that power and to deflect magic that's used on them."

Gavin had a sense from the old thief that there was something within what he said that troubled him.

"In order to keep her safe, we have to figure out what we're going to do. We could return her to the Captain"—Gavin looked over, and he could tell from Alex's face that she didn't want that—"or we keep her safe."

"We have to keep her safe," Gaspar said.

"There may be a way to do so," Wrenlow said.

"How?"

"Well, think about that other job you were offered."

Gavin frowned. "The egg?"

"Right. The other job. There were other enchanters. Isn't that what he said?"

It's possible that we might be able to hide her there, but even if we did, is that necessarily safe?

He didn't know. Alex was still too young to be off on her own, and unless she had somebody to protect her, they weren't going to be able to ensure her safety.

"What about your family?" Gavin asked.

"My family is gone," Alex said.

"What happened to them?"

She looked over, holding his gaze, and she shook her head. "They're gone."

"What does that mean?" Wrenlow asked.

Gavin glanced over and shook his head slightly. "Don't."

"What? If her family is gone, then we can find them. I mean, I have resources within the city I can use and leverage to do that. I'm sure Gaspar, having been in the city as long as he has, has resources as well. Between the two of us, we should be able to find what happened to her family. Even if they were removed."

"Don't," Gavin whispered.

"Gavin—"

"They're gone, kid," Gaspar said, leaning forward. His voice was harsh and rough, and he glared at Wrenlow.

Wrenlow didn't seem to take the hint, and he ignored it.

Gavin sighed. "Were you there when it happened?"

"No. Well, I heard it."

"I'm sorry."

"What did she hear?" Wrenlow asked.

Jessica stood and tapped Wrenlow on the arm. "Why don't you help me in the kitchen and gather some food and drinks. I think the rest of the crew is needing to visit."

"I suppose. I still want to know what she's talking about."

Jessica gave him an annoyed look, and she flashed a smile at Alex before guiding Wrenlow away.

"I'm sorry about him," Gavin said. "He doesn't always see what's obvious."

"And he provides your intelligence?" Alex asked.

"He's smart, but it doesn't mean he's *smart*."

"Sounds like the two of you are quite the pair," Gaspar said.

"Careful," Gavin said.

"Or what? You're going to continue to harass me?"

Alex laughed softly. "What happens if she comes back?"

"Seeing as how we stopped her for a little while, we don't have to worry about that just yet."

Though Gavin doubted they would have much longer.

"What I don't really understand is why she would've needed me to get you out of the Captain's fortress," he said. "As powerful as she was, I would've expected that she'd have been able to rescue you herself."

"It wouldn't have been a rescue," Gaspar said.

"Fine. Not rescue, but break her out. Why did she need us?"

"There are protections around the fortress," Alex said.

"You were aware of them?"

"The Captain warned me. He told me I wasn't going to be able to do much there. He said it would get better."

"That your magic would get stronger? More controlled?"

Alex shook her head. "I don't really know."

Gavin leaned back, crossing his hands in front of him while thinking. The man had enchantments, that much

Gavin was certain of. The Captain's indestructible nature suggested that those enchantments were powerful and that somebody was creating them for him.

"What else can you tell us about your time there?" Gaspar asked.

"I was only there for a few days. They fed me, and then he had people working with me."

Gaspar frowned. "What do you mean they were working with you?"

"They were testing me. I think he was trying to see how much I knew."

Troubling. There had to be a reason she'd been brought there, and a reason the Captain knew about her. None of this made any sense to him.

Jessica came out of the kitchen carrying a tray of food and drinks, which she set on the table in front of them.

Gavin got up and tapped Gaspar's shoulder. "I need a word."

Gaspar joined him, and they headed to a table in the back corner of the tavern.

"Something about this isn't adding up," Gavin said.

"It's about time you saw that."

"Have you been able to figure out what's going on?"

"No, but I share your concern," Gaspar said.

"What do you think it is?"

Gaspar looked over to where Alex sat quietly at the table. "I don't know. You said she was powerful when she attacked you?"

Gavin nodded. "That was controlled magic, Gaspar. I

don't know how much experience you had with that in your previous occupation, but this was someone who was in control of what they were doing. I had to use every bit of focus I had to withstand it."

"Are you sure it was your focus that helped you?" Gaspar asked.

"What else would it have been?"

"You know you have other potential."

"Let's not go into that now," Gavin said.

"Are you afraid to?"

"I'm not afraid to get into it, but I think we have a more pressing matter at hand."

"And I think they're connected," Gaspar said.

Gavin took a deep breath. "Possibly." He couldn't deny that there might be something more taking place. "If so, we still need to know what they intended."

"In that, we agree." Gaspar frowned. "Your friend does have a good idea though."

"Which is?"

"This other job you were offered. This Zella," he said, frowning again as he did. "I can't help but think that we might be able to borrow some information from that job."

"Borrow?" Gavin asked.

"Perhaps that's not the right word, but we might be able to find this group of enchanters and uncover more about the Mistress of Vines," Gaspar said.

"It sounds to me like we know all that we need to about her."

"Are you sure about that? She almost single-handedly

took down all of us. Think about what she was able to do to you. You, a man trained to fight and control himself, someone who has the ability to handle all sorts of different dangerous scenarios, was nearly overpowered by this Mistress of Vines."

"She surprised me," Gavin said. He hated admitting it, but it was true that she'd surprised him and nearly overwhelmed him, though he wasn't going to tell Gaspar that.

"Of course she did. She's powerful."

Gavin breathed out slowly. "It won't happen again."

"I hope not."

He glanced over at Gaspar. "So are we going to find this group of enchanters?" He looked around the tavern, locking eyes with Wrenlow for a moment before he turned his attention back to his notebook and began writing.

"It sounds like it," Gaspar said.

"Good. I need the coin," Gavin said.

Gaspar looked over, his expression darkening. "What?"

Gavin shrugged. "The job would pay an additional third when I find Zella."

"If she's there, you need to be cautious. We don't know anything about this jade egg."

With everything else that had been going on so far, Gavin knew better than to get locked up in another job. Alex had been enough of one, and now that he had another…

He sighed. "That's where we need to start. Find the egg. Find the enchanters. Help Alex."

Gaspar clenched his jaw. "You might be right."

"You don't have to sound like it hurts you to say it."

"It does hurt to say it. I don't like the idea of you being right. Been right too much these days," Gaspar growled.

Gavin smiled at him. A rare compliment from Gaspar. "You know, I *am* right more often than I'm wrong."

"I find that hard to believe," Gaspar said.

"I think you want to work with me more than you're letting on."

"See? Now you're just proving how often you're wrong."

Gavin chuckled as he shook his head. "Where do we start?"

Gaspar sighed. "As much as it pains me, I feel like we need to go back to Desarra."

"Why Desarra? Because she was the one who got us the plans to the Captain's fortress?"

"That… and another reason."

"What other reason?" Gavin asked.

"I'm not going to share everything with you, boy." Gaspar left him and headed over to the table.

Jessica wandered over and joined him. "Thank you," she said.

"What for?"

"For protecting me."

"You knew I would," Gavin said.

"And for protecting her."

"Why wouldn't I have protected her?"

She smiled. "You could have let this Mistress of Vines

take her."

"You know I couldn't have," Gavin said. "I don't really know what to make of all of this, but I'm not much of a fan of people with magic tossing it around and harming those without. I've had a few experiences with magic users."

"More than just Yoran?"

Gavin nodded. "More than just Yoran."

"I figured. You handled the El'aras attack much better than anyone else would have. I guessed that you had some experience."

"Unfortunately. More than what I would've liked."

"What has it involved?"

"Mostly it's involved trying to keep from drawing notice."

"It's been more than that," she said.

"Before I came to Yoran, and really before I even partnered with Wrenlow, I spent time wandering, which brought me to other places. Yoran isn't alone in banishing magic, though they do a better job than most cities. There are still places that welcome magic. They embrace it. Most of them aren't even all that far from the city. Places where they use magic to protect their people—and where they use magic to rule."

"You have experience with it."

Gavin shook his head. "I've tried to stay away from those places. The man who trained me warned me against spending too much time there. They were dangerous. Not just to outsiders, but to people trained like me." Now that he'd started to wonder about the nature of his abilities, he had to question whether Tristan had known about his potential for magic and if that was the reason he'd been warned to stay away.

"Have any of your jobs dealt with magic like this?" Jessica asked.

"You mean like my most recent jobs have?"

"I suppose so."

Gavin shook his head. "Not many. Well, there was one, but it didn't go so well."

She raised an eyebrow. "What happened?"

"Let's just say that I didn't complete the mission."

"No?" Jessica started to smile. "What exactly happened?"

"I was hired to take out a dangerous ruler. I didn't finish the job."

"So they're still in charge?"

"No. Thankfully, I at least pushed them out of the city, but there's always the risk that they might return." He frowned. "I don't like it when I can't finish the job."

"What about what's happening here?"

Gavin took a deep breath and let it out slowly. "I don't like having jobs that are incomplete. Even when they deal with magic." He glanced over at Alex. "She beat me, you know."

Jessica chuckled. "Are you sure it was her?"

Gavin shrugged. "At the time, I thought it was, but now having seen this Mistress of Vines attack, I'm not even sure anymore. Maybe it wasn't Alex."

"I can't imagine what that's like," she said.

"It's not as bad as you'd think. There are some uses of magic that are quite outstanding. Think of all the enchantments you have. I don't know much about what Yoran was like before all of that was banished, but I can imagine there were plenty of enchantments that allowed power and amazing things to happen."

"There were. There were also dangerous and deadly things."

"Such as?"

"People disappearing. Battles in the streets. Sorcerers fighting sorcerers. Did you know that before the Captain, the person with the most power in the city was a sorcerer?"

Gavin smiled tightly. "That's not surprising. That's been the case in many of the cities I've seen. And the Captain isn't without his magical connection. He might not be a sorcerer"—though Gavin wasn't entirely sure if that was true or not—"but he certainly has enchantments. He has his own connection that enables him to maintain his standing in the city." He had no idea how extensive that magical connection might be, nor did he know just what the Captain did to keep that position.

Even though the Captain had enchantments, his guards didn't. That surprised Gavin.

If this was all about sorcery and all about using magic in ways that were hidden, then why wouldn't the Captain have kept others with him with that kind of power? Why would he have been the only one to have enchantments?

"I don't think Gaspar likes getting back into this," Jessica said, leaning across the table and shifting so that she could look at both Gavin and Gaspar.

Gavin glanced over at the old thief. "Getting back into the magical world?"

Jessica nodded slowly before turning her gaze back to him. She smoothed her hair back with one hand, and her brow furrowed.

Was she thinking about how much she still had to do to clean up the tavern?

"In his mind, he was done with it before," she said.

"Is that why he and Desarra can't be together?" Having seen the two of them, it seemed strange to Gavin that they couldn't. They obviously wanted to.

"I don't know. It's more complicated than that, and don't you go pushing me for more answers, Gavin Lorren. I don't have them. I just know. And I know you don't need to be pushing Gaspar when he doesn't want to share."

"He wants to go back to her for the job."

"He does?" Jessica asked, watching Gaspar closely.

"I think he believes she has something to offer us so we can figure out what's taking place. He thinks Desarra might be able to help us find where these other enchanters are."

"What do you believe?"

Gavin shrugged. "It doesn't really matter what I believe. I'm willing to do whatever it takes to finish this job." Maybe he could finish both jobs.

"Then what?"

He looked over at Jessica. "You want me to stay."

"I didn't say that."

"You didn't, but you don't have to. I can see it in your eyes."

"Are you sure about that, Gavin Lorren? Are you so sure that you can see my thoughts? Do you know what I want?"

"I know you're the reason the rumors were spread throughout the city."

"And I've told you that I'm not. You can choose whether or not to believe me, Gavin, but I'm not responsible for that. If somebody wanted to spread rumors about you as a tracker and to force you into doing these things, you'd better start looking into why."

She stormed away, and Gavin sat there for a moment, frowning to himself.

Maybe she was right. It was possible that he did need to look at things in a different way.

If it wasn't Jessica, who was responsible?

There was no doubt in his mind that somebody had spread the rumors. That was what Davel Chan had said. Perhaps that was where he had to go.

He looked around the tavern. Wrenlow brought him a tray, and Gavin picked at the food and drank his ale.

His mind tried to work through everything. He didn't come up with any answers, but that didn't change how troubled he felt.

CHAPTER FIFTEEN

The cleared section of the main room of the Dragon made it easy for Gavin to practice. A fire smoldered in the hearth, giving a hint of light, and he moved through his patterns in the space he'd cleared out in the room. He needed to keep his skills sharp. There was a time when he wouldn't have needed practice. There was a time when he never would've worried about losing any of his skills, but that had been before he had come here.

That had been before he had stayed in Yoran for as long as he had, and now he felt as if his skills were starting to diminish, if only a little bit. He didn't want to those skills to diminish. He'd worked incredibly hard to acquire them, suffering for much longer than he ever would have believed that he would've been willing to do, to gain those skills.

Which was why he had to work at them, honing them

for him to remember how to flow from movement to movement.

"You couldn't sleep, either?"

Gavin spun out of a Noru fighting stance and turned to see Wrenlow coming down the stairs, pausing at the bottom of the stairs and looking out at him. He held a lantern in one hand and rubbed sleep from his eyes with his free hand. His notebook was tucked up under his arm, and a pen was stuffed behind one ear.

"It's not a matter of not being able to sleep," Gavin said.

"You're down here, though."

"I'm down here," Gavin agreed.

Wrenlow took a seat at one of the tables, and he kicked back, resting his heels on a chair next to him. "Don't let me keep you."

Gavin grunted. "You intend to watch?"

"I don't get to see you fight that often, so why shouldn't I see you practice?"

"You don't want to see me fight," Gavin said.

"I don't necessarily want to be a part of the fighting," Wrenlow said, smiling slightly, "but at the same time, I don't want to be left out of it, either."

Gavin paused and grabbed his shirt off the chair, and he dabbed at his forehead. "Do you feel left out of it?"

"I know my role, Gavin."

"That wasn't the question," Gavin said.

Wrenlow shrugged, and he set his book in front of him, and pulled the pen out from behind his ear. "I can't deny that I would be interested in learning a little bit more."

"You want to learn how to fight?"

Wrenlow looked over, and rested his elbows on the table, staring at Gavin for a moment. "With all the things that we do, I'm bound to end up getting in trouble sometime. It wouldn't hurt to know a little bit more about how to defend myself if it came down to it."

Gavin took a deep breath, and he nodded.

He should have thought about that before. Wrenlow wasn't wrong. Gavin did ask quite a bit of him, especially finding information, and learning how to find dangerous people in a city like this put him into a very different type of danger. Without any enchantments, other than the one that allowed them to communicate, Wrenlow wouldn't be able to do much.

"Would you prefer we find enchantments that would allow you to fight more effectively?"

"What good are enchantments if I don't have the skills to use them anyway?"

"Even an enchantment for speed is useful," Gavin said. He moved to the table where Wrenlow sat, and he rested one hand on the chair, leaning toward Wrenlow. "If you have an enchantment, you can run."

"You don't run."

"I don't run," Gavin said. "But then again, I'm trained not to run."

"You don't even use any enchantments."

"Again, I'm trained not to use them." He dabbed his

forehead. He'd been working for the better part of an hour and had managed to get through quite a few different fighting styles, flowing from one to the next, often times mixing different styles together. That was how he would best ensure that he stayed sharp. "I try not to use enchantments. I was taught that if you come to rely upon enchantments, you might find yourself using them at the wrong time."

"What's the wrong time?"

"Basically, you find yourself relying upon them, and if you do that, and the enchantment fades, you could suffer."

Wrenlow pulled his book toward him, and he shook his head. "So, you want me to learn to use enchantments, and if I were to need them, I might find them not available?"

"How often do you really think that you're going to need enchantments?"

"How often are you going to send me after information about people like the Captain?"

"You didn't have any trouble finding that information, did you?"

"Not that time, but…"

Gavin pulled the chair out and took a seat. "What's really on your mind?"

"We've been dealing with an awful lot of magic," Wrenlow said.

"That's what you're concerned about."

Wrenlow shrugged. "Shouldn't I be? Considering everything that we have gone through, and all the dangers that we've faced, don't you think that I should be a little bit concerned about how much magic that we have suddenly been facing? First it's your sorcerer friend—"

"He is not my friend."

"He *was*."

"I thought so," Gavin said softly.

"And then there is his mentor, or whoever that was, whoever was trying to call you into gathering him. Now we have another sorcerer."

"I'm sorry," Gavin said.

"You don't have to be sorry. It's just the reason that I'm asking for a little bit of help. Maybe some training." Wrenlow grinned slightly. "We've dealt with quite a few different sorcerers over the time that we've been together."

"I've tried to stay away from sorcerers," Gavin said.

"Ever since you dealt with that crazy bastard in Noral."

"He was the worst," Gavin said, shaking his head. "He tried to hire me to take out his rival."

"I don't think he believed you could actually do it," Wrenlow said, chuckling and shaking his head. "I mean, who would believe that somebody without any magic could take out somebody with magic?"

"Maybe he knew I had more than I knew," Gavin said.

Wrenlow arched a brow. "Maybe," he said. "And how is that going?"

"You mean how is it going with me trying to figure out whether I have any connection to power?"

"Something like that."

"I've been struggling," Gavin admitted. "I don't know if I can control it."

"You've moved past the idea that it's not magic?"

"I don't know that I have much choice in believing that is not magic," Gavin said. He glanced over to the book, and he reached for it, but Wrenlow smacked his hand away, arching a brow at him. "I have been able to do too many things with that power that are probably magical. And now I don't even know."

"It's useful, though."

"Maybe," Gavin said.

"Think about some of the things that you dealt with before. Can you imagine what we would have been able to do had we known that you had that kind of power? We had that one sorcerer in Kevlin who was more than even you could handle."

Gavin shook his head. "The Tanran."

"That's right. I forgot about his name."

"Or hers," Gavin said.

"If you say so," Wrenlow said. "Either way, we couldn't even find him or her. You got hired to take him out, and then he goes and disappears on you."

"Again, I'm not so sure that it's a matter of him disappearing so much as it was me just not learning where to find him."

"You gave up on that job awfully quickly," Wrenlow said.

Gavin leaned back, closing his eyes. That had been a difficult time. The sorcerer had been skilled. He hadn't even gotten close to finding the Tanran. He'd been asked to take care of a dangerous and deadly sorcerer, and as he had gotten close, the sorcerer had simply disappeared; moving on. Over the years, Gavin had caught word of the Tanran a few other times, but he had never attempted to pursue.

"None of that matters," Gavin said. "I don't even know if that job would've gone any easier had I known I had a connection to magic."

"It couldn't have gone any worse."

"No one died."

"Not at your hand," Wrenlow said. "Others in the city did, though."

Gavin leaned back, looking around the inside of the Dragon. It was dark, and other than the lantern that Wrenlow had brought down, there was little light. He been sparring using the light coming off the hearth, but that was barely enough for him to see much of anything. He hadn't needed to see much of anything, though. For the kind of work that he needed, it was mostly by feel. At this point in his fighting, that was how he had to practice. Instinct, more than anything else.

"Why couldn't you sleep?" Gavin asked, looking back to Wrenlow.

"Probably the same as you."

"I doubt it," Gavin said.

"Fine. I guess I don't have the mysterious magic that you do, nothing that keeps me awake the way that your strange magic has suddenly started to keep you awake, but

I do understand there's something going on. And I've been trying to figure out the connection between all of this. I feel like the answer is right there the edge of my ability to understand, I just have to find it."

Gavin chuckled. "If anybody's going to find it, it's going to be you," he said.

"Thanks, I guess," Wrenlow said.

"I know you feel like you need to fight in order for you to have some value to what we do, but that isn't where you bring me the most value."

"I just want to help," Wrenlow said. "And I don't want you to feel like you have to take pity on me."

"I don't."

Wrenlow arched a brow at him.

"I'm not saying that I *didn't*," Gavin said, and he laughed. "When I first found you, you were pretty pitiful."

"I was, wasn't I?"

"You got better."

"I've gotten exposed to things that I never would have imagined that I would be a part of," he said. "And there are times when I still don't even know what to think of some of this."

"I hadn't brought anybody else with me before you," Gavin said.

"Why not?"

Gavin closed his eyes. "One of the aspects of my training was that I needed to manage on my own."

"No one can be on their own forever," Wrenlow said.

"I was taught to be on my own," Gavin said.

"Did you like it?"

"What was there to like?"

"Your training. Everything that you went through. You haven't talked much about this mentor of yours recently. Not since Anna told you that he might be alive."

"I don't know what there is to say about him," Gavin said.

"You never really talked about him before, either."

"Because he was gone," Gavin said.

"You don't talk about the dead?"

"The dead don't need us," Gavin said.

"The dead don't need *you*," Wrenlow said, laughing softly. "You can't kill someone who's already dead, can you?"

"No," Gavin answered.

"What will you do if you find him?" Wrenlow asked, looking to Gavin and watching him. "That's what you intend to do, eventually, isn't it?"

Gavin breathed out slowly, and he looked around the inside of the Dragon. "I think I'm getting too comfortable here," he said.

"What's wrong with comfortable?"

"It means that I'm getting complacent," Gavin said.

"You're still the greatest fighter in the city."

"I was once much more than that," Gavin said. He took a deep breath, letting it out slowly, and shook his head. "But maybe I have to be content with being the greatest fighter in the city. At least for now."

"You want to be the greatest fighter in the world?"

Wrenlow started to laugh. "You do know the world is kind of a big place. And I can't imagine that you could find a way to be the greatest in the entire world. There are others who have innate magic. Think about the El'aras. They wouldn't have any trouble with somebody like you."

Gavin arched a brow at him. "I handled the El'aras."

"I suppose you did," he said. "Sometimes I forget about that."

"We shouldn't forget about that," Gavin said.

"Have you tried calling her?"

"What makes you think that I will?"

"I saw the way that you are looking at her when she was here," Wrenlow said. "I didn't say anything to Jessica, if that's your concern."

"That's not my concern."

"Not while you are here. But eventually, won't it be? She gave you the marker to get a hold of her."

"She gave me the marker, but I haven't used it."

"You could," he said.

"For what purpose?" Gavin rested his elbows on the table, looking at Wrenlow, holding his gaze. "What purpose would there be in me calling to the El'aras, and drawing them back here? They were here for some other reason, hiding the Shard, or to stay away from the rest of their people. I don't even know. And I don't even care. Just so long as they don't give me a reason to go after them, I shouldn't get caught up in it."

"You shouldn't?"

Gavin shook his head.

He tried to ignore the fact that Anna had claimed he was part El'aras. He didn't know anything about his own past before he had trained with Tristan. That was the only thing that he could really remember. That and the fires that had claimed his parents.

He took a deep breath and got to his feet. "Come on," he said to Wrenlow.

"Come on?"

"You wanted to fight."

"Now? With you?"

"You have to fight with me to learn," Gavin said.

"Are you going to hurt me?"

Gavin frowned. "Are you going to give me any reason to?"

"I just want to learn to protect myself."

"There are a few different fighting styles that might be effective for that," he started. "I can help you with them. But I have to warn you, I can be a painful instructor."

"I believe it." Wrenlow got up, and he set his pen down next to his book, and he glanced to the lantern before stepping into the cleared space in the Dragon. "How did you learn so many different fighting styles?"

"Tristan taught me most of them, but I've learned a few more since I left him."

"How can you learn a fighting style so quickly?"

"Many different techniques borrow from each other," Gavin said, shrugging. "And that makes it easy for you to connect the techniques. When you learn one, and discover its strengths, you can start to work on its weaknesses, as well. When you know enough different fighting styles, you can use the weaknesses of one style, augmented with the strength of another, and ideally, you become unstoppable."

"The greatest fighter in the city." Gavin lunged toward Wrenlow, who jumped back, laughing. "Fine. I will give you the greatest fighter in this part of the kingdom. How about that?"

He shook his head. "You know, I never wanted to be the greatest fighter before."

"What did you want to be?"

Gavin frowned. *What would I have wanted to be?*

He hadn't even given it much thought.

Before he had gone to Tristan, he had never wanted to be a fighter. He had never wanted to learn to fight. Then again, with as few memories as he had of that time, he didn't know if he had always been destined to be a fighter. Maybe this was always going to be who he was. There was no denying the fact that he was skilled.

"I don't know," he said.

"I thought I was going to be a scribe," Wrenlow said.

"You *are* a scribe."

"I'm more than that," he said.

"Most of the time," Gavin said, laughing softly. He brought his hands up. "We're going to start with the Jasap style. It is one that's all about flow. It's easier to learn, hard to master, but useful since very few people have seen it, and those who have are unlikely to attack you."

"And this is one that Tristan taught you?"

"One of them."

"Did you ever beat him?"

"I don't know," Gavin said, stepping back and taking his opening fighting stance.

"How is it that you don't know?"

"I don't know what was a test and what was not," he said.

"Why not?"

"Because much of what he did to me was a test." He stepped forward, nodding. "Now are you going to keep talking, or are you going to fight?"

"You don't often talk about your past, so I was thinking maybe I would keep talking," Wrenlow said, grinning.

"If you want to be even somewhat competent, you're going to have to be able to stop this," Gavin said, darting forward and striking outward.

Wrenlow stood fixed in place.

Gavin pulled back at the last possible second, grazing Wrenlow across the chest.

"You have to do a little bit better than that."

"I didn't know that was going to be the first attack," Wrenlow said.

Gavin smiled tightly. Maybe he *did* need to work with Wrenlow, if only so that he could help him not be completely helpless if he were attacked. Gavin couldn't afford to lose him. Not with everything else that they were doing, and with what was taking place in the city. He needed Wrenlow to be able to gather information. And it wouldn't do for Wrenlow to get hurt in the process. He was a friend. Gavin didn't have many of them, and couldn't afford to lose one.

"I'm going to start a little slower with you this time," Gavin said. "Watch where my hand goes."

Wrenlow nodded. Gavin moved slowly, much more slowly than Tristan had ever been with him, and he pushed that thought aside.

Why did I need to be as forceful as Tristan had been with me?

He could be kinder and gentler in his instruction.

Wrenlow was his friend, after all.

And maybe it was long past time for Gavin to teach him.

CHAPTER SIXTEEN

The street looked emptier than it had when Gavin had come the first time. The air was cool and crisp, typical for the city. Shops all around had started to come alive, and while there wasn't much activity along the street itself, there was plenty within the buildings he passed on the way to find Davel Chan.

There was no answer when Gavin knocked on the door in the early morning. He pounded on it, trying to get the man's attention, but still he didn't come to the door.

Standing back, Gavin unsheathed the El'aras dagger slightly, but there was no glow to the blade. Davel wasn't here using magic, but that didn't mean he wasn't here at all.

Gavin tested the door. It was locked. He didn't have Gaspar's ability at breaking into locked areas, but that didn't stop him from trying to get past the door. He jabbed the dagger into the doorframe and pried. The

El'aras blade was incredibly strong, and it made the wood around the door scream in protest. The door popped open.

Gavin stepped into the house. He paused a moment, letting his eyes adjust as some of the light from the street drifted into the room. Everything looked the same as last time.

"What are you doing here?"

Gavin spun, holding the dagger out from him.

Gaspar stood in the doorway.

"I figured I'd start with my other employer and see if I could come up with anything to help us figure out more about the jade egg job."

"He was here?" Gaspar asked. He began to sweep through the room, quickly surveying everything, opening and closing doors, sorting through things.

When Gavin had first seen Gaspar go through this process, he'd assumed that it was because of Gaspar's background as a thief. Now he couldn't help but wonder if perhaps there was a different reason.

Gaspar had been a constable. Gavin wouldn't be surprised if the constables hurriedly searched houses like this with the ability to find magic users.

"There's nothing here," Gaspar said.

"I know there's nothing here. I looked."

Gaspar arched a brow at him. "I figured I would take a look myself. You have a tendency to miss things."

Gavin shook his head. "And you have a tendency to be an ass."

Gaspar laughed. "Your other sorcerer friend had a lair beneath his home. Do you think there might be something here?"

"I don't really know," Gavin said with a shrug. "It's possible. Of course, if he does, that means this man has magic that's more potent than I think."

"Should we look for it?"

Gavin headed toward one of the back rooms. He paused for a moment in the doorway and didn't see anything on the floor. No sign of a trapdoor.

He shook his head. "There's nothing here. We could go to Cyran's lair and see if there's anything there."

"Do you think there might be anything more than what you already observed?"

Gavin shrugged. "I don't know. Other than what's in the lair? When I was there, I was more concerned about getting out and returning to the Dragon. I was a little preoccupied, worrying about what might happen to the rest of you."

"I see. Maybe while we're working together we can work on increasing your observational skills."

"You'd take me on as an apprentice?" Gavin asked, offering a hint of a grin. Maybe he could get Gaspar to talk about his other apprentices.

"Doubt you'd be able to help me nearly as well as you helped your previous mentor." Gaspar motioned for him to move. "Well?"

Gavin shook his head and headed back to the street toward Cyran's home on the outskirts of the city. Gaspar stayed with him, saying nothing. They reached the home, and Gavin looked around before opening the door.

A blast of power exploded toward him.

Without really thinking about what he was doing, Gavin drew on his core strength. He let it flow up from some deep part of him, and it crashed into the explosion. Each time that he reached for it now, it was as if there were some pool of reserve energy sitting deep within him. All he had to do was dig into it and pull it through him.

He had no idea what it was, and if it were magic, then so be it. At this point, it mattered little to him what he used, just so long as it was effective.

Gavin scrambled to his feet and drew the El'aras dagger.

Gaspar pressed behind him. "What was that?" he whispered.

"It seems as if the Mistress of Vines decided to prepare for the possibility we might return," Gavin said.

"Are you sure it was her?"

Gavin looked along the street. There had been so much trouble in this home. "I don't really know anymore. Given what we've gone through, it seems reasonable."

"It's also reasonable that Cyran, or whoever he was working with, came back," Gaspar said.

Gavin shook his head. "I don't think that was him."

"But you don't know."

"We can't know that."

Gavin held the dagger out from him. As he walked slowly forward, he could feel the energy of the explosion.

It left his skin tingling, every bit of him on edge. He frowned and moved into the room.

There was nothing.

"Well?" Gaspar asked.

"There's no sign that anybody's been here," Gavin said.

"Good."

Gaspar hurried into the room, and he quickly began to examine it. He pulled open cupboards and flipped through things, moving with that same practiced style. Gaspar didn't seem to pause in front of anything either. He simply kept moving, and Gavin didn't see anything else in the room.

"I looked already. I think he moved anything of value before he left."

"Only he didn't leave. He was captured," Gaspar said.

"Captured, but he thought he had removed me as a threat at that point. That's why I think he would have taken everything."

Gaspar continued to sort through things, and he came to a locked cupboard. After pulling out a lockpick and trying to pick the lock, he looked over at Gavin.

"That doesn't mean anything," Gavin said. He hadn't seen it when he'd gone through the first time—or he hadn't paid any attention to it.

"A locked cupboard in the middle of all of this? You don't think that means anything?"

"It wasn't in his sorcerer's lair."

"Maybe it's not anything magical," Gaspar said.

There was nothing particularly unique about it, except

that it was locked where the other cupboards were not. Gavin tested it by pulling on it.

Gaspar laughed. "If it was unlocked, I would've pulled it open. I think you have to do something to it."

"I have to *do* something? You're the thief. At least, you're a thief now."

Gaspar shot him a side-eyed stare. "Is it going to be like that?"

"It's not like anything. I recognize there's a story you're not telling me. I figure you'll get to it in your own time."

"No time," Gaspar said. "Especially since we both got our secrets."

"Yours deals with what you went through *here*. I think your history as a constable makes a difference."

"Not anymore. What I was has no bearing on anything we have to do."

"I think knowing that you had history with the constables has some bearing. Actually, given what we've seen, I think it has considerable bearing." Gavin stepped back from the cupboard. "Just open it already."

"You don't think that I've tried that?"

"Not really. I've seen you pick locks before."

"I've already tried to pick this lock," Gaspar said. "It's your turn."

Rather than continuing to argue, Gavin stepped forward. He held the El'aras dagger out. It started to glow.

"What did I say?" Gaspar said.

"That's enough."

"It has magic. I thought it might."

"You only thought it might because you weren't able to open it," Gavin said.

"That's reason enough."

Gavin jammed the dagger into the cupboard. The blade flashed briefly, and the cupboard popped open.

Gaspar pushed past him, smiling tightly. "See? What did I say?"

"It's not that I did anything. It's more the El'aras blade that did it."

"You go ahead and tell yourself that all you want."

Gavin looked over Gaspar's shoulder, trying to see what was inside the cupboard. There were bottles of powder. Gavin reached over Gaspar and ignored as Gaspar swatted at his hand, trying to slap him away.

"Why would he keep these locked in here?" Gaspar asked.

"Because they're dangerous. Or valuable," Gavin said.

He could think of several reasons why these powders would've been locked up. He thought back to when he'd visited Cyran here and what he'd seen then. Cyran had made a tea.

Had he been standing by this counter?

"Grab them," Gavin said.

"We don't know what they are," Gaspar said.

"We don't, but I think we need to take them with us. If they were important to Cyran, then they might be important to us."

Gaspar studied him for a moment before shrugging

and grabbing the vials. He stuffed them into his pocket and then looked around. "I don't see anything else here."

"I don't either. We can go down to the lair, but I don't know what we're going to find there." Other than the artifacts that were there, though that depended upon them knowing what to use them for.

Gavin led him to the back room and pulled the trapdoor open. He paused in front of it and looked down the ladder. The dagger didn't glow. Perhaps that should've reassured him, but after what he'd experienced when he'd been down here before…

He sheathed the El'aras dagger and unsheathed the sword, holding it at the ready.

Gaspar looked over at him, frowning. "Do you think you're going to need that?"

"Who knows, but I want to be prepared for the chance she might be here. This is the only thing that worked against her."

Gavin headed down the ladder and paused, swinging the sword out in front of him. He waited for it to glow, but no light came from its blade, so he didn't have to be as concerned about any potential attacker coming at him. He lingered there a moment but didn't see anything more.

Gaspar followed. "What is this?" he asked.

"What do you mean?"

"The rubble here."

"That's the ceiling." Gavin pointed to the collapsed ceiling overhead. "She tried to crush me."

"I can't even imagine what you did to get through here."

"I used the sword."

Gaspar frowned again, staring at the blade. "I think you and I are going to have to talk about this lack of magic you have."

Gavin chuckled. "There's nothing to talk about."

If it was magic, then he would have to learn how to control it. It wouldn't be sorcery, which involved techniques and spells and other sorts of power that Gavin simply didn't have. Whatever he called on through the core reserves he possessed was different, something intrinsic to him, which was different than how sorcerers called magic, and even more different than how enchanters placed magic onto items. If only he had an opportunity to talk to somebody he could trust.

Maybe even somebody he couldn't trust.

Anna might help, but that involved calling her through the enchantment she'd given him. So far, he'd been reluctant to do so, mostly because he didn't know how she'd react if he were to use it.

Gaspar shook his head. "You keep saying that you don't have any magic, but…"

Gavin paused, tracing his hand over one of the stones. He grabbed one the of rocks by the side and grunted as he tried to lift it. He finally abandoned it.

They climbed over the debris in the small passageway until they reached the door at the end of the tunnel. Gavin rested his hand on it and pulled upon that energy within him. He summoned that reserve of power the way he had before, and he yanked on the door. It came surging open.

This time, Gavin could feel exactly what he did. There was something within him that exploded, some source of power, and it combined with whatever energy was on the door to enable him to open it. He stared at the other side.

"This is his lair," he said softly.

Gaspar stood in the doorway, sweeping his gaze around. He didn't step inside. Rather, he remained at the threshold, a strange expression in his eyes.

"What is it?" Gavin asked.

"When I was in my other role—"

"You mean when you were a constable?"

"I never came across a sorcerer's lair. We knew they created them, but we never found one. We spent countless hours searching. We found many of their homes, but never anything like this. We *should* have found this though."

"I hadn't looked closely enough," Gavin said. Gaspar arched a brow at him. "Besides, Cyran hadn't been here that long."

"This was once the home of a sorcerer named Mesmer. He was removed about twenty years ago, and the home was empty since then."

"Why didn't you say that before?"

"Because it didn't make a difference. There were plenty of people who moved into old sorcerers' homes. Back in the day, there probably were several dozen sorcerers throughout Yoran. Hell, they even had a school here for a time."

Gavin's eyes widened. "Really?"

"All of that ended when Tagus took power."

"Why?"

"He abused it. It didn't take long for there to be a rebellion. I think Tagus thought he'd be able to survive the rebellion better than he did. Unfortunately for him, there were others who had their own sort of power."

"Other sorcerers?"

"No. The other sorcerers were concerned about Tagus. They had different factions, and none of them were particularly willing to take him on. It was the enchanters. They weren't nearly as powerful as sorcerers, which allied them with others in the city without power." Gaspar smiled tightly. "I think that most of the enchanters believed they would be permitted to stay in power, such as it were, but they didn't realize that the magic they possessed would eventually draw the attention of those who had their own magical power. Ultimately, the enchanters were the reason for their own downfall."

Gavin smiled. "I imagine that didn't go over well."

"Not particularly, but seeing as how the enchanters had been building up the constables with devices to allow them to withstand magical attacks, there wasn't much they could do. In the end, the enchanters who remained within the city decided to move underground. That is, until the constables began to hunt them." Gaspar looked around the room. "There was a time when I would've given anything to find a place like this."

"Why? So that you could advance your career?"

"I was already advanced enough," Gaspar said. "There was a time when I believed we had to remove the threat of those with power. I believed it was my responsibility to ensure that others who possessed magic were no longer a danger to the city."

"You don't feel that way anymore?" Gavin asked.

"I don't feel a commitment to the city, if that's what you're asking."

"I don't know what I'm asking."

Gaspar finally followed Gavin into the room.

The only thing Gavin could make out was that a sense of power remained here. He paused at one of the shelves with various strange artifacts on it. Gavin beckoned for Gaspar to join him. "What do you think of this?"

"It looks like he was collecting other items of power."

Gavin looked around. Erica hadn't cared that Gavin had brought her here. In fact…

"It makes me wonder if the Mistress of Vines knew about Cyran and hoped I would bring her here." That would have indicated a greater level of forethought than he would expect out of her.

Unless she'd been aware of him for longer than he'd known.

"Maybe, but if she wanted that, why would she have attacked you when she did?"

"I don't know," Gavin said.

As he looked all around him, he didn't see anything that made much sense. The items in here were all strange, though even "strange" didn't quite suit them. There were bowls and paintings. Some of the artifacts were sculptures; little figurines that looked intricately designed. Others were nothing more than loops of rope, stacks of books, or even empty jars.

What had been inside of them?

Nothing here gave him any answers. In fact, he only had more questions.

"None of this is going to help us find the Mistress of Vines," Gavin said.

"Do we want to do that, or do we want to find these other enchanters?"

"This isn't going to help with that either," Gavin said.

Gaspar looked around. "No, I doubt it will. If we had someone with magical knowledge, we might be able to use this better, but without that…"

"What do you suggest?"

"I suppose we could regroup at the Dragon and see what the others might've come up with. Your friend has been proving himself," Gaspar said.

Gavin smiled at how difficult it was for Gaspar to admit that Wrenlow had been finding out information. "I'll be sure to let him know."

"Oh, I'm certain you will."

"We need to keep Alex safe," Gavin said as he looked around. "But she might know something about the items here."

"Do you trust her enough to bring her here?"

Gavin shook his head. "I don't think we should."

"Good. When I first met you, you struck me as appropriately suspicious, so if that had changed, I was going to start worrying."

"I don't know enough about her." He thought about the beating he'd taken. "She seemed too willing to stay in the fortress. At least, her attack on me suggested that she was."

"Which makes me question her motivations," Gaspar said.

"It's all so damn unusual," Gavin muttered.

He headed toward the door and took one more look around. There were dozens upon dozens of different magical devices here, but none of them were things with an obvious use like the sword, which Cyran must have kept it contained to keep it from getting stolen.

Gavin took a deep breath and shook his head. "We need to find others with magic. We need to be able to search for those…"

"What is it?"

"That's it." Gavin should have considered it before, but he'd been caught up in everything he'd been doing.

"What is it?"

"I think I know how we can look."

"Oh, do tell," Gaspar said.

"The constables. We need their enchantments."

CHAPTER SEVENTEEN

The street was mostly empty. Gavin had sheathed his sword, and as he hurried along, he tried to ignore Gaspar's grunts as they hurried through the streets.

"Do you have to make that much noise?" Gavin asked.

"How much noise would you like me to make? I've heard you sleeping. You snore as loud as a bear. You do everything loudly," Gaspar said.

Gavin ignored him, sweeping his gaze along the street, looking for any sign of movement from whoever that might be out there. Once they found the constables, the next step would be to sneak up on them and incapacitate them.

"I still think this is a terrible idea," Gaspar said.

"Your objection is noted." Gavin glanced over to him. "When you were with them, did you have any items like *that*?" He hesitated to mention the constables too loudly. He never knew who might be listening. Gavin didn't think that anyone was out here following them, but if there was, he didn't want them to know that they were intending to go after the constables.

"When I was with them, they were just getting started."

"Getting started hunting those with magic?" Gavin asked.

"There was less understanding about what they were doing."

"I don't know. It sounds to me from what you've said that there was a pretty good idea about what they were doing."

"I don't think they understood the consequences," Gaspar said.

Gavin turned to look at Gaspar behind him and shook his head. "What consequences do you think there really have been through all of this?"

"When it comes to missing out on these opportunities for other power, there are consequences."

Gavin shrugged. He had seen places different than this, places where magic was used more openly. In his mind, that was one of the benefits of Yoran. He didn't think that those who ruled in the city had any greater justification for their power, but at least they weren't using magic as a reason to rule.

"So you don't have one of these enchantments," Gavin said.

"If I had one, don't you think that I would have offered it?"

"I think it depends on what you might get out it."

"You can think anything you want. I've been far more helpful with you than I have with anyone else in the city."

"What do you mean by that?" Gavin asked.

"You think you're the only person who's come thinking they can disrupt the typical patterns here? But you get things done. You've been useful. So for that reason alone, I've helped you. And it's a far sight more than I've helped anyone else, so be thankful."

Gavin watched him a moment, debating whether to thank him or argue with him. "You do know I'm not trying to disrupt anything."

Gaspar grunted. "You're not trying, but you're still doing quite a good job of it. Damn it, but the things taking place within the city are things that need to change. The fear of magic has been unreasonable." He said that quietly, and his gaze darted around the street, almost as if he was afraid that somebody else might hear what he was saying. "At the same time, I also realize I'm not in any position to make those changes," Gaspar added.

There was something in what he said that suggested to Gavin that Gaspar *wanted* change. Probably because of Desarra, but maybe there was more to it. He'd never pushed to find out what Gaspar did on his jobs, but he made it sound like he had some noble purpose.

"There are ways you could help," Gavin said.

"Maybe, but that involves me wanting to. I wanted to ensure that those I work with are safe, and you, *boy*"—he added the "boy" more aggressively than he usually did—

"have made it very clear that you aren't always concerned with that."

"I want to keep the Dragon safe."

"You say that, but maybe stop bringing danger to it."

Gavin opened his mouth before shutting it again. Danger continued to follow him to the Dragon, despite his intentions. "I'm not trying. It's just that bad people keep coming to it."

"Because of you."

There was movement from a crowd at the end of the street, and Gavin headed toward it. He was looking for a crowd; anything that might suggest constables. In the last few days, they had been a constant presence, so he expected that they would be here. So far, he hadn't seen any.

"Why do you think we're having a hard time finding them when we want to?" Gavin asked.

"The constables don't have any sort of supernatural ability," Gaspar said. "They aren't magical."

"They *do* have enchantments though."

"Be careful how loud you say that."

Gavin looked at him. "Why? Because you fear that the constables will hear us?"

"Yes."

"I thought you said that their enchantments were only to help them detect magic."

Gaspar shook his head. "There are many different kinds of enchantments. You think that just because I was a constable that I'd be privy to all their secrets, but that's not the way it works. I don't know about all of the enchantments the constables have. Possibly the ability to listen, or perhaps something else."

In the distance, there was more movement from the crowd of people along the street. He saw something, though it didn't seem to be constables. "Come with me."

Gaspar sighed loudly as Gavin hurried up the street.

He had no idea if he was heading in the right direction, but as he raced forward, Gaspar kept pace with him. The old thief breathed heavily, and Gavin couldn't help but feel as if he were doing it intentionally.

They reached another intersection, and Gavin found what he was looking for: three constables who were stopped in front of a home. He hesitated, motioning toward them so Gaspar knew they were there too. A few others were out in the street with them, but they looked as if they attempted to avoid their notice, speeding along the street.

"I can see them," Gaspar said.

"Yes, but you're also old. How am I supposed to know what you can see?" Gaspar turned to him, and Gavin chuckled again. "Easy. I just wanted to make sure that you saw them."

"You need to cut out your jabs."

"When you do, then I will."

"Fine," Gaspar said.

They hurried along the street. Gavin stayed near the buildings, a row of homes with several shops. The homes were all squeezed together, narrow buildings that stretched two to three stories high, and though they were better maintained than some in the city, they were still run-down. One of the homes had a shattered window in the upper level, and it had been boarded over. Another's door was askew.

Why would they leave the door ajar?

Still another building had evidence of scorch marks along the outside, though it hadn't been completely burned. It was like a fire had come through but had been put out just in time.

Signs jutting out from the buildings marked the businesses. This wasn't the typical merchant section of the city, so the buildings here had once been homes and were later converted into businesses. The owners probably lived above their shops.

When they caught up to the constables, Gavin looked over to Gaspar. "What do you suggest?"

"This is your plan."

"How many of them will have this enchantment?"

"I don't really know."

"For someone who worked with them, you're not a lot of help."

"I never promised I would be."

Gavin had seen constables in pairs before. This was the first time he'd come across a trio. He'd have to incapacitate all three to determine who might be the one with the item he needed. Doing that while also making sure that he wasn't seen was going to be tricky.

"How about we just follow them for a while," Gavin suggested.

"If you say so," Gaspar said.

"If we attack them now, then we run the risk of them seeing us."

"It's more than just *them* seeing you." Gaspar motioned to the people in the buildings nearby.

Gavin frowned as he followed the direction of Gaspar's gaze, and he realized that the old thief was right. The people here would potentially betray them. Reporting to the constables what happened might earn them a level of protection for themselves.

He moved toward the constables, staying as hidden as he could. There didn't seem to be much of a pattern behind what they were doing. They paused in front of several buildings, standing there for a moment before moving on.

"I think they're detecting magic," Gavin whispered.

"Probably," Gaspar said.

"How do you think it works?"

"Probably the same as any other enchantments."

"How?" Gavin asked.

"You don't have experience with enchantments?"

"I have this," he said, tapping on the enchantment that allowed him to communicate with Gaspar and Wrenlow. The enchantment that Anna had given them was different than the one that Gaspar and Wrenlow had shared. There was still a chain that connected the ear piece to the primary enchantment but the metal was a darker silver, and it had a stranger weight to it. "But I don't have others."

"Given the type of work you do, I would've expected that you'd want access to enchantments," Gaspar said.

"They can be dangerous to rely upon."

Gaspar continued to frown at him. The constables turned a corner, and Gavin hurried ahead, trying to keep up with them. He positioned himself so that he could watch the constables. In front of this building, they paused for a little bit longer. A different idea came to him.

If they followed long enough, the constables might help them uncover an enchanter. From there, Gavin and Gaspar could use that knowledge to figure out where the other group of enchanters would be.

Still, all of it would take too much time. He had no idea how long they were going to have with this, only that he suspected that the Mistress of Vines would make her next move soon. She wasn't afraid of anything they might do—and she wanted Alex for some reason. Perhaps they should release Alex to the Mistress of Vines and see what happened. Gavin looked over at Gaspar, and he doubted the old thief would agree to something like that.

The constables moved on.

"They haven't found anything," Gavin observed. "I suspect the sorcerers in the city are much better at hiding their presence."

"We don't have many of them here. It was a wonder that your friend stayed for as long as he did."

"You keep calling him my friend, but you *do* remember him attacking me."

"Fine. Your old friend? Is that better?"

"A little bit," Gavin muttered.

"We've all got friends like that," Gaspar said.

Gavin looked over. Could the old thief actual be trying to make him feel better?

They made their way along the street and watched as the few people who were out continued to move away from the constables. The constables stopped at another building and lingered in front of the door. This time, they did something different—they opened the door.

It was a slightly smaller building than some of them, only two stories high, and it had been maintained recently, painted with a deep green. The shutters were neat and tidy, and all of the windows were intact. It had been well cared for, which meant it likely was somebody's home.

"They found something," Gavin said. He ran forward.

"What are you doing?"

"Now's our chance."

"Now?" Gaspar asked. "They're inside someone's home. If they… I see."

"Good. Then you can help."

Gavin reached the doorway. He paused, glancing along the street, but he didn't see signs anyone out there was paying attention to them. Darting forward, he reached for one of his knives but changed his mind.

The El'aras dagger.

He had no intention of killing any of the constables. Doing so would only draw their attention to him. That is, unless he killed all three of them. Gavin didn't want to do that either.

But he wanted to be ready for the possibility of magic used around them. If the constables had detected anything in this home, he needed to be cautious. The blade didn't glow. That reassured him, though he still questioned what the constables had detected.

He stayed as low as he could and grabbed the nearest constable. He wrapped his hand to cover the man's mouth and jerked him back, slamming his free hand into the side of his neck. The constable collapsed.

When he was down, Gavin dragged him away.

Gaspar looked over. "What did you do to him?"

"He should be out for a little while," Gavin whispered.

It was a brutally effective technique—and one he hadn't used in quite some time—but in close quarters, it was the right move to use. That left two constables.

"Check him. See what you can find," Gavin said.

Gaspar nodded. It was a wonder he didn't argue.

Gavin sprinted forward, and he found the other two constables searching a back room. He snuck up behind the nearest one, quickly wrapped his arms around to silence him, and dropped him with the same technique he'd used on the first.

He spun to avoid detection, but the remaining constable noticed him.

Gavin lunged. He tried to keep his head down and

twisted as he lunged, wanting to get to the constable without him noticing what Gavin was doing. He wrapped his arms around the constable's throat and held tightly. The constable struggled, thrashing for a moment, but Gavin used his strength and brought him down.

He waited and held on until the constable was completely immobilized. Gavin dragged one of the constables back to the room. When he returned, he reached for the other constable.

The blade of the El'aras dagger started to glow.

Balls.

The constables must have detected something.

Was it a sorcerer, or was it an enchanter?

Either way, Gavin didn't want to get caught. It would be better for him and Gaspar to grab the enchanter and get back out into the street, but first they had to find the enchantment. It could be anything.

Gavin had experience with enchantments, and had seen how they could be utilized to devastating effect. Practically *anything* could be enchanted, but the type of enchantment depended upon the particular skill of the enchanter. Each enchanter had an ability to perform very specific enchantments, though Gavin didn't know if that ability depended upon what they placed the enchantment upon. Sorcerers could use enchantments as well, and were often even more skilled, but sometimes the strangeness of an enchanters ability made their kind of power unique.

Gavin hurried across the room, dragging the other constable. "See what you can find," he whispered.

"What are you going to do?"

He held out the dagger. "Look."

Gaspar frowned at it. "Then we need to go."

"Just because there's magic here doesn't mean there's anything we need to be concerned about," Gavin said. "Hell, if the constables had broken in because there was something dangerous here, maybe this is exactly the place we need to be."

Gaspar turned his attention to the constable.

Gavin stayed low and moved back into the other room. Maybe there was a trapdoor. If so, that meant a sorcerer was here.

He examined the inside of the small room. It looked to be a bedroom, though other than the bed and a table, there was no clothing and no signs that anybody spent much time here. He backed out, and he looked around. An outline on the wall caught his attention, indicating a section that was a little off. Without the glow of the El'aras dagger, he likely wouldn't have even seen it. He probed at it, pressing the dagger into the wall, searching along the corners.

The wall popped open.

Power exploded toward him.

Gavin braced himself, and he brought the El'aras dagger up, which deflected the explosion and caused the energy to split off to either side. He darted forward, holding onto the dagger. It continued to glow, though it was fainter than it had been before.

He stepped into a massive room, larger than he

would've expected from the other side. It opened into a large chamber with a low ceiling. Pillars of stone held up the ceiling, and Gavin had a difficult time seeing to the far side of the room. Shadows loomed in the distance, and though a lantern hung on one of the nearest pillars, there was no light emanating from it.

The room extended through the neighboring buildings. Whoever occupied this place had most of the block.

Something slammed into him again. The impact reminded him of the beating he'd sustained when Alex had attacked him while trying to escape from the Captain. He spun in place with the dagger, but he didn't see anything there. There was nothing other than the darkness.

There had to be someone here.

Gavin moved forward carefully. He held out the dagger, trying to illuminate the room. There were shelves along the walls, and the items on the shelves reminded him of what he'd seen in Cyran's sublevel.

He turned quickly and realized what it was. A sorcerer's lair.

Enchanters didn't have anything quite like it. They didn't need to. Sorcerers required the space and the solitude to carry out their spells and incantations to create power.

He almost chuckled, but the power slammed into him again, knocking him back. It wasn't painful, not the way even Alex's attack had been. Whoever used their magic at him wasn't nearly powerful enough to do any real damage.

"If you don't stop what you're doing now, I'm going to bring the constables in here," Gavin said.

Power surged against him again.

"I said, if you don't stop…" Gavin held out the dagger. He didn't see any movement, nothing that would give him any sense of what he'd detected, but he couldn't shake the irritation within him. They were continuing their assault.

"Fine. If this is what you want to do, then don't blame me when the constables drag you off to…" Gavin had no idea where they took magic users. Perhaps he should ask Gaspar about that.

The assault faded.

"Good. I knocked out the three constables that came to your home. I don't know who you are or where you are, but step forward so I can see you."

Gavin waited for a moment. A small figure stepped out of the shadows, and his breath caught.

A child.

CHAPTER EIGHTEEN

Gavin stared at the child. He looked to be no more than twelve, with thin cheeks, dark hair, and hollowed eyes that had seen more than they should at his age. He'd heard of sorcerers claiming children before, but usually that was because they detected potential for sorcery and because they were willing to train them. Sorcery was a complicated art. He didn't know enough about it to understand all of the details involved, but those who practiced sorcery needed incredible training. He didn't expect a child to have the necessary training, or even the mindset, to handle the skills sorcerers were able to learn.

Which was why he should have known Alex *wasn't* a sorcerer.

"What's your name?" he asked.

"Kegan," the child said.

Gavin studied him, trying to gauge an age. Maybe

twelve. Thirteen. Similar to Alex. "What are you doing here?"

"I'm hiding. You said the constables were there?" The boy looked past Gavin, peering beyond the border of the sorcerer's lair.

"Hiding from what? It can't just be the constables."

"They would take me away," the boy said.

"The constables are searching for people who use magic," Gavin said. Of course, the boy was exactly what the constables were looking for, based on what Gavin had experienced of his power. Only, he couldn't imagine if the constables expected to find somebody this age.

They would've anticipated facing off against a sorcerer, someone of power who posed a real danger to them. That had to be why they brought three constables to bear.

"Are you going to bring me in?" Kegan asked.

"I don't care about magic," Gavin said.

"You don't?"

"I'm not a constable. Now, what I do care about is you attacking me the way you did."

"I thought you were one of them." He took a step off to the side, and in the pale light of the dagger, he looked beyond Gavin. He was watching the space outside of the lair, searching for something on the other side.

"They're unconscious. For now. I don't know how long they'll stay that way. Unless you give me some answers, they might start to come back around."

"Who are you?" Kegan asked.

"My name is Gavin Lorren."

The boy's eyes widened. He recognized the name, though Gavin wondered if he knew him as the assassin or from the rumors that had spread. If it was the latter, then the boy wouldn't be afraid of Gavin. If it was the former…

"What are you doing here?"

"I came looking for the constables."

"You're *attacking* them?"

Gavin glanced behind him for a moment before turning his attention back to Kegan. "Not as a general rule, but they have something I need."

"What do they have?"

"It doesn't matter."

Gavin looked around the room. He watched Kegan out of the corner of his eye, though he kept his focus on the rest of the room, searching for signs of somebody else here.

"How long have you been here?" Gavin asked.

"Not long."

"Where's your master?"

Gavin didn't really know what sort of arrangement the sorcerers had, but he suspected that there was a master and apprentice type of role. Gaspar had said that there'd once been an attempt to have a sorcery school within Yoran. Gavin couldn't even imagine such a thing. In all the places that he'd visited, there'd been nothing like that. Most places were willing to accept sorcery as a necessary evil, but they *did* view the people who used it as something dark. They didn't care for sorcerers. He had enough experience with them and with their magic to agree with that sentiment.

"He is going to return soon," the boy said.

Gavin smiled. "Then we'll wait." He motioned for him with the dagger. "Why don't you step out here? I don't need you to attack me again."

"How were you able to endure it?"

"Your little punches? You need to work on the intensity of your blows if you want to do any real damage."

"You shouldn't have been able to tolerate it," Kegan said.

"I think you're giving yourself far too much credit. I don't know much about magic, but I have the sense that you have some potential. Still, you need to perfect it."

"Perfect what?"

"How you're attacking. You need to focus it. A lot of those small blows could be honed into something more tightly controlled. If you did that, then you might've been more effective harming me."

What was I doing telling the boy this?

He didn't need to help develop a sorcerer who knew how to use their power. Of course, this boy didn't have enough strength to be able to harm Gavin. Yet.

"I've used it before, and it works."

"On constables?" Gavin asked.

The boy stared at him. "Yes."

"Only constables?"

"What's that supposed to mean?"

"Well, I figure somebody like you would need to practice. And if you're practicing only on constables, then you aren't learning what you need of your power." Gavin shook his head. "Trust me. I've had plenty of training, and I know you need a diversity of challengers to ensure that your techniques are effective."

"What do you know about magic?"

"Nothing." He jabbed with the dagger again. "Get out here."

Kegan eyed him for a moment before heading through the doorway. He stayed away from Gavin. He looked young, though there was still something about him that wasn't quite young. It was a strange feeling that Gavin couldn't put his finger on. Maybe the boy was older than he appeared. There were plenty of children who looked younger than they were. He hunched forward as he walked and glanced at Gavin. Wide set eyes glowered at him.

The dagger started to glow more brightly.

"If you're going to try anything..."

Kegan shook his head.

Gavin swore under his breath. He wasn't alone.

He darted off to the side and moved just in time. Something swirled past him. He suspected a magical attack, rather than anybody managing to creep up on him. Still, the idea that Kegan—or whoever he was working with—had surprised him was worrisome.

Gavin was equipped well enough to handle those sorts of things. And somehow, the boy had surprised him. No, *distracted* him.

He tapped on his enchantment. "Be ready. There's a boy coming your way who has some potential, but he isn't alone."

"What kind of potential?"

"Alex potential."

Gavin crouched down, sweeping the dagger around. He needed to figure out the source of the other attack. He hurried through the room, staying low, and debated whether it made sense for him to keep the El'aras dagger out. His knives would likely be more useful, but if he sheathed the dagger, he wouldn't have the advantage that it offered. He needed its light to be able to see.

He moved forward into the large room. He had thought that it was enormous when he'd first seen it, but now that he was here, it seemed even larger than he'd believed when the door first opened. It wasn't as well hidden as the one beneath Cyran's home, but perhaps it didn't need to be.

The doorway that had blocked it had been effective. Had Gavin not had the glow of the El'aras dagger, he might not have ever noticed that there was anything here.

He stayed low and crept forward, then turned when he reached the far end of the room. There was a shadowed form across from him.

Gavin lunged. His elbow connected with something, and he toppled farther forward than he'd anticipated.

It was another child.

Crap.

Gavin rolled to the side, holding out the dagger. This

child was a little bit older than Kegan, but still couldn't be out of their teens. They were unconscious.

Gavin grabbed the boy and slung him over his shoulder, carrying him toward the entrance of the lair. He stepped out and found Kegan watching Gaspar, who simply stood over the three constables, a short knife in hand.

"I found a buddy of his," Gavin said, carrying the other child out and setting him near the constables. He glanced over at Kegan. "Do you have anybody else in there?"

"Mekal?" he whispered.

The boy was older than Kegan, with a hint of whiskers growing on his cheeks, the earliest wisps of a beard. They had the same wide set eyes and the same shock of dark hair. Mekal looked taller and thicker than Kegan, like an older version of him.

"He's fine. Well, he will be. He needs to wake up."

"I didn't take you for the kind to attack children," Gaspar said.

"I wasn't attacking a child… that's not right. I *did* attack a child, but I didn't know I was," Gavin said.

"Who is he?"

"You got me. He was in the back of the room. Kegan came out first, so I suspect this one had been teaching him."

Gavin looked over at Kegan, who was staring at Mekal. "Is that right? Has Mekal been teaching you?"

"Our master is going to return home any minute."

"Are you sure about that?" Gavin glanced over at the

constables. "I could wake them up and give them the news. I'm sure the constables would be most impressed with what you've just told me. I'm sure they might even have something to say about your master's return."

"Don't," Kegan said, moving toward him.

"Then start talking."

"We live here. It was our parents' home."

"What happened to them?" Gavin asked, already on edge. He worried about what the boy was going to say, but he already had a suspicion.

"Do you think this is the first time that constables have come to our home?" Kegan said with an edge of arrogance.

"What do you mean?"

"They come every few weeks. Most of the time, we have enough notice and we can hide. Sometimes we have to run."

"Run?" Gavin asked.

"If they come inside."

"Like they did today."

"We didn't detect them," Kegan said. "I don't know how."

Gavin glanced down at the constables before turning his attention back to the boy. "How do you detect them?"

"They aren't subtle," he said. "They come looking for those who have abilities, and they want to drag them off, but they..." He shook his head and wiped away tears that had formed in his eyes.

Could that be what the constables were doing?

He could imagine that they were going door-to-door, checking out the old homes of sorcerers or even enchanters.

"Were your parents sorcerers?"

Kegan shook his head quickly. "They didn't have enough power."

Enchanters then.

Enchanters had a weaker form of magic. The type of magic they called upon was similar to that of sorcerers, but not nearly as potent. Enchanters had to harness their power, focusing it into items that could be used in other ways, such as Gavin's first communication device. It was how some people had enchantments that allowed them strength or speed or, in the case of the Captain, impenetrable skin.

"Your brother has been teaching you?" Gavin asked.

"He's been trying to show me as much as he can, but he doesn't know enough. There are—"

Kegan cut off, and Gavin smiled. "There are what?"

"Nothing."

"Were you about to say that there are others you've been working with?"

Kegan's eyes widened slightly. "No. I wasn't going to say anything like that."

"Listen, boy. If you know something about other enchanters, I need you to share it with me now."

"I'm not going to tell you anything."

"Even if I do something to your brother?"

Gavin pulled out the El'aras dagger and twisted it. The

blade glowed softly, so he knew that Kegan was still holding onto some magic, though not nearly as much as he was able to.

"What are you going to do to him?" Kegan asked.

"It depends."

"On what?"

"On what stories you've heard about me."

Kegan shook his head. "I don't know anything about you."

"That's too bad." Gavin crouched down.

Gaspar shot him a hard look. "What are you doing?" he whispered.

It came through loud and clear through the enchantment. That was interesting. It was another use for the enchantment he hadn't even considered before. Perhaps he should have thought about that before now. He imagined that Anna had realized the potential of the enchantment in such a way.

Perhaps they needed to call upon the El'aras. They had power, and Anna had lived in Yoran for quite a while—long enough that she might know what was taking place here. The El'aras in the city would have to have known about others who used magic, wouldn't they?

"Just watch," Gavin whispered. He held the dagger out and jammed it into the ground next to Mekal. He touched Mekal on the shoulder. "Wakey, wakey."

Mekal started to stir, and when he opened his eyes, he looked up at Gavin. The El'aras dagger started to glow more brightly.

Gavin shook his head. "I don't think that's a good idea." He placed his hand on Mekal's chest, keeping him from sitting up. "You should know that we have your buddy—brother—Kegan over here. He's been telling us some very useful information, but he doesn't want to tell me anything more about where you've been learning magic." Gavin leaned close to him. "Now, I'm not a constable, but I *am* someone who needs information."

"Who are you?" Mekal asked.

His voice trembled as he did, and Gavin wished this weren't necessary. He needed this information so he could keep Alex safe. And it might be more than that even.

"Your brother knows who I am. That's all that matters. Now, why don't you tell me a little bit more about where the two of you have been training. If you don't, then I might have to find a different place to stick this dagger."

Mekal looked up at him, and he didn't say anything. He trembled, and the power that he was holding onto started to build.

The glow of the El'aras dagger intensified. Gavin reached for the blade, and he held it above Mekal's eyes. "You see this?"

Mekal nodded.

"This tells me that you're trying to call upon power. This is my little enchantment that allows me to know what the two of you are doing."

At the mention of "enchantment," Mekal's eyes twitched.

"See," Gavin continued, "I have a feeling the two of you

know all about enchantments. And that's the information I need right now."

"This is where you're going with it?" Gaspar whispered.

Mekal stared at Gavin. "Go ahead and do what you need to do to us. We can't reveal the others."

It was almost enough to make Gavin regret his choice. Here they were being heroic. Defiant. "I have no interest in harming your other buddies. We're looking for a group of enchanters. All I want is for you to tell me who might know where to find them."

"I…"

Gavin slammed the dagger into the ground again, and it sank all the way to the hilt. The blade's glow winked out, leaving them in darkness.

He leaned toward Mekal. "Listen. I knocked out these three constables in your home. Now, I didn't know the two of you were here, and for that I apologize. I suspect they're going to come back."

These two were in more trouble than he'd realized. Had he known that there were children here, Gavin might've tried a different approach. He would've tried to draw the constables out, and then he would've attacked them in the street. Even if they had noticed him, it would've been better than having them think that Mekal or Kegan had attacked them.

"All I need is a name. Or, even better, where to find Zella."

With that, he pulled the dagger out of the ground and held it up close to Mekal's face.

The boy turned his attention toward the dagger, his eyes still wide. "Why do you want to find Zella?"

"Because she might be able to help me."

Mekal turned his head, glancing over toward Kegan. "I'm sorry, Kegan."

With that, Mekal started to pull upon more power.

Gavin *felt* it. It was the first time he'd felt anything like it. This was more than just seeing the glow of the El'aras blade. He felt something deep within, almost as if his proximity to Mekal connected them and gave him a sense of what the boy was doing.

Gavin leaned over him, and he touched the El'aras dagger to Mekal's neck. "Stop," he said.

Mekal trembled. "What are you going to do to me?"

"I'm sure that your imagination can come up with many different things that I might do."

"You're despicable," Gaspar whispered.

"You know I'm not going to hurt him," Gavin muttered, trying to keep it under his breath.

"Still. This is a child."

"A child sorcerer." Or powerful enchanter. Gavin no longer knew if he could tell the difference. "Where do I find Zella?" he asked Mekal.

"I can't tell you."

Gavin sighed deeply. "I'm afraid that's not the answer I needed. Unfortunately for you, I think that—"

"I can show you," Kegan said.

Gavin glanced over, holding his arm completely still. He could hold this position for hours if needed. He'd tortured men in a similar way before, creeping a knife toward them only a sliver at a time. In Mekal's case, he didn't expect to need to actually penetrate the skin, though the boy was tougher than Gavin thought.

"Where is she?"

"I can show you. Just don't hurt him," Kegan said.

"If you try to mislead me, if you try to do anything other than show me where she is, then he goes first," Gavin said, nodding to Mekal. "Then you."

He got to his feet, grabbing Mekal and jerking him up to stand. He glanced down at the constables. "What should we do with them?" Gavin asked Gaspar.

"You're the one who knocked them out."

"I did, but I didn't really think anything through. With these two kids here, we can't let them come around."

"You're not killing them here," Gaspar said.

Kegan stared at him. "You're going to kill them?"

"I can't have them waking up and finding the two of you," Gavin snapped.

"There might be something else we can do," Kegan said.

He crouched down in front of them, and before Gavin could react, power built from him that caused the dagger to glow brightly.

"You really shouldn't do that," Mekal said.

"Quiet. If he was going to kill them…"

"What's he doing?" Gavin asked Mekal.

"He's changing their memories."

"He's doing *what*?"

"It's not really very effective. All he can do is obliterate the last day. In time, he might be able to do more than that, but…" Mekal shook his head.

Power that was able to erase memories like that would be incredible.

"Why didn't you use that against me?"

"If they fight it, it doesn't work," Kegan said.

"You need them sleeping. Unconscious," Gavin mused.

"Pretty much." He looked up at Gavin. "It isn't the first time I've used it on constables."

Gavin smiled. He'd thought that Mekal was the only strong one, but Kegan had a little bit of steel within him as well. Despite himself, Gavin found that he liked these two.

When Kegan was done, he stood. "If they wake up here, they're going to have questions."

"I can deal with that," Gaspar said.

He lifted one of the constables and carried him out into the street, leaving Gavin with Mekal and Kegan. Both of them looked at him, and the dagger continued to glow.

"You'll find that I'm fairly resistant to magical attacks," Gavin said. "You can try me if you want, but Kegan found that his battering magic didn't really work on me. So if you want to have a go at me, Mekal, feel free. I don't think you're going to like the outcome any more than you liked the outcome when I crashed into you the last time."

Mekal turned away.

Gavin smiled to himself. "Go close your door," he said to Kegan.

Kegan hurried off, and he sealed off the door leading to the back room. As Kegan disappeared, Gavin looked over to Mekal, watching him. The boy said nothing, though he frowned at him. The room was mostly empty, and now that a lantern had been lit, Gavin could see more clearly. It didn't push away the shadows in the distance of the room, and there was still quite a bit of darkness, but it was better than it had been. The air was stale, leading Gavin to think they hadn't opened this room very often.

Kegan returned and joined Mekal. "What are you going to do to us?"

"All I need to know is where to find Zella. After you tell me, you're free to go."

"Just like that?"

"Just like that. Why are you hiding here?"

Mekal and Kegan shared a look, but neither of them answered.

"You're going to wait here, so you might as well tell me what's going on," Gavin said.

"Nothing has gone on," Mekal said. "Until you came here."

Gavin chuckled, glancing to where Gaspar had brought the constables. "That's not quite true."

"What do you intend to do with Zella?"

They cared about her, which meant he could use that, though he didn't love using somebody they cared about against them. These were children, regardless of how mature they might have become after losing their parents.

"Why do you need to find Zella?" Kegan asked.

"Because I was hired to."

Kegan's eyes widened. He *had* heard rumors about Gavin. They weren't the ones that Jessica had been spreading—they were the rumors about his real job. It surprised him that Kegan would've heard anything about it.

Gaspar returned, and he carried one of the other constables out. Kegan and Mekal didn't talk. They watched Gavin; suspicion in their eyes. There was power coming off of one or both of them, and the El'aras dagger glowed continuously.

"You may need to be careful with how much magic you're pulling on," he said to them.

"We can hide it," Kegan said.

"Obviously, you can't hide it completely. Otherwise, you wouldn't be concerned about the constables."

"They've been coming here because they know about us," Mekal said.

"Right. And they have some way of detecting magic. So I'm sure that they'll come after you."

The door opened as Gaspar came in, and he reached for the remaining constable.

"I think it's time for us to go," Gavin said. "And it's time for the two of you to lead us to Zella."

Kegan and Mekal shared a nervous look before heading out the door.

CHAPTER NINETEEN

They left the house and moved to the street, heading toward the north part of the city. Kegan and Mekal were only one step ahead of them, and Gavin kept waiting for them to try to run. He could stop them if they did, but he figured it would make a scene. Hopefully, his threat that he'd come after them would keep them from doing anything else.

"They're afraid of revealing Zella," Gaspar whispered.

"I know. Either she's incredibly powerful or she's someone they care about."

"It could be both."

"It could be," Gavin said.

"It's interesting how they were able to hide," Gaspar said.

"I find it interesting that they have the ability to obliterate memories."

"Not much use if they can only do so for short times," Gaspar said.

"No, but in times like this, it has its uses."

They turned a corner. In the distance, he caught sight of a pair of constables. He took a step forward and nudged Kegan and Mekal. "We're heading this way," he said, motioning for them to follow down a different street that was empty.

"What was that about?" Kegan asked.

"Constables. I figured you wanted to keep your use of power away from them." He said it low, and he arched a brow as he leaned in. "Otherwise, if they detect your magic…"

"If they detect magic, they may blame *you*," Mekal said.

Gavin smiled. There was that steel again. "Maybe. Then again, maybe not. Even if they were to detect it from me, I've trained enough that I'm able to take care of a couple of constables." The words hung in the air a moment. "What about you? Do you think you might be able to handle a pair of constables out in the open? A little bit dangerous, I would say. I'd also think that you wouldn't want to risk it."

Mekal glared at him.

Gavin couldn't help but smile back.

When they reached the next intersection, Gavin indicated for them to stop. "Which way?"

Kegan motioned along the street, waving his hand wildly toward the north. He glanced over at Mekal and held his gaze for a moment, something passing between them. It put Gavin on edge. He already knew they had some way of using power and had heard a little bit about the nature of their magic, so he knew to be careful with them. If they were to use their power against him, he didn't have complete confidence that they wouldn't be able to overwhelm him—especially out here in the street where they had an opportunity to run.

"This way, but the constables were also the way we need to go," Kegan said.

"We should be able to weave around them," Gavin said.

They turned, following the street. He hoped that it didn't look suspicious, but with him and Gaspar following behind the two boys, it might look questionable or even lecherous.

"Did you find anything on the constables?" he asked.

"Nothing of use," Gaspar said.

"They should have some way of detecting magic," Gavin said.

"That was my suspicion, but I didn't see anything."

If not, then how were they searching through the city for other magic users?

He didn't see other constables. As they moved along the street, he was lulled into relaxation. They turned a corner, and Kegan and Mekal started to quicken their steps. Gavin hurried to keep up.

He leaned close to them. "Try to run, and I will find you both."

Kegan stiffened and almost stumbled, then slowed

down a step. Mekal took another moment before he slowed.

"Better," Gavin said.

They reached a building two doors from the end of the street. It was a simple wooden structure like so many that he'd passed, and there was nothing about it that would set it apart. They turned toward it.

"Here," Kegan said.

"This is where we'll find Zella?"

"If she lets you," Kegan said.

"If she lets me?" Gavin glanced from Kegan to Mekal, smiling and shaking his head. "How powerful do you think she is?"

"Powerful enough she won't fear you," Mekal said.

Gavin chuckled. "You really should think about being a little more careful with your mouth." He pushed them forward, motioning for them to head to the door.

"What do you expect us to do?" Kegan asked.

"Knock. Do whatever you do to let Zella know you're here."

Mekal stared at the door, holding one hand above the knob, concern building in his eyes. He didn't look over at Gavin, who wondered if he needed to be more wary than he was. Zella was an enchantress, and one the boys respected, but it was more than that.

They feared her.

"She already knows we're here," Mekal said.

"How do you know that?" Gavin asked.

"She would've felt us. She's probably felt you. Chances are good that she's—"

The door opened, and Kegan gasped. Darkness greeted them from the other side.

Gavin held out the dagger. Of course it glowed.

"Go on," he said, nudging them.

Kegan and Mekal stepped into the building.

As Gavin headed toward it, Gaspar grabbed his arm. "I think we need to be careful here."

"This is what we're after."

"I don't know if finding this egg makes that much of a difference," Gaspar said.

"It's more than just finding the egg. If we can find this enchantress, she can help us locate the Mistress of Vines," Gavin said, keeping his voice in a low whisper. "That's what you care about. That's the job you were hired to help with."

Gaspar frowned. "I wasn't hired for any job."

"You took the job with me. It means you were hired for it." Gavin stared at the doorway. "This is just a secondary job, but…"

"But what?"

Gavin glanced over at him briefly. "But I'm starting to get the feeling that they're connected."

He stepped into the room. Power tried to slam into him, but he was holding onto the El'aras dagger, and the magic seemed to curve around him. Kegan and Mekal turned toward Gavin. Both of them were staring, jaws clenched.

"It's like that, is it?" Gavin asked. He could see faces in the darkness beyond, though he wasn't able to count how many were there.

He sighed as the power continued to push in on him. Behind him, Gaspar cried out.

Not only were they attacking me, but Gaspar too?

Gavin had some natural resistance to magic somehow, and the training that he'd undergone with Tristan had fortified that.

Gaspar didn't have that same benefit.

"Stop it," Gavin said, turning his attention to Kegan and Mekal.

They were the only ones in the room that he thought he might be able to get through to. He suspected that the other two dozen or so in the room were also young, at least as young as Mekal, and possibly as young as Kegan. The only one he didn't know about was Zella.

But considering that these two knew her, was she just as young?

"You aren't going to like what happens," Gavin said.

"You might've been able to overpower the two of us, but you won't be able to do so with all of us," Kegan said.

Power continued to squeeze him. They were right. If he did nothing, they were going to be able to overpower him. Gavin summoned his core reserves, thinking about what he'd done in the past when magic was used against him. Not just with the Mistress of Vines, but even before then.

With Tristan.

He thought about how he'd broken through Tristan's leathers, ropes, and finally chains. He thought about what he'd done when he'd broken free of the magical bindings Cyran had attempted to use on him.

All of those memories filled him, and that energy came up from deep within. It bubbled up from some buried pool of power that lingered inside of him, and all Gavin had to do was tap into it. Doing so was difficult now, especially when he could feel that power fading, but he needed to summon it.

He needed to decide whether he was afraid of the power within him or whether he would embrace it. Gavin pushed it out from inside him. It exploded, causing a burst of energy.

The El'aras dagger surged with light that was almost overwhelming.

With that light, Gavin counted seven faces in the room with him. Two of them were Kegan and Mekal, but the others were young, much like he'd suspected. All of them were children, and he guessed they were all using magic on him.

In that brief moment, he hesitated. He had no idea if his ability to break chains, to break through magical bindings, would cause them any harm. He didn't necessarily want to hurt them. He just wanted answers.

It was too late for him to withdraw it though. Gavin didn't have any control over the magic. If it *was* magic.

That energy burst from him and exploded away,

unleashing a ring of power that collided with the attackers. They were thrown back.

Gavin darted toward Kegan, grabbing him and then Mekal, and he threw them further into the room. He snarled at them. "Where is Zella?"

Mekal looked at him, his eyes wide. "How did you—"

"No more games," Gavin said. "If you know who I am"—and he suspected that Kegan, at least, knew who he was—"then you will tell me where I find Zella. If you don't, I'm going to go through this room and carve through every single person here until I find her."

Gavin put every bit of anger and rage into the comment as possible. He tried to fill it with as much power and as much passion as he could to make them believe he was willing to do this. There was some distant part of him that might even be willing to do it. It was the part of him that had trained with Tristan. His mentor had wanted him to gain that skill and know how to be a killer, and that part of him flared up as he sneered at these two.

"Don't. Please." Kegan tried to fight, and he shook.

"You might find that magic comes a little bit slower to you now," Gavin said softly. His voice was a dangerous growl. "It's been my experience that those who are around when I break the chain of magic take a little while to recover. I suspect you will find you're no stronger than the Mistress of Vines."

Kegan whimpered.

"Do you recognize that name?" Gavin asked. "Would you like me to bring you to her? I'm sure she would be thrilled to know children who play with magic that shouldn't."

"Enough," a voice said from the back of the room.

Gavin dropped the boys. He released the rage that filled him, and he turned toward the voice. A dark figure greeted him. She was young like the others, with black hair that faded into the shadows. Still, he detected an intensity from her. Gavin strode forward, holding the El'aras blade out. It only glowed softly, not nearly as bright as it had been before. That was one of the detriments of breaking through their magic. Now it was too dim to see.

"Zella?" he asked.

"Who are you?" she whispered.

"I was hired to find you. It sounds as if you have something my employer wants."

"I don't have anything. Please don't hurt us."

Gavin looked around, and he noticed the fallen faces of what amounted to be children. Most of them were similar in age to Mekal, thankfully. There were only two who were younger, Kegan and another girl, but all of them were still far younger than what he would have expected from sorcerers.

"I'm not going to hurt anyone else unless you give me a reason to. So don't give me one."

"What do you need?"

Gavin watched her carefully. What he'd said to Gaspar was not untrue. Even though he had rescued Alex, he still didn't know whether that was the only part of the job he needed to complete.

But was it a job?

Erica had betrayed him and wasn't *really* an employer. Maybe the only thing he really considered a job was a task that needed to be completed.

With the Mistress of Vines, he was determined to complete it. He wouldn't let her beat him.

There was something more taking place. He just had to understand what it was—and why *he'd* gotten pulled into it.

"You stole something from my employer," he said.

"I didn't steal anything."

"Unfortunately, he feels differently. And he feels strongly enough that you did that he hired me."

"What do you think I stole?"

"He called it a jade egg."

Her eyes narrowed. "I didn't steal it."

"Really? Like I said, he felt differently. Enough to pay. And, unfortunately for you, he's paying well. So if you do have the jade egg, it'll be far easier for you to simply tell me where it is so I don't have to drag that knowledge out of you. If you don't have it, then…" Gavin smiled, trying to look as dangerous as he could. "I'm not really sure what I'll do. Perhaps I'll see how much you share with me as I jab this dagger into your belly, curving it as I'm—"

"Enough," Gaspar said from behind him.

Only, Gaspar wasn't right there. He shouted it into the enchantment, loud enough for Gavin to hear the anger within his voice. Gavin glanced over his shoulder at Gaspar. The old thief watched him, anger and violence flashing in his eyes.

"Sorry. You're right," Gavin muttered. "Let's make this easy," he said, shifting tactics. "All I need is the egg. Once you hand it over, I can be out of your home. I don't need to do anything different. I don't need to harm you. I don't even need to reveal your presence to the constables. All I need is the jade egg. Once you provide that, you won't ever see me again."

Though he had to worry that they might come after him. They did have power, after all. Perhaps not as much as sorcerers, but they were skilled nonetheless.

He was playing this all wrong. He could feel Gaspar's eyes on him and the irritation within them.

Gavin didn't care. At this point, the only thing he cared about was finishing this part of the job. He didn't even have to turn in Zella. He'd been paid enough and could be paid even more, he realized, especially given the terms of the agreement.

"I thought the point of this was to see what we could find out," Gaspar whispered through the enchantment.

Gavin ignored him. Even though that was part of the plan, there was something more he wanted. If he were able to get the jade egg, then not only would he earn enough money to leave Yoran, but he also could finish two jobs here. Wasn't that better? Certainly Gaspar should be able to understand that.

"I don't have it," Zella said.

"Where is it?"

"I don't have it, but…" She looked all around her, her gaze lingering on Kegan and Mekal for a long moment before turning back to Gavin. "I can help you find it."

"Good."

She motioned for him to follow. Gavin went along with her, heading down the hallway. It was much like what he'd seen in Kegan and Mekal's home.

The others joined her and stayed close, as if they intended to protect her in case Gavin tried to do anything. Considering the way that he'd attacked, he doubted there would be anything they could do to prevent him from harming her if he decided he wanted to.

Gaspar stayed behind Gavin by only a step. "I don't like any of this," he muttered through the enchantment.

"You know, you *are* the reason I took this job."

"This isn't the job you took."

"It's all tied together," Gavin said. The more involved he got, the more certain he was.

The hall ended at a door, and Zella used a burst of magic to open it. Through the El'aras dagger, Gavin was aware of the way the power pushed out from her and into the door. She motioned for him to follow.

He passed through the doorway and noted a strange tingling wash over him, which suggested there was some sort of magical energy here. He couldn't see anything that confirmed it, and he waited for a moment.

"You can come in further," Zella said.

Gavin sighed before following her inside. Gaspar walked in next, staying close.

The room was different than some of the other lairs he'd been in. There were shelves all around, several tables, and a rug in the middle. Gavin wondered if the rug would be removed to reveal a trapdoor beneath it much like Cyran's had. She stopped in the middle of the room, looking around. There was something in her eyes that suggested this was a place of value to her.

"What is this place?" Gavin asked.

"I'm a collector," Zella said.

"A collector?" Gavin paused in front of one of the shelves filled with sculptures. Some of them were tiny figurines, others were bowls, and still others looked to be creatures crafted out of dark metal. There was something to these he hadn't realized before. As he held his dagger up, he sensed power. The blade glowed softly, taking on a hint of pale white light. Many of the sculptures reminded him of what he'd seen in Cyran's lair.

He spun, facing Zella. "Don't try anything."

"You've already made it clear that nothing I could do would work."

"What is all of this?"

"These are enchantments we've collected," she said.

Gavin looked around. "Enchantments?"

"All of them. We've been taking them from the constables."

Gavin glanced over at Gaspar, whose brow furrowed. Gaspar headed toward the shelves opposite Gavin, and he began to search along them in his quick but methodical way.

"Just from the constables?" Gavin asked. There was an enormous number of enchantments here.

"Primarily, though we've taken some from others." She looked over at him. "Some of these enchantments allow us to be stronger or faster, and they give us an advantage."

Gavin smiled to himself. He could imagine the youngsters carrying these enchantments, and he could easily imagine how they were able to hide the fact that they were the ones responsible for taking them.

Who would guess it would be those like Mekal and Kegan?

They looked too young to pose much of a threat. The constables would underestimate them.

Had he not found them when the constables did…

He turned to Kegan, suddenly understanding. He let out a long laugh, ignoring Gaspar watching him. "They didn't just find you," Gavin said. "You were drawing them in."

Kegan turned away, but Mekal continued to look at him defiantly.

Gavin smiled to himself. "What do you think you can do by disarming the constables of their enchantments?"

"They have to have a limit to how many enchantments they have."

"Why must they?" Gavin asked.

He studied the shelves. Some of the objects were simple, such as rings, necklaces, and bracelets. Others were devices, like bowls or boxes or even statues. If these were all constables' enchantments, they had incredible reserves of them. Not that he was surprised by that. Everything he'd seen of the constables suggested they had access to considerable power. They would have to, in order for them to be able to keep peace and push out the sorcerers and enchanters.

"Everything they have is tied to what they stole from our masters," Zella said.

She might've appeared young, but there was something about the way she said it that suggested she might be older than what he gave her credit for. Gavin looked at her anew. Studying her, *really* studying her, he tried to better understand why that was. Maybe it was simply that he'd assumed her to be a certain age.

Gavin had lived a hard life, and his training with Tristan had made things more difficult for him. Because of that, he looked older than he was. Not that he needed any help with that. He'd been scarred through his fighting and through his travels.

"You all trained with the enchanters who were taken?"

"Not taken," Zella said. "Slaughtered. They bargained with our people, and then they slaughtered them."

"So you just think you're taking everything back?"

"Should we not?" She raised her hands, spreading them out in front of her, and she turned in place, looking around the room. "Everything here was created by those who partnered with the constables. Partnered with those who led Yoran at the time. The sorcerers were dangerous. Our people recognized that, and they were willing to work with them, to help them stabilize the city. Even as we did, they were planning and plotting against us."

Gaspar looked over with a troubled expression on his face. "We need to be careful," he whispered.

"Why? That was over a decade ago."

"Yes, but I recognize some of these items. They are powerful. As strong as you are, you still need to—"

The dagger started to glow.

Gavin frowned. "What are you doing?"

"I'm afraid, Gavin Lorren, I'm not going to let you harm any of my people," Zella said.

He realized too late that something had been placed behind him. It was a small figurine that looked like a wolf carved out of black metal, which reflected the light coming from his El'aras dagger. The wolf started to shift, shimmer, and then it began to grow.

Gavin shook his head. "This is a mistake."

"Mistake or not, you came here. You attacked my people. I suspect you would—"

Gavin lunged and stabbed the El'aras dagger into the growing wolf's back. He had no idea if it was even going to work, but as he jabbed it down, the dagger flashed with another burst of white light. The sculpture shattered.

Somebody nearby cried out. Gavin spun, turning to the others in the room. Many of them went racing toward the shelves on the walls.

"If you want to keep anyone from getting harmed," he whispered through the enchantment, "you need to help."

"What do you want me to do?" Gaspar asked.

"You were the constable. Figure it out." Gavin darted forward, turning toward Mekal and Kegan first. They were heading for one of the shelves, reaching for enchantments.

Gavin flipped, the energy of it carrying him up and over them. He kicked softly, though with enough force to incapacitate, and he caught Mekal in the forehead. The boy stumbled backward.

Kegan grabbed something off of the shelf and held it outward. Gavin braced himself, holding the El'aras dagger out from him. The dagger absorbed the brunt of the attack, sending the power streaking off to either side.

He shook his head. "You're making a mistake."

Kegan held out whatever he'd grabbed, forcing it toward Gavin. "No."

Gavin dropped low, twisting his legs in a scissoring technique, and he caught Kegan and flipped him to the ground. The boy's head crashed into the stone and bounced. The sound was almost sickening, but hopefully he hadn't fallen so hard to have crushed his skull.

At this point, Gavin wasn't even sure *how* he needed to feel. They looked like children, but he had a sense that perhaps they weren't children at all. Magically enhanced in some way...

But was that all they were?

With other magical beings, they *looked* human. The El'aras looked mostly human, but they were not. There were others in the world that looked... different. Most of the enchanters he'd met *were* human.

But could there be something else? What did I really know about enchanters, other than the fact that Alex was one?

And Alex was with Jessica. Wrenlow. Imogen.

Gavin tapped on the enchantment, and he quickly whispered, "Wrenlow, if you're paying any attention, you need to be careful with Alex. I don't know what sort of enchantments she might be hiding from you."

There wasn't any response, but that didn't necessarily mean anything. It was possible that Wrenlow was tied up with whatever research he was looking into at this point. He hoped that Alex hadn't escaped them, and he hoped she wasn't doing anything right now.

Gavin shifted, turning toward several of the other enchanters. Three of them converged on him, and all of them held items in hand. Gaspar snuck around the backside of the room.

"Listen. All I need is the jade egg," Gavin said, looking past the three enchanters approaching and trying to get Zella's attention.

"What makes you think I'm going to provide you with the jade egg?"

"What is it?"

"Something we've been trying to reclaim for years," Zella said.

"Why?"

She shook her head at him. She nodded toward the others, making a motion with her hands. They were facing Gavin, but they reacted to the motion she made.

Could that be another enchantment?

This place was a storehouse of enchantments, and he could imagine how they might be used.

Hell, he wanted to go through everything in here to see what there might be. Despite what he'd told Gaspar about not wanting or needing enchantments, there was still value in them, like with the enchantment he communicated to Gaspar and Wrenlow through. He could think of other enchantments that would be equally valuable to him if he were given the opportunity to use them.

He turned toward the three oncoming enchanters. He was prepared for whatever they might do to him. But he wasn't ready for how quick they were.

They streaked toward him, and Gavin did the only thing he could think of.

He jumped.

Training kicked in at that point. While in the air, he spun and stretched his legs out from him on either side, and the momentum carried him around. One foot struck the shoulder of one of the enchanters and sent them spinning off to the side. The other missed, but as Gavin came back down, he chopped with his arm, slicing toward them. The blow was hard enough that he knocked one of the enchantments away from the attacker.

He darted forward, using a burst of power from his core reserves, giving him a hint of speed. When he slammed into the third enchanter, they collapsed.

Gavin raced forward, holding onto the El'aras dagger. Resistance pushed against him, but he ignored it.

Then he reached Zella.

He pressed the dagger underneath her neck and held her tightly from behind. "Call them off."

As he looked around him, he could see the other enchanters getting back up, turning toward him. Some of them, including Mekal, remained down. Still, Gavin worried that even a few enchanters organized would be more than what he could withstand.

"I'm not calling them off. They're doing what they are instructed to do. They are protecting me. Our people. Our—"

Gavin shoved a little harder than he intended. The El'aras dagger cut the skin of her neck. Blood trickled down the blade, causing the glow to surge brighter.

"Call them off," he hissed.

Zella stiffened. "You wouldn't hurt me."

"Who do you think I am?"

"Gavin Lorren. The tracker." She flicked her gaze up to him, though it lingered on the dagger. "I know Davel Chan hired you to find the egg."

"You got the name right, but you don't have the occupation right." He pushed her forward, thrusting her toward the others. Gaspar stood behind him.

Gavin focused on the core energy within him.

"I'm Gavin Lorren. Assassin for hire."

CHAPTER TWENTY

The enchanters stood across from him, some of them trembling, but Zella held her gaze on him, unmoving and seemingly unconcerned. The room was quiet and still, and Gavin could practically feel the tension building within it. He could feel the energy here and knew that the moment he took a step forward, everything would shift.

He held his gaze on Zella but also paid attention to the others around him. He didn't need to watch to keep track of them. He counted seven other enchanters surrounding him. Given their number, there was a reasonable danger to him.

Which meant he had to finish this quickly.

"Where is the jade egg?" Gavin asked.

"I told you where it was," she said.

"No, you told me that you don't have it."

"I don't have it anymore. I used it."

"What did you use it for?" he asked.

"Payment."

"What sort of payment?"

"It doesn't matter." Zella crossed her hands in front of her, and the El'aras dagger started to glow again.

Gavin shook his head at her, jabbing the dagger forward. "I think we have well established that your magic isn't going to work on me the way you want it to, so you might as well stop attempting to call on it. Don't give me any more reason to attack you."

"You can't defeat all of us."

"I already have. And I'm not opposed to cutting you all down, but not before I get answers."

Gaspar came up behind him. Gavin flicked his gaze over to him, looking to see what Gaspar might do or say, but he remained silent.

"What kind of answers do you need?" Zella asked.

"To start with, I want to know more about the jade egg. What is it?"

Davel Chan had made it sound as if it was something only slightly valuable, but maybe it was far more valuable than he'd let on. If that were the case, Gavin needed to figure that out before he returned it.

Of course, the man *had* been willing to pay upwards of thirty gold crowns.

"It's an enchantment," she said.

Gavin grunted, careful not to move the dagger. "I gathered that."

"It's a powerful one. Using the jade egg, even someone

without the natural enchanter ability can place new enchantments."

"I don't think that's how it works," Gavin said.

"It was created by the enchanters from decades ago. They wanted to give the constables something to use so they could create their own enchantments. They poured much of their energy into making it. The egg was how they knew they could defeat the sorcerers. It was a dark and violent time for those within the magical community," she said.

"What happened?"

Zella stared at him. "A sacrifice."

Gavin shook his head. He could imagine what kind would be involved in it. Creating magical items often required sacrifice, and though he didn't necessarily know all that much about magic, he knew enough to understand that it didn't come free.

Magic always required something of the user.

In the time he'd wandered, he had experience with many magic users. Most of them had willingly sacrificed whatever they had to in order to get the power that they wanted. "I've seen how magic can require a sacrifice," he said softly. "Unfortunately, I have far more experience with magic than I would like."

"How have you survived it?"

Gavin shrugged. "The one who trained me ensured that I would survive anything." He watched Zella. They had gone through something, but she wasn't going to reveal it to him.

What would Cyran have been willing to do in order to gain more power?

Gavin had seen that he was willing to sacrifice everything to grow in power, including his friendships that were the connections he had to his past.

"I imagine that your masters—or parents," he said, watching them and trying to determine whether or not that was true, "stored something of themselves into the enchantments."

Zella stared at him. "Yes."

"What did they give up?"

"Their magic."

Gavin didn't know that such a thing was possible, but if they had poured their magic into the jade egg, then he could understand why Zella and the others would want to get it back. And he could understand why Davel Chan would be willing to pay thirty gold crowns for it.

An item like that would be invaluable.

"How did they give up their magic?"

"By pouring it into the egg, which absorbed it and gave those without power the ability to cast enchantments. It's limited and requires time to replenish, and it's no different than using magic normally. In creating the egg, they allowed the constables the ability to enchant anything they needed to defeat the sorcerers."

Gavin glanced over at Gaspar. "Did you know this?"

"All I knew was that there was an item of power. I knew they had access to enchantments, sometimes many more than I would've expected. I would never have imagined anything like that."

"Where's the egg now?" Gavin asked Zella.

"As I said, I offered it as payment."

"Payment?"

"Yes."

"What kind?" Gavin had an idea though.

"The kind of payment that means our people will finally be safe."

"You mean safe from the constables."

She stared at him.

"Fine. You don't have to tell me, but I have a feeling that your payment ended up in the hands of the Mistress of Vines and that you're the reason I was sent to the Captain's home."

He had a rising suspicion that he'd seen the enchanters steal the egg from the constables. That was what he'd seen with the wagons, which meant that the egg hadn't been out of their hands for very long. It also meant that Davel Chan was with the constables.

And even more than that, he had a feeling he might've been used in more ways than he'd imagined. The lack of reaction from Zella's face suggested that he was right.

He looked at the others. "Don't get in the way."

He started toward the door, and Gaspar followed.

"What are you doing?" Gaspar whispered through the enchantment.

"Leaving."

"You're leaving, with all of this here?"

"Yes."

Gavin reached the door and turned, holding out the El'aras dagger. He could feel the energy within the room, though he couldn't tell where it was coming from. The only thing he could determine was that there was a sense of power here. The El'aras dagger continued to glow with a soft white light, filling the room with it.

Gaspar shook his head. "Are you sure about this?"

"What do you want me to do?" Gavin asked. "Clean them out? If she's right, and if the jade egg is the source of the constables' enchantments, then all of these were created by the constables."

Zella nodded slightly.

"And I don't disagree that the power belongs to them, I just disagree with how they've been getting it back. The way they've attempted to use me," Gavin said.

"What do you intend to do?" Gaspar whispered.

"Finish the job."

He stopped at the door and looked back at them. "Stay out of my way."

"Or what?" Zella said.

"Or you're going to see just how far I'm willing to go to finish all of my jobs."

Gavin headed through the building and stepped back on the street. He took a deep breath before stalking off.

Gaspar caught up to him. "What do you think you're doing?"

"I'm going to have words with Davel Chan."

"We were there already. There was nothing."

"We were there, but I don't think there was actually nothing."

"Why?"

"Because I'm pretty sure I was hired by constables," Gavin said.

He hurried back toward the home where they'd found Mekal and Kegan. Gaspar stayed with him, quiet until they reached the home.

"Where did you leave the constables?" Gavin asked.

Gaspar motioned for him to follow, and they rounded a corner into an alley. Gavin crouched down in front of one of the constables. He had a rounded face, soft chin, and ruddy cheeks. He *looked* soft. Soft men often cracked.

The others were leaner, and one of them even had a scar on one of his cheeks, suggesting he had some experience with fighting. This was the kind of man Gavin would respect but wouldn't necessarily be able to get answers out of as quickly as he wanted. Besides, he figured the first man was the one who led them.

Gavin shook him. Then he waited. The constable didn't come around.

"See if you can't wake him up," he said to Gaspar.

It was one thing to be offered a job, but it was another for Gavin to take it so foolishly and ignorantly that he hadn't paid attention to who was hiring him. This had happened too often in Yoran.

Gaspar reached into his pocket and pulled something out, resting it underneath the constable's nose. "Why do you think Davel Chan is a constable?"

"The money," Gavin said.

"How much did he offer you?"

"Thirty gold crowns."

Gaspar grunted. "That's... considerable."

"It is, and I thought the reason he was willing to pay so much was only because he had me going after someone with magic. Now I wonder whether or not it was simply because he has an unlimited supply of coin."

"Not unlimited."

"Mostly though," Gavin said. "I realize it comes from the taxes charged, and the people of the city are the ones paying, but..."

The constable started to come around, and Gavin leaned forward, pushing Gaspar off the side. He crouched down next to the constable and held the dagger underneath his neck.

He looked directly into the man's eyes. The constable stared back.

"There you are," Gavin said, leaning close. "You have a dagger under your neck. And a knife to your groin," he said, shifting the other knife. "Trust me when I say I'm not afraid to use either of them. Your answers will determine which end of the blade you experience. Do you understand?"

The constable didn't say anything.

"You can blink once if you understand."

The constable blinked.

"Good. Now I'm going to pull the dagger at your throat away a bit, but I'm not going to remove it altogether. I expect answers. Nothing more than that. If you strike me as being misleading in any way, you're going to find pressure on one of the blades. I decide at the time which one it is." Gavin started to withdraw the dagger slightly, and he stared at the constable. "What's your name?"

"You're making a mistake. You would dare to attack constables of—"

Gavin shoved the knife forward but not by much. He had enough control over the blade that he could tell it wasn't going to slice all the way through the man's groin, but enough to give him a haircut.

"Listen," Gavin said. "We can do this many different ways. I'm perfectly content to have you continue to chat away at me, but know that I have all the time in the world. You are off in an alley, and the longer you talk, the more likely it is that my hand is going to slip. Is that what you want?"

The constable stared at him.

Gavin nodded. "Better. Name."

"James Thierry."

"Good. Now that I've got that established, I have a few questions for you. First question: Do you know the name Davel Chan?" A hint of tension fluttered the corners of the constable's eyes. Gavin had his answer, but he wanted to know what James might say. "No answer? Fine."

He shoved again, sending the blade into James's groin. The man screamed, the sound sharp and high-pitched.

Gaspar was there in an instant, clasping his hand over James's mouth.

"Thanks," Gavin said, looking over at Gaspar.

"You see, I don't like that answer. The next one might anger me even more. Do you know the name Davel Chan? It's a simple question, and in my mind, it would have a simple answer. All I'm asking is for you to tell me whether or not you know the name. I'm not asking you to tell me where to find him."

"I know the name," James said.

"That's what I thought. Now, the next question might be a little bit harder for you considering how difficult the last one was. *Where* is he?"

James said nothing.

Gavin offered a tight smile. He pressed the dagger forward into James's neck. Blood dribbled down the edge of the blade.

James winced, trying to pull away, but Gavin held steady and even pressure.

"Again, I didn't care for that answer."

"He didn't answer," Gaspar said.

Gavin glanced over his shoulder at Gaspar, who was glaring at James. "You're right." He turned back to the constable. "I didn't care for that lack of answer. Now, where do I find Davel Chan?"

"He's not the kind of person you find."

"What does that mean?"

"He finds you," James said.

Gavin sighed and shook his head. "How do I have him

find me?"

The constable smiled at him. "If he finds you, then you're dead. Is that what you want?"

Gavin shoved a little bit further with the dagger, and James cried out again. "Listen. I've told you what I want. How do I get him to find me?"

One of the other constables started to stir, and Gavin twisted quickly and kicked him in the head, knocking him out again.

James's eyes widened, and he glanced over at his partner. "What are you going to do to them?" he asked Gavin.

"That depends on what you do for me. All I need is an answer. How do I get Davel Chan to find me?"

"You don't want him to find you. If he does, you'll be dead."

"And I've told you that I don't necessarily care."

"I have a ring," James said.

Gavin shook his head. "I don't need money from you. You won't be able to buy me off."

"No. It's a ring I use to call him."

Gavin flicked his gaze to Gaspar. "I thought you took everything off of them."

"I did."

Gaspar reached into his pocket, and then he pulled out the items that he'd taken off of the constables. He held them in one hand. James blinked a few times.

Gavin reached into Gaspar's palm and plucked a ring free. "This one?"

"That one helps me—all of us—if we need reinforcements."

"And it reaches Davel Chan?"

"Yes."

Gavin started to squeeze it.

Gaspar grabbed his wrist. "Are you sure you want to do that? If this man is who it sounds like he is, then you'll be drawing the attention of the constables to you. *All of them.*"

"If he's who it sounds like he is, I've already drawn their attention." Gavin flipped the dagger, and he slammed the hilt into James's forehead, knocking him out again. He straightened, sheathing the knife but holding onto the dagger and the ring. "What do you propose?"

"If you're going to draw the head of the constables here, I don't want to be here," Gaspar said.

"You don't need to be."

"Gavin—"

Gavin shook his head. "No. This was the job I took. I'm the one who got drawn into this. I'm the reason Davel Chan is even involved in anything. Why don't you go back to the Dragon and make sure everything's safe. I haven't heard back from Wrenlow, and I warned him that Alex might not be quite as innocent as we think."

"Why would you say that?" Gaspar asked.

"Because I suspect she's with the other enchanters. So I warned him, and seeing the way Imogen was able to hold off the Mistress of Vines, I'm not as concerned as I would've been otherwise," he said. He watched Gaspar for some reaction or a sign, but he didn't give one. "Regardless, I figure somebody needs to go back to make sure that everybody's okay."

"You aren't going to be able to take on all of the constables."

"Who said anything about taking them on?"

Gaspar's gaze drifted down to the fallen constables before looking up at Gavin. "Don't do anything foolish."

"I thought you said everything I do is foolish."

"Maybe," Gaspar said. He nodded at Gavin, then he started off down the alley.

Gavin looked at the fallen constables and squeezed the ring, thinking it would somehow activate the enchantment. He slipped it onto James's finger so he could activate it when he came around, and then he darted toward the back of the alley. The space between buildings shrunk as the alley stretched on, and he used it to scale the sides of the buildings.

Once he was on the roof, he hurried forward, racing to where he could see the constables. He looked down and watched.

It wouldn't be long.

The only question was whether Davel Chan would come himself or whether he would send other constables.

All Gavin could do was wait.

CHAPTER TWENTY-ONE

The constables hadn't stirred. It had been nearly an hour, and there was still no sign of movement along the street to suggest that anyone was coming this way. So much for the enchantment being able to call Chan.

Gavin was tempted to return to the Dragon. Gaspar might need his help, though he would use the enchantment to call Gavin if he did. That he hadn't…

He lay in place, debating what to do. An irritating thought came to him. Perhaps James hadn't told him the entire truth. It was possible that the ring could summon Davel Chan, but it was also possible that he'd misled Gavin. If he had, Gavin still could use him.

So he waited.

It wasn't too much longer before the constables started to regain consciousness. They moved slowly, and he could hear one of them starting to stir the other.

Gavin stayed hidden on the rooftop, not wanting to reveal his presence just yet. He didn't know who was the first one to come around, but the voice didn't sound like James.

Finally, another one grunted. "Where is he?"

This was James. Gavin was certain of it.

"Where is who?" another asked.

"The bastard who tried to cut my balls off."

Someone chuckled but silenced quickly. "What happened?"

"I told you," James said. "The bastard had a knife to my throat and my balls. He threatened me."

"What did he want?"

"He wanted to know how to find Chan."

"What did you tell him?"

"I told him about the ring, dammit. Why would it matter? If he wants to summon Chan here, then let him."

"I don't see Chan."

Gavin shifted so that he could look. In the position that he was in, he could make out the outlines of the constables, but he couldn't see what they were doing.

"No. He didn't come."

"Do you think he got the message?"

"I don't know."

The figure who looked like James limped toward the end of the alley.

Gavin smiled to himself. He thought he'd been a little bit more cautious with the knife to the groin, but perhaps he hadn't been as cautious as he'd thought. The constables reached the end of the alley, and they paused while looking out.

Gavin followed them, creeping along the rooftop. Thankfully this section of the city had roofs that weren't nearly as sloped as in other parts, which meant he could stay up here. At the end of the alley, he flattened himself to look down. The constables moved along the street.

He slipped down, dropping to the ground, and he started forward. Movement behind him caught his attention.

Gavin spun, whipping the El'aras dagger around.

Five constables were there. Davel Chan was among them.

The other constables were all of a similar size; average build, average height, and average appearance. They had on the gray pants and jackets, each of them armed with a sword, their dark blue cloaks fluttering in the wind. Then there was Davel Chan. He was shorter than the rest, wider, and perhaps more dangerous.

Gavin grinned. "Here I thought you'd abandoned them."

"That was you?" Chan asked.

"I was the one who sent the message."

The constables remained arranged around the alley, as if trying to block him from going down it. Gavin wasn't blocked from the street, though he suspected they had other ways of preventing him from going anywhere. If he was right, then there were also constables that moved along the street toward him.

He didn't have much time before he'd have to resolve this. Either he was going to have to fight through them, or he was going to have to come to terms with them. At this point, given how he'd been used, he was tempted to do the former.

It wasn't the smart move.

Tristan had trained him better than that. Gavin could fight through five constables, but if they were enchanted, then it would be harder than he thought.

"Did you find it?" Chan asked.

"Really? That's all I get?"

Chan regarded him with a frown. He looked more confident than when Gavin had seen him before. "If you knew you were hired by the constables, would you have taken the job?"

"Probably not."

"I didn't think so. Your reputation is such that I figured you would refuse, and considering how important this item is to us, we wanted to ensure it was recovered. Where is it?"

Gavin flashed a wide smile. He shifted to glance in either direction. James and the other two constables had stopped at the end of the street. They were looking in his direction. He didn't have to turn around to know that there would be other constables there too.

"I think the terms were another ten gold crowns when I found Zella."

"You found her."

"That's what you hired me to do."

"If you found her, then you have the egg."

Gavin shrugged.

"We have you outnumbered, Lorren. Do you really want to fight your way through us?"

"You might have me outnumbered, and given what I've learned, you're heavily enchanted as well." He watched and waited for any sort of response, but Davel stared at Gavin, his face neutral. "You don't want to deny it?"

"What's there to deny?"

"I guess I thought that the constables would deny using enchantments."

"We've never denied that."

"Well, let me just tell you that I incapacitated an entire gathering of enchanters, so your paltry collection of enchantments is unlikely to pose much difficulty to me."

Davel simply stared at him. This was a different man than Gavin had met when he'd gone to his home. That man had seemed uncertain and easily manipulated. Of course, he'd made sure to come off that way. He'd played Gavin.

Gavin shook his head. He flicked his gaze down the street that was now emptying out. The people who'd been there were clearing, and the constables would be all that remained. Even if he had the jade egg, it was unlikely he would get out of here easily.

"Where is it?" Chan asked.

"You aren't sticking to the terms of the agreement."

"I'm modifying them."

Gavin shrugged. "Then I'm going to modify my response to them."

"I don't think that's wise."

"And I don't think it's wise for you to have challenged me."

Davel started to chuckle. "You really think quite highly of yourself."

"I know what I'm capable of. I'm guessing you don't know that, though, which is reason enough for me to feel confident I'll get past you." He smiled. "Anyway, the agreement was another ten gold crowns when I found Zella, which I have. And then a remaining ten when I recover the jade egg."

Chan smirked. "Fine. I'll give you the ten gold crowns as we agreed." He reached into his pocket, and he pulled out a pouch and tossed it toward Gavin.

Gavin crouched down, using the opportunity to search along the street and survey how many other people were there. His survey showed five coming from his left and another four coming from his right. That didn't count James and the two other constables still there.

Quite a few. Just for him.

He lifted the bag and hefted it for a moment, gauging its weight. "Are you sure it's ten?"

"I might've been a little generous with you."

"That's kind, but it doesn't change the terms."

"Really. Then you're going to tell me where you found Zella."

Gavin flashed a smile. "Those weren't the terms."

"The terms were that you would get ten gold crowns when you found Zella. Now tell me where she is."

"Again, that wasn't our agreement. And seeing as how you were the one who wanted to change the terms of our agreement, I don't want to give you any reason to continue to change them."

"Lorren—"

Gavin smirked. "Thanks for the gold crowns. I might have to pass on completing the rest of the assignment."

"You aren't going to get out of here. If you know where to find Zella, then—"

"I know how to find her, and I have a good idea *why* you want me to find her. You need the egg back so you and your constables can continue using your enchantments. I'm not so sure I'm going to have any part of that, especially not if it's going to allow you to attack those who have any magical potential."

"You aren't from Yoran. I'll let that much slide. You don't understand the nature of magic within the city. You don't understand the danger that exists here."

"I might understand it better than you do. Besides, the constables were pretty useless when the city was attacked by a sorcerer not that long ago."

Davel's eyes narrowed.

Gavin cocked his head to the side, noting the steadily approaching constables. They weren't rushing toward him, which suggested they were trying to take up positions around him. He was going to have to act quickly if he was going to do anything at all.

"You didn't know about that, did you?" he asked. "You had a sorcerer active in the city. From what I understand, it's been quite a while since you've had *any* sorcerers active here, and that kind of oversight wouldn't look very good for the constables."

"What are you getting at?" Davel asked.

"You have *another* sorcerer active in the city."

"We would know."

Gavin scoffed. "Like you knew about the first one?"

"There wasn't another sorcerer."

"I beg to differ. In fact, there were two, though one of them didn't really step foot in Yoran, so I suppose that doesn't count."

Davel glared at him.

"It doesn't count, does it?"

"No."

Gavin readied to move. He would have to fight a little, though hopefully not so much as to hurt anyone more than he had. "Do you have some sort of agreement with sorcerers that keeps them from Yoran?"

"Only if they wish to live," Davel replied.

"I'll take that as a yes. That's what the egg is for?"

It had to be more than just to provide enchantments. That might be part of it, but enchantments alone wouldn't be enough to make it as valuable as it seemed to be to everyone.

"With the power of the egg, we've prevented sorcerers from gaining traction within Yoran. You don't know what it was like when they were here before."

"I can imagine," Gavin said softly. Having seen sorcerers rule elsewhere, he knew it was never pretty.

"If you can imagine, then you know the only way for the city to be safe is to keep sorcery at bay."

"By using enchanters. A weaker form of the same damn magic."

"It's not the same," Davel said.

"You can tell yourself that. It doesn't make it true."

Davel glared at him.

Gavin just shook his head. "Anyway, the sorcerer active in the city now goes by the name of the Mistress of Vines."

Gavin watched him, trying to gauge his reaction, but it was difficult. Davel's blank expression as he stared at Gavin was surprising. He was far more neutral than expected.

Not just neutral, but skillfully so.

Impressive.

"Given your lack of response, I'm guessing you've heard the name before, and that tells me that you aren't altogether surprised she's active in the city. Interesting."

"You've seen her."

"Seen her? She hired me."

Davel stared. "You're working for the Mistress of Vines?"

"I didn't know I was, and even now, I'm not so sure I want to be, but she did ask me to protect someone, so…" Gavin shrugged. "I figure I need to do that much at least."

"Who did she ask you to protect?"

"Client confidentiality. I'm sure you can understand. I don't imagine you want too many other people knowing that you hired me to recover the egg. For that matter, I doubt you want too many other people knowing you lost the egg in the first place."

"I didn't lose it."

"No? Then who did? Someone must have taken it."

Davel stared at him.

"Your constables are pretty good at being neutral like you. James thought he was going to get away with that, too, didn't you, James," Gavin said, raising his voice to carry down the street. Out of the corner of his eye, he saw James hesitate. Gavin smiled. "I didn't mean to hurt him. I was trying to gather information. Seeing as how you used me, I figure you'd understand."

"What did you do to him?"

"Nothing he won't recover from. I don't think I permanently maimed his balls, though honestly, sometimes I lose track."

"Enough," Davel said. "If you know how to find Zella and the Mistress of Vines, then you need to tell us."

"Or what?"

"I think you know."

Gavin took a deep breath and let it out slowly. "Why did you hire me?"

"What was that?"

Gavin flicked his gaze around again. He didn't have much time left. "Why did you hire me?"

"Because you have a reputation as being someone

who's incredibly skilled and who can work with magical items. I'll admit, I hadn't heard much about you before, but the information came from a reputable source."

"What source was that?"

Davel said nothing.

Gavin almost shook his head. If all of this was because of rumors spread around the city about him, and maybe by Jessica... "So you heard I was a tracker. That was it."

Chan frowned at him. "Is that not the case?"

"Unfortunately for you, no."

Gavin focused on the core reserves of power, that magic he *might* possess, and he summoned it as the constables came toward him. He burst forward with a jump.

The jump carried him up and over the constables, back toward the alley. He landed and spun, and he dropped the nearest two constables with a kick. He slammed his fist into the next constable, turned around, and drove a punch into another. By the time the constables reacted, he'd already knocked out the fourth one.

It left only Davel Chan, who stood watching him. There was a hint of amusement in his eyes. He drove forward.

The man was fast. When Gavin had faced the enchanters, they had moved quickly, but this was something else. His enchantments were incredible. He darted forward so fast that Gavin could barely keep up.

Gavin scrambled to follow the movements, and he was

forced down the alley, blocking each attempt, trying to parry each blow.

"Where is the egg?" Chan asked.

His fighting technique was exquisite. He varied between three different techniques: Sudo, a fairly common fighting technique but no less effective; Ishan, a technique well suited to such close-quarter fighting; and Jonal, a fairly rare fighting technique Gavin hadn't seen too many others use. It was abrupt, brutal.

And lethal.

Thankfully, Gavin had trained in all of them and knew how to counter them, but he also knew other fighting styles that complemented them that were incredibly effective.

Even in the close confines, he didn't struggle. He could block, and it was only Davel's superior—enchanted—speed that he struggled with. Gavin continued to focus, thinking about the nature of the techniques he was using, and he fell into the fighting pattern.

He'd fought faster and more skillful opponents before. He might not have the speed Davel possessed, but he had experience and knowledge. If they were out in the open, he might not be able to withstand the attack, but here in the alley with walls on either side of him, he was protected. He could use the close quarters to overwhelm everything Davel did.

"Not a tracker, are you?" Davel asked.

"I think you would have discovered that had you done

more research. Of course, had I looked into you, I might've learned a little bit more about you as well."

"It seems both of us were misled."

"Only I wasn't the one who misled you."

"No? You were certainly eager enough to take the job."

"I should've known better," Gavin said.

"Yes. You should have."

"I do have to thank you. You've given me enough money to leave Yoran and not have to worry about finding another job for a while."

Davel shook his head. "You aren't going to get out of here until I have that egg."

"And I'll be honest. I don't know if I can give you the egg back."

Gavin blocked a blow that came right at his forehead. It was quick, a sharp jab that was a misdirect. He spun, and the wall prevented him from getting out of the way.

Davel twisted, swinging his hip around. With the speed he operated at, it looked almost lazy.

Gavin knew it was anything but. He dropped, pushing off of the wall, sliding forward and bringing his fist up. Davel rotated, catching Gavin's fist between his thighs and squeezing. Gavin flipped back up and kicked toward Davel, driving his foot at the man's shoulder.

The move freed his hand, and he spun around, trying to position so that he could see Davel. But the shift had put the other constables between him and escape.

Davel stood in front of him. Either Gavin was going to have to overpower him, or he was going to have to find a way out. He'd already used energy from his core reserves, and there was only so much power remaining. He didn't want to risk depleting too much of that power until he knew more about what Davel was capable of.

"I need the egg," Davel said. "I'm sure you can understand why it's valuable to us. If you faced a sorcerer in the city, then you understand just how important that is."

"Obviously the egg isn't so important to you. Otherwise you wouldn't have lost it."

"And I said we didn't."

"No? Somebody stole it from you?"

Davel didn't say anything.

Gavin tried to prepare for anything that Davel might do to him, but he wasn't sure what it would take. He twisted again, and he focused on his attack. He'd have to find a way to escape by using the energy he had left.

The constables behind him approached slowly.

He was ready for anything.

Or so he thought.

Davel shifted his attack and barreled toward him. Gavin barely jumped in time. Had he not been already calling upon his core reserves, it may not have been enough. He managed to launch in the air, but he didn't have the space to maneuver and kick.

He grabbed for a low overhang and pulled himself up to the rooftop. Crouching there, he looked down at Davel.

"You aren't going to be able to get away from there," Davel said.

"You don't know that," Gavin said.

"I know better than you."

Davel jumped and reached the rooftop quickly, which surprised Gavin again. He was enchanted. *Heavily* enchanted.

Knowing what he did now and how the jade egg was the key to enchanting the constables, Gavin imagined that Davel used it frequently, drawing upon the energy of more and more enchantments to secure his position. It was the kind of thing someone who wanted to maintain power would do.

Gavin backed away. The roof wasn't all that sloped, but it also wasn't stable enough that he could fight effectively. He was going to have to move carefully. He crept along the rooftop and carefully maintained his footing. Then he slipped.

He slid toward Davel, and the constable reached for him. Gavin twisted and spun his feet, trying to spiral around as quickly as he could. The twisting caught Davel off guard. Gavin kicked and caught Davel in the thigh, knocking him down.

Gavin used the leverage to push off. He scrambled back, up the roof, standing at the peak of it. He ran as he saw Davel starting to stand back up.

He didn't like racing across the rooftops. The pitch was unstable, and he called upon his core reserves as he ran as quickly as possible, but there were limits to that power. Limits to how much he could summon and limits to what he could do.

He slipped again, and he slid down the side of the

rooftop. Gavin cried out, scrambling for grip. His hand caught something, and he pushed the pain away as his flesh tore.

He finally came to rest and hurried to his feet. He looked behind him, and Davel was following him at almost a leisurely pace. Still, despite how it appeared, the man moved faster than the average person.

Gavin didn't know if he would be able to outrun him on the rooftop. Even in the street, he didn't know if he could outrun Davel, who obviously knew how to find him. He needed to find another place of safety.

"If you're listening, we need to be careful. Davel Chan is heavily enchanted," he said.

Gaspar's voice came through. "I warned you."

"What about the others?"

"They're fine."

"All of them?"

"All of them."

Gavin exhaled. "We need to find a safe place. At least until we get through this. The constables know about the Dragon."

"There you go again," Gaspar said.

"What?"

"Putting the Dragon in danger."

"You know I don't do it on purpose."

"Which makes it all the worse."

"Do you know of any place that might be safe? Somewhere the constables won't be able to reach?"

There was silence for a long while. Gavin continued to

race along the rooftops, sliding every so often and recovering, then looking behind him. Davel Chan continued to follow, though there was now enough distance between them that Gavin thought he might be able to get away.

Once I got down into the street, then I could run, but to where?

The city wasn't safe for him anymore, not until he was able to figure out what he was going to do.

"I might know a place," Gaspar said.

"Why do I get the sense this isn't going to be something that I'll like?" Gavin replied.

"It has nothing to do with you. It has everything to do with me."

CHAPTER TWENTY-TWO

Gavin approached the home in the darkness. He moved slowly, looking over his shoulder every so often for the constables that might be after him. As far as he could tell, he had lost them long ago. The street was quiet, and his gaze lingered along the shops. He watched the reflection in the glass of the shop windows. No signs of anybody following him.

That should reassure him, but at this point, nothing did. He wouldn't put it past Davel to have some way of tracking him.

Gavin pushed the gate open, and he paused on the pathway leading up to the home. In the darkness, he studied it. It was a massive formal home with well-manicured shrubs leading up to the door. Lights glowed in each of the windows, giving a warmth to it. He watched for any movement in the windows. Nothing. He stayed in the shadows near the shrubs, watching and waiting,

He sighed.

Had I beaten Gaspar here?

Not likely, but he wasn't sure. All he knew was that coming on his own and waiting wasn't something he wanted to do with Davel hunting him. Maybe he *had* made a mistake by engaging the constables.

Or by going after the jade egg.

Or by taking the job to rescue Alex in the first place.

As he waited, he continued to look out into the night, checking the street. This was the kind of place that the constables wouldn't think to search. There was no reason to do so. The home was too nice, and places like this generally were left alone. When he was content that there was nothing around him, Gavin headed toward the door, and he paused as the door opened.

Jessica greeted him. She shook her head slightly. "She's gone."

Gavin frowned at a bruise on her cheek. "What happened?"

"We were making our way over here when they grabbed her. It happened so quickly that Gaspar couldn't do anything. Imogen neither. They both chased, but the people were too fast."

Gavin squeezed his eyes shut and sighed. "Enchanted," he whispered.

"That's what they said." She tipped her head toward the door. "Gaspar is in there. He's in a bit of a mood."

"I'm sure he is." Especially if they'd failed to protect Alex. "You're safe?"

"We're safe. All of us are."

"I'm glad."

Jessica glanced past him into the night, then turned her attention back to him. "You shouldn't have taken on the constables."

"I gathered that."

"He said you attacked them?"

"I did a lot of things," Gavin said.

He waited another moment, and Jessica seemed to debate before pulling the door all the way open and letting him in. Gavin stepped inside the immaculate home. Marble tile gleamed beneath his feet. Statues lined the walls, and paintings hung there as well.

From the outside, he knew it would be a place of incredible wealth, but it was beyond what he could have imagined. It wasn't anything like some of the manor homes. Those were formal and lavish in their own way, but this was old wealth. This was money.

Gavin stood in place, looking at the walls and the portraits and the sculptures. He turned to Jessica. "Who is Desarra?"

"You know who she is."

"I know *who* she is, but who *is* she?"

"You're going to have to ask Gaspar that, if you want to know."

Gavin followed her along the hallway, and they reached the doorway of a massive room. An enormous hearth crackled with a warm and cozy flame in the back of the room.

Wrenlow jumped up and hurried over as soon as Gavin entered. "You made it."

"You didn't think I would?"

"I wasn't sure whether or not you'd get into any more trouble."

"I would've alerted you had there been something."

"The way you alerted me before?" Wrenlow asked.

"I told you something was going on."

"You did, but only after you'd already attacked them. If you'd said anything to me sooner, I might've been able to—"

"You wouldn't have been able to do anything," Gavin said. He patted Wrenlow on the arm and smiled. "Where is he?"

"He's in there. He's not very happy about all of this," Wrenlow said.

"I don't think he wanted me to know he was married before, and now that we all know, I think it's troubling him." Gavin looked past Wrenlow but didn't see Gaspar. He could hear his voice though. "What about Imogen?"

"She's out patrolling," Jessica said as she closed the door and joined them. "She figures she isn't a known entity, and that gives her the ability to patrol for anything concerning."

Gavin nodded. Imogen had already proven that she wasn't concerned about the fights they'd experienced or fearful of the potential for magical attacks.

Was there something more to that?

Maybe Imogen had some connection to magic herself,

though he hadn't seen anything from her to suggest it. As far as he knew, she was no more magical than him—or at least no more magical than he'd once believed himself to be.

Gavin followed Wrenlow into the room and saw Gaspar, who sat near the hearth, talking quietly to Desarra. She was a lovely woman, with her dark hair braided and tied by a loop of blue ribbon. She had on a bright yellow dress that accentuated her figure. A young girl was across from her, watching the conversation. She had similar dark hair and pale blue eyes that widened when Gavin entered the room.

"What's this about?" he asked.

"Ever since Gaspar got here, he'd been telling Desarra about what happened to the two of you. She's concerned," Wrenlow said.

Gavin looked at the girl and withdrew his El'aras dagger. It was glowing. He smiled to himself.

The girl had magic. At least, he believed it was her and not Desarra. For all he knew, it could be either one. He walked over to them, stood behind Gaspar, and watched the girl. It wasn't always easy to know when magic users were drawing on their power.

"Are we sure it's safe here?" Gavin asked.

The others turned toward him. Gaspar frowned, his expression angry.

"Why wouldn't it be safe?" Jessica asked.

Gavin turned his attention to Gaspar, holding his gaze. "I don't know. It should be safe, shouldn't it, Gaspar?"

"Watch it, boy."

"I just want us to be certain that we're all on the same page here. Are we sure?"

"I'm sure," Gaspar said.

"Gavin?" Wrenlow asked.

"It's nothing," Gavin replied.

Desarra looked over to Gavin and then to Gaspar, who nodded once.

"Wrenlow, why don't you and Jessica go with Olivia," Gaspar said.

The girl stood up, and Desarra smiled at her. "Where would you have me go?" Olivia asked.

"See if you can gather some food," Desarra said. "I'm sure they're hungry, especially considering what they've gone through today."

Olivia looked at Gavin. For a moment, the El'aras blade surged more brightly. Now he knew with certainty.

"I would love to see the kitchen. You know, I'm something of a cook," Jessica said with a wide smile. She grabbed Olivia's arm and led her away.

Wrenlow glanced over at Gavin, who nodded in the direction that Jessica and Olivia went. It would be better for Wrenlow to go with them. He shrugged and followed them out of the room, leaving Gavin with Desarra and Gaspar.

"Now, do you care to tell me what's been going on?" Gavin asked.

"You don't need to know anything," Gaspar said.

"Look at him," Desarra said. "He already knows. You aren't going to keep anything from him at this point."

Gavin shrugged. "She's not wrong. Olivia is an enchanter, isn't she?"

"It doesn't matter," Gaspar said.

"It does because it at least answers a few questions I have."

"What do you think that answers?" Gaspar asked, his voice rising. There was tension within him, almost as if ready to explode.

"It explains a little bit more about why you left the constables." Gavin made a circle around the chairs, and he took a seat across from them. "Let me tell you what I suspect." He unsheathed the El'aras dagger. "I suspect that the two of you were happily married. Something happened. I've been trying to figure out what that might've been, especially considering how the two of you still seem to care about each other. Maybe regardless of what you might claim, Olivia is your daughter," Gavin said, nodding to Gaspar. That answer didn't feel *quite* right given what he'd seen. "You discovered she had potential, and it drove you out of the constables."

"Careful, boy," Gaspar said.

"How close am I?"

"You aren't close at all."

"Then tell me."

"You don't need to know," Gaspar said.

Gavin took a deep breath and smiled. He sheathed the El'aras dagger and shrugged. "It was worth taking a shot.

The other possibility is that she's older than she appears. From what I'm guessing of the enchanters, they're all considerably older than what I believed at first. If that's the case, then it's possible Olivia is your sister," Gavin said, nodding to Desarra. "Gaspar learned of it and wasn't able to protect her."

Gaspar glared at him.

"Fine. Make me keep guessing. I can go on like this."

"Don't," Desarra said, raising her hand.

"I don't really want to. Honestly, when it comes to these sorts of things, I'd rather just be told."

"He doesn't like to talk about it."

Gavin nodded. "I gathered that. He doesn't like to talk about much."

"In this case, he *really* doesn't like to talk about it," Desarra said.

Gavin leaned back in his chair and watched Gaspar. "Let's get to a real question then. How safe are we here?"

"Safe enough," Gaspar said.

"Are you sure? Because I want to make sure we don't have to worry about the constables finding us here."

Gaspar's brow furrowed. "I'm sure."

There was something more taking place here than Gavin understood, but perhaps none of that mattered. At this point, the only thing he needed to know was what they were going to do about the jade egg. "At least tell me what's going on here."

"You're the one who took the job. Why do I need to help you understand it?" Gaspar asked.

"We can't stay here indefinitely. The constables are after us. This is only going to get Desarra and Olivia into the same mess we're in."

"You don't have to worry about us," Desarra said.

"Why?"

"You just don't."

Olivia used magic fairly openly, enough to make the El'aras dagger glow, and Gavin had a sense that Desarra was completely aware of what she did. "All right. You'd both better start talking."

"Watch it," Gaspar said.

"What's there for me to watch? I've been running around the city, dealing with constables attacking, and trying to find this jade egg so the other enchanters can free their families' power. All while trying to figure out what role Alex had to play. Now she's missing, and—"

"Is that what they told you?" Desarra asked, leaning forward.

"What do you mean?"

"Is that what the others told you?"

Gavin sighed. "Which others are we talking about? At this point, I'm dealing with quite a few different groups, and I don't even know which ones you're getting at."

He had an idea though. He suspected that she knew far more about these young enchanters—and about everything that was taking place—than she was letting on.

"The enchanters told me they wanted the jade egg for the Mistress of Vines so they could free their families," he said. "They claim she's the only one who knows how to release the magical energy within it."

Olivia returned, and Gavin glanced behind him toward the kitchen. He thought that she'd gone with the others, but she must have snuck back in. At this point, she deserved to be a part of the conversation.

Desarra and Olivia shared a look, and neither of them spoke.

Gavin chuckled. "I take it that isn't quite right."

"No," Olivia said.

"So what's the truth of the matter?"

"You wouldn't understand," she said.

"Try me. I think I might understand more than you give me credit for."

"Watch it, boy," Gaspar growled.

Desarra rested her hand on his arm, and she shook her head. "It's okay, Gaspar. He's been helping. He should be a part of this."

"A part of what?"

"They didn't get the jade egg to the Mistress of Vines so she could release their families. They're gone, unfortunately," Desarra said. "The jade egg is an item of magic, and whoever possesses it would be able to unsettle others of considerable power."

"It's my understanding that it allows the constables to make enchantments," Gavin said.

"It can help make enchantments for the constables, but that's not its only purpose. The egg contains collected magic, and in the right hands—or the wrong hands—it allows someone to use it against another person who has power."

Gavin frowned and looked from one to the other. "The Captain. Why?"

"Because he's been holding power over the city."

"He might be powerful, and he might have misused some enchantments, but—"

"Not misused," Olivia interrupted. "He's been buying off those who have the ability to place enchantments and forcing them to serve." There was heat in her voice, anger that seethed just beneath the surface.

Gavin looked over and frowned. He thought about the enchantments that he'd experienced when he'd broken into the Captain's home. They had been more than what he'd expected.

Within Yoran, there weren't all that many people with enchantments. Having them was an admission of a link to magic that most people didn't want, especially somebody who was as well-connected as the Captain would be. The fact that he had magic and was willing to use it so openly suggested that not only was he not concerned about his link to magic, he could use it without repercussions.

"How's the Captain tied to the constables?" Gavin asked.

"He's bought a measure of influence. Not with all of them, but with enough. He uses that influence to maintain his hold over the city, or at least his role within the city. And he doesn't fear the constables taking away his enchantments because doing so would reveal theirs," Desarra said.

Gavin shook his head. "That doesn't make sense. The constables aren't afraid of revealing their own enchantments."

There was so much about Yoran he didn't fully understand. There was a history here he wasn't privy to, one that people like Gaspar—and, he suspected, Desarra—fully understood.

"Let me get this straight. The Captain uses enchanters to place enchantments on whatever he needs," he said. "The constables look the other way, but at the same time, they search for those with magic. And now Zella and the others with her are somehow involved."

"Zella and the others have always been involved," Olivia said.

"Why?"

"Because they're the ones who have suffered the most."

"What do you mean?" Gavin asked.

"Do you think Alex is the first one who's been rescued? The Captain has captured others over the years. Not all of them escape, but many of them do. Even with the enchantments he's able to place, he struggles to hold them, partly because they're incredibly powerful in their own right."

"What about Alex?"

"She was taken."

"I know that," Gavin said.

"She was part of the group that attacked the constable

caravan. They were the ones who took the jade egg in the first place," Olivia said. "Her ability is…"

"What about her ability?"

Gavin had seen it was powerful, but it had to be more than that.

"She can tap into enchantments. Make them stronger."

He breathed out. That explained many things. "And since the jade egg is an enchantment…"

It would be why the Mistress of Vines wanted her.

Alex could make the egg *much* more potent.

"She was captured like so many others have been," Olivia said.

Gavin looked to Olivia. "You were captured once."

Olivia said nothing.

"How did you get out?" he asked.

"There's one thing the Captain understands," Olivia said softly.

"What's that?"

"Money."

Gavin glanced at Desarra, then turned back to Olivia. "How long ago were you held?"

"It's been a while," she said.

Gavin frowned and glanced at Gaspar, who made a point of ignoring him. "So you were once there. I take it that's how you got the layout to the Captain's home?" He looked at Desarra.

She nodded.

"Then what's going on with the Mistress of Vines? If these others have used her to get to Alex…"

It still didn't make complete sense to Gavin. Alex was able to augment the jade egg, and somehow the Mistress of Vines was responsible for it. She was the reason that Gavin got involved in the first place. She'd wanted him to get Alex out—which meant she would use the egg. The enchanters had said that the Mistress of Vines would help free their families and somehow release the energy trapped in the jade egg. They'd finally have a sense of safety that their families had not had for years.

"What is she really after?" he asked.

"The same thing they are," Olivia said.

"And what exactly is that?"

"They want to remove the Captain."

"Why remove him? It sounds to me like he's not opposed to the use of magic."

"Not opposed to it, but he'd also rather keep the status quo. Given how much power and authority he has, he'd much rather ensure he keeps it rather than allowing others to have any."

"Why would he even care? It seems as if he's only willing to work with enchanters..." Gavin started to smile.

How much had Anna known about the Captain?

She had spent some time in his fortress. He didn't really know what she knew, but he questioned whether or not she'd even been aware of it. Perhaps she had known. Maybe that was the reason she'd gone to the fortress in the first place. Or perhaps it was because she could use magic more openly around him.

If only he had a chance to speak with her. Given everything that had occurred in the city since taking on these two jobs, Gavin should've taken the time to reach out to her.

"He's an enchanter, isn't he?" he said.

The timing made sense. He hadn't pieced it together before, but now that he started to think through it, he thought he understood. The time when the Captain had risen to power. The reason behind him building such an incredible fortress. That few knew anything about him.

"Did you know?" he asked Gaspar.

"I've suspected. None of us really know. That's one of the things I've looked into since I left." He looked over to Desarra. "The bastard keeps an element of mystery around him."

"So even though he must have been a part of the sorcery war, he somehow managed to position himself in such a way that he gained even more power after it? This despite the fact that the constables removed all of the enchanters with any power?"

"Sometimes even those without power," Desarra whispered.

"Why didn't you tell me?" Gaspar asked.

"What would I have said? That he's used his authority to harm us? That he's an enchanter?"

"I would have cared," he said.

"It was better this way," she whispered.

"Better for who?" Hurt filled Gaspar's eyes.

There was no answer, and Gavin turned away.

"So," he said after giving them a few moments of

silence, "the Captain has held a position of authority in the city, using enchantments he's not supposed to use, and he continues to cause difficulty for others who have power. That about right?"

"It's more than that," Desarra said. "He doesn't have much magic on his own. That's why the constables left him alone. They knew that much about him."

Gavin nodded in understanding. "He doesn't have much power on his own, but he uses the other enchanters he's buying to gain strength. Is that what he's doing?"

"As far as we can tell," Desarra said.

"And then he learned of Alex?"

Could the Captain want the egg for himself?

It would be a complicated ploy, and one Gavin wouldn't expect to work.

"I didn't know who she was at the time," Desarra said, looking over at Gaspar. "When you wanted the layout, I thought it was for another one of the enchanters who'd been taken. It had been a while since he'd managed to purchase one. They don't allow him to purchase too many, but…"

Gavin leaned forward. "Who is she? I mean, other than her ability to augment enchantments."

She had to be significant otherwise. He tried to think about why that would be the case, but he wasn't sure.

"She's Zella's daughter."

Gavin got to his feet and started to pace. He glanced over every so often, and his mind worked through everything that he'd learned. Strange for a city that disliked magic this intensely to have so much within it.

Why should this city be so different than any others that I'd been in?

Some were more open and welcomed the idea of magic, recognizing its value. In others, the sorcerers were a part of the community, and they worked with the people rather than trying to subjugate them. In still other cities, it was more like the way Yoran had once been. The people had been conquered, and they lived under the rule of a sorcerer. There were some like Yoran was now, where magic was expelled. In all of them, there was always an undercurrent of power. Gavin should've expected this city to be no different.

Gavin paced in front of the fireplace, looking all around the inside of the room, trying to piece together everything he'd heard and everything they'd implied.

What did I need to do now?

Gaspar and Desarra talked quietly.

Gavin looked at Olivia. "If the Captain keeps taking—"

"Not taking. Buying."

Gavin nodded. "Buying other enchanters, then what are they interested in?"

"They're interested in freeing those who have been purchased," she said.

"It's not just about freeing them though. It's about something else, isn't it?"

"Yes," she whispered.

"What?"

"There's a reason Zella was willing to offer the egg to the Mistress of Vines," she said.

He leaned forward. "What?"

"They want revenge."

"Revenge for what the Captain's doing?"

"For all of it. The Captain primarily. They view him as responsible for not only the capture of people like Alex and others but also what happened to their parents."

"Why?"

"Because he was one of them. He betrayed them. And they're hoping the Mistress of Vines will finally get that vengeance."

"I suppose I can understand that," Gavin said. Maybe this was just something he needed to leave alone. Vengeance was a motivation he well understood. "Then we wait until it plays out."

"You can't," Olivia said.

"Why not? I don't really care if the Mistress of Vines or the Captain has the fortress."

"All they want—*we* want—is the freedom to use our magic without fear."

"So you convinced the Mistress of Vines to help."

"When they took Alex…"

Gavin shook his head. That had been the tipping point for the enchanters. Either that, or the Mistress of Vines propositioned them. He didn't know which.

"If they attack, if the Mistress of Vines succeeds, there will be open war within Yoran again," Gaspar said, looking over to him. "I've lived that before. I don't want to see it again. For as bad as he might be, the Captain did accomplish one thing. The magical war ended."

"Only because the constables were using enchantments to hunt those with magic," Olivia said.

"The alternative was worse," Gaspar said.

"Are you sure?"

They were both right. He'd seen it. Gavin had been through a few places where there'd been a battle between those who had magic and those who did not. It was never easy, always brutal and bloody. The time when he'd been hired to remove the Tanran had been the worst, but there had been others.

Gavin looked over at Gaspar. "You got me into this. You're going to help me finish it."

"Finish what?"

"If I know sorcerers, she wants the egg for more than just to help the enchanters." Power, of some sort. It was just learning what kind of power. "So we have to reclaim the jade egg."

CHAPTER TWENTY-THREE

Gavin sat by the fire with hands clasped together, looking around the room for a moment before returning his attention to the crackling flames. Olivia sat next to Desarra, both of them talking quietly to each other. Gaspar had slipped out, looking for more information.

Gavin's mind raced as he struggled with the various scenarios. To get Alex back, he'd have to stop the Mistress of Vines, though he had no idea whether he could. She was a powerful sorcerer, and skilled enough that he would need help.

"What is it?" Wrenlow asked, leaning forward and watching him. He held a book open in his lap and was jotting down notes, though nothing in the book would probably help when it came to what they needed to do.

"I'm just trying to come to terms with something I resisted over the years," Gavin said softly.

"What's that?"

Gavin looked over at his old friend, who watched him with concern in his eyes. He suspected Wrenlow knew just how dangerous this was going to be, though they'd gone into dangerous situations before and come out on the other side just fine.

"I've resisted taking enchantments with me."

"You have not," Wrenlow said, shaking his head. "You've taken as many as you think you need."

"You mean this?" He tapped on the earpiece and shook his head. "This is as far as I've gone. I'm talking about a different kind of enchantment."

It was a measure of the difficulty they faced that Gavin was willing to take one now. Wrenlow didn't even see that from him.

Maybe it was for the best.

"What kind?"

"Similar to the ones the constables have used."

"The... no. Gavin, you can't go back there."

"I know I shouldn't," he said, though maybe he should. There was no reason that he couldn't break into Zella's home and take some of her enchantments. They would be a challenge to get to again, but the issue wasn't so much about what he could do as it was knowing whether or not they would even work. He'd have to figure out what the enchantments did. He didn't have enough information, which put him in danger. "There might be another way for us to get the enchantments we need."

Gavin didn't know if the enchantments in Cyran's

sorcerer's lair would be useful, but doubted it. Not unless he knew what they were for.

"What, then?" Wrenlow asked.

The door opened and Gaspar slipped back in and headed over to Gavin. "Time to get moving."

"Now?"

"She's making her play. The fortress."

Gavin squeezed his eyes shut. "She didn't even wait. After getting Alex back, she's going to go straight at him."

Gavin got to his feet, and he walked over to the table where Olivia sat with Desarra.

"This is going to be a break-in," he said, looking to Gaspar. "Your kind of plan."

"We've already done that," Gaspar said.

Gavin nodded. "Right, which as we know is a bit dangerous, but this time we'll know a sorcerer is there."

"I seem to remember you thinking the girl was the sorcerer."

"I've thought many different things during this whole scenario. None of them have been accurate, but that hasn't been my fault. I've gathered as much information as I can to try to get through this."

Gavin took a seat at the table, looking over at Desarra and Olivia. Both of them watched him. He couldn't shake the resemblance, but given what he knew about enchanters, he wondered something.

"Why do all enchanters look younger than they are?" he asked. They needed to prepare, but this was a question he wanted answered.

Gaspar frowned at him. "What?"

Gavin nodded to Olivia. "Her. I suspect all of the enchanters that I've met, including Zella, look like they're still in their teens. They appear young, though I have a feeling that none of them are quite as young as they seem."

Desarra shook her head. "They *are* young," she said.

"I don't know. Something about it isn't quite right."

"It's tied to the war," Olivia said softly. She glanced at Desarra, then stared off into the distance. "During the attack, something happened. Nobody really knows, but all enchanters found that we were stuck in time." She swept her hand down from head to toe and shook her head slowly. "Not that we really understand it. Even now, we still don't."

"So you're stuck as you were?" Gavin asked.

Desarra shook her head softly, but Olivia nodded.

"Yes. It gives us the opportunity to move places where we wouldn't otherwise." She smiled tightly. "Many saw us as less of a threat."

Gavin frowned. "Which means you *are* sisters."

Desarra's eyes twitched slightly, and Gavin knew he was right.

Gavin turned to Olivia. "For us to do this job, I need your help."

"She's not coming with us," Gaspar said.

"I'm not asking you," Gavin said to him. "And I'm not asking her to come with us. I just need her help."

"What do you need?" Olivia's voice was soft.

"I assume that your parents were enchanters as well,"

Gavin said. He glanced from Desarra to Olivia, and the slight tension in the corners of their eyes told him all he needed to know. "Which means they poured part of themselves into this jade egg, no differently than any of the other enchanters."

Olivia nodded.

"Why them, and not anyone else?" Gavin asked.

"What do you mean?" Wrenlow asked. He got up from where he was seated and sat down next to Gavin, watching him for a moment before turning to look at the other two. "Who else are you concerned about?"

"It's not so much a concern," Gavin said. "It's more about understanding." He rested his elbows on the table, looking from Desarra to Olivia. "If your parents were enchanters, why is it that they were pulled into creating this egg, but not anyone else?"

"They protected us," Olivia said. She looked over at Desarra. "And they wanted us to protect the others, but…"

"But there was only so much you could do," he said, looking at Desarra.

She nodded slowly.

Gavin turned to Gaspar, but the old thief was looking away from him. There were answers here, if only Gavin could dig into it and figure out what they might be. He had a feeling Gaspar wouldn't share anything with him anyway, but that didn't change a whole lot for him.

"So when Olivia was captured…"

"It was my responsibility to get her back," Desarra said.

"I see."

"What do you see?" Wrenlow asked.

Gavin shook his head. "Nothing clearly, and I get the sense that they don't know either. Only that those who have enchanter abilities found themselves stuck as children when their parents created the jade egg." Whatever magic had been used had shifted things for them. He had no idea what to make of it, only that it had been powerful enough to keep them from progressing in age or appearance. "What about those who have been born since?"

"There haven't been many," Olivia said.

"Why?"

"Look at us," she said, looking down at herself. "We look like children, and yet…"

Gavin smiled at her. "I know what I was doing when I was a teenager."

Gaspar swung his gaze over to him. "What were you doing?"

"Training mostly, but I did have breaks in my training. A growing boy has needs, you know."

"I know too much about your needs," Gaspar said.

Now the enchanters weren't growing anymore. It fit with what he'd seen, though, and it helped him feel better about his attack on people like Kegan and Mekal. They weren't children. Not really. They looked young, but he had to tack on years since the war to help him recognize just how old they might actually be.

"What about this egg?" Gavin looked over at Desarra before turning his attention to Olivia. "Will the Mistress of Vines use it to start a new war? If you brought in a sorcerer to deal with all of this..."

Olivia shook her head. "She promised to use it to help."

"For what purpose?"

"To break what happened to us," she said softly.

They viewed it as a curse. Of course they did.

"You didn't know she'd go after the Captain?"

She shook her head.

"I'm going to do what I can to get it back, but I can't make any guarantees," he said.

"You owe them more than that," Gaspar said.

Gavin shot him a hard look. "You're the one who put me on to this job in the first place. I wouldn't have taken any of this."

"That's not true," Wrenlow told him quietly.

Gavin sighed. Wrenlow was right. He might have taken the job anyway. Gavin wasn't a tracker, even though he'd been hired that way, and yet he also couldn't stand by if somebody was suffering and he had some ability to help.

"Now that we have that established," Gavin said, "I was hoping that you might be able to offer us an enchantment."

"What sort of enchantment?" Olivia asked.

"I'm looking for anything that might help us. What sort of specialty do you have?"

"Specialty?" Gaspar asked.

"Enchanters tend to have comfort zones," Gavin said, ignoring Gaspar's pointed look in his direction. "Which means that Olivia probably has certain things that she's more comfortable with. I've seen two enchanters who turn small figurines into weapons."

"Mekal and Kegan," Olivia said, nodding. "They've used those to protect us over the years."

"So they have," Gavin said. "And I have a feeling they don't have other skills beyond that, except for Kegan's memory ability."

"Some, but you're right. They're more comfortable with that technique."

He leaned forward. "What about you?"

"Mine aren't terribly impressive. I can make things happen more quickly."

"What do you mean?"

"I can help flowers grow, or I can make time speed up, or at least seem to."

"Can you make *us* faster?"

Having seen something similar with the constables, and in particular with Davel Chan, Gavin couldn't help but wish for something that might give him that advantage. If he could move more quickly, or at least appear to, he could take on any power that might be there.

"There might be something that I can do," she said. Olivia headed over to a cabinet, pulled out a box, and brought it back. She set three bracelets down on the table. All were made of gold or silver, and far more ornate than anything Gavin would wear. They were probably incredibly valuable too. Maybe not thirty gold crowns valuable, but still valuable.

"What are these?" Wrenlow asked.

Olivia held his gaze for a moment and smiled, then looked back down. Gavin chuckled softly. Leave it to Wrenlow to get involved with a woman who looked like she was fifteen but was probably thirty-five.

"I should be able to enchant these bracelets. I can only do two or three at a time." She looked at Gavin. "After that, it will take me a few days to recover."

Whatever she could generate would be all they would have.

"Do you have any way of determining what other enchantments might do?" he asked.

She shook her head. "Not really. That's not my skill set. There are some who can know the purpose of an enchantment just by holding it, but unfortunately, that's not me."

"Like who?"

"Zella."

Gavin grunted. That wasn't going to be of much use. He let out a long sigh, and she picked up one of the bracelets, cupped it in hand, and closed her eyes. There came a flash of light from between her hands, and she handed the bracelet to him.

"Try it on," she said.

The bracelet had changed during the process of enchanting it. It was still silver, but now it was a plain band, no longer ornate. He slipped it onto his wrist, and it fit perfectly, as if made for him and only him.

He got up and then took a step.

As soon as he moved, he could feel the difference. Something within the bracelet seemed to give him the ability to control how quickly he moved. He darted around the room, avoiding the chairs and the table. He nearly crashed into the hearth before skidding to a stop and taking a seat back at the table.

"That will work," he said.

"I don't know how many times you can use it," she said. "Unfortunately, my enchantments have a limit."

"If it gives us the ability to use that even a little, that's more than what we had before," Gavin said.

She picked up another bracelet and squeezed it. As before, there was a flash of light. When it faded, she held it out. Wrenlow reached for it, but Gaspar stretched across the table and batted his hand away. He grabbed the bracelet and slipped it onto his wrist.

"I think we both know it'll be more useful for me," he said to Wrenlow.

Wrenlow frowned. "What about me?"

"I can try to make a third," Olivia said.

She grabbed the third bracelet and cupped it in her hands.

"It might be better for Imogen," Gavin said.

"Imogen won't take it," Gaspar said.

Gavin ran his finger along the surface of the bracelet. "Is that because she doesn't need it? Or because she has some other way of accessing power?"

Gaspar stared at him. "I don't need to answer that."

One of these days, he was going to have to find out Imogen's secret. There was a secret, regardless of what Gaspar wanted him to believe. For all Gavin knew, maybe Gaspar *wanted* him to believe that there was a secret.

What if she was simply highly trained, the same way I am?

There had to be more to it. He'd seen her fight the sorcerer, and she had handled herself quite well. She'd managed to withstand a sorcerer's attack without struggling nearly as much as somebody without any sort of natural defense would. He still suspected that there was something more to her that gave her those advantages.

"Here," Olivia said. "I don't know if it's complete, so don't rely on it too many times, but maybe it will protect you."

Wrenlow took the bracelet from her, his hand lingering near hers for just a moment before he slipped the bracelet on his wrist. "Now I can be like you," he said to Gavin.

"I'm not so sure that's what you should aspire to," Gaspar grunted.

"Would you leave him alone?" Gavin said.

"Fine. How about we get going?" Gaspar asked.

"Just like that? No plan?"

"What's there to plan? You and I are going in. Wrenlow will spot for us," he said, nodding to Wrenlow, "and Imogen will clean up anybody who's outside and coming toward us. Does that sound like a reasonable plan?"

"Reasonable enough," Gavin said.

"Good. I'm glad you're not going to argue with me about that as well."

"When have I ever argued with you about your plans?" Gavin asked.

"Oh, I don't know. How about every single time the two of us are forced to work together."

Gavin chuckled. "We aren't forced to work together. We can stop at any time." He looked at the others with him—his team. They were risking themselves with him. Wrenlow was right. He didn't have to do things alone. "Let's go get the egg and stop the Mistress of Vines."

CHAPTER TWENTY-FOUR

Gavin stalked along the street outside of the Captain's fortress. He'd been here not that long ago and for a very different reason. Now he was coming here to somehow protect the Captain and to defend the fortress.

Lights glowed in windows, which illuminated the entirety of the building. It looked imposing in the darkness. If he didn't know any better, he would think that there wasn't anything that the Mistress of Vines would even be able to do against the Captain. But given her power and the support she would likely have from the other enchanters, she would be an effective opponent.

Gavin had seen fighting similar to what would likely happen here. When magical attacks occurred in places with similar views of magic as Yoran, things became dangerous.

He had to help. He didn't know if he had enough

understanding of his own power to do so, but he had to try. Rather than the El'aras dagger, he held onto the sword. It had a bit better reach, and he'd seen how intense its effect was when it came to cutting through magic. That was what he needed now.

Gavin didn't know what else he could do, but he had to believe the sword might carve through anything that would come toward him. He lingered in the darkness near the wall around the building.

"Are you ready?" Gaspar whispered through the enchantment.

He didn't know where the other man was. He was somewhere distant, far enough along the wall that Gavin would have to search for him, but in the darkness it was difficult to see anything.

"As ready as I'm going to be. You do know what happened the last time we came in here."

"You came out with the girl."

"I got beat up with magic. I'm not that excited about the prospect of the same thing happening again."

"Then don't get beat up," Gaspar said.

Wrenlow laughed in the enchantment.

Gavin looked behind him. Wrenlow sat atop the wall, the knife he clutched in hand catching a little of the moonlight. "You aren't a lot of help."

"Sorry," Wrenlow muttered.

"Don't mind him. He's just irritated he's not quite as skilled as he'd like us to believe. I guess that means we're equal."

Gavin grunted. There were times when he wished that he could reach through the enchantment and throttle Gaspar.

"I'll keep watching," Wrenlow said.

"Let me know if you see anything coming along the street."

"As I said, I'm watching."

It was just the three of them.

Gavin glanced at the bracelet. It fit his wrist almost as if it had been made for him—another effect of the enchantment, he suspected. Gaspar wore a similar one, and together they were enhanced with speed.

Would this give us enough of an advantage over the Mistress of Vines?

There was only one way to find out.

The wall loomed in front of him. Gavin climbed carefully. The enchantment was strange. It was odd for him to feel the increased effects of speed, and it took some time for him to be able to compensate for that. Olivia had told him this enchantment would last longer if he only drew a little from it. The opposite was also true; he could draw more power, but the enchantment would drain more quickly.

He'd faced Davel and saw how having an enchantment that would allow him to move more quickly would be beneficial. He didn't necessarily want to rely upon enchantments, but having trained without them, Gavin thought something like this might help, if only for tonight.

He moved in the darkness, heading toward the

fortress. As quiet as he could, he tried to creep along the ground, and he kept his head down as he moved. In the distance, the fortress continued to loom closer and closer.

"Where are you?" he whispered to Gaspar.

"Not far."

"You need to get moving."

"We aren't going to take any additional action until she reveals her presence," Gaspar said.

"What if she's already inside?" Gavin asked.

"There has been no sign of that."

They'd been watching for the better part of the night, long enough that if the Mistress of Vines had moved on the fortress, they would have seen it. She hadn't recovered Alex long enough to have acted any sooner. It was likely that she now had the jade egg and was already moving.

Unless she wanted to take time to plan, but that didn't strike him as the kind of thing she would do. Something about the night felt off to him.

He moved closer to the building. There still wasn't a sign of any activity in the yard. Gavin held onto the sword, keeping it pointed downward, and was about to say something to Gaspar when the blade surged with white light.

"Something changed," Gavin whispered.

"What is it?"

"The sword. It's starting to glow."

"She's moving," Gaspar said.

"Either that, or she's already here."

He didn't know if she had some way of appearing

without them seeing her. Given how little they were able to surveil all of this, Gavin suspected she might've been able to show up without him even being aware of it. Had they a larger crew, it might not have been so much of an issue, but given how few of them there were, there was a limit to just what they were able to watch.

He focused on the intense glow from the blade.

Gavin turned slowly and felt a strange resistance against the sword that was coming from behind him. "Be careful," he whispered. "There's something back there."

He started to creep backward toward the wall. There were shadows behind them, and he used the sword to light his way.

"To your right," Gaspar hissed quickly.

Gavin spun, holding out the sword. There was movement, and the sword burst with more light, glowing brightly. Whatever was out there pulled on considerable magic.

He darted forward, sweeping the sword in front of him. "I don't see anything."

"Straight ahead," Wrenlow whispered.

"You can see it?"

"Not well, but there's something moving across the yard."

Gavin had to trust in these other two. He stalked forward with slow, careful steps. As he went, he braced himself for the possibility that there would be some sort of magical attack. He lingered for a moment, sweeping his gaze around in the darkness, but he saw nothing.

"Are you sure—"

Power struck him.

Had he not been holding onto the sword, the power might have blasted over him. As it was, the blade seemed to absorb most of the power, keeping it from harming him. Gavin embraced that power and carved through it.

The sword swept over that attack, and Gavin darted forward again. He still didn't see anything out there, but he could feel energy and movement in front of him. He didn't need to see it now. Gavin could *feel* what was taking place.

In the distance, he could make out the dark shadows of three figures.

Not the Mistress of Vines—but enchanters.

She'd brought them into the fight as well.

Of course she had.

She'd probably convinced them they needed to be a part of this. Considering the Captain had been abducting enchanters and forcing them to serve, they had every reason for revenge.

He still didn't know why the Mistress of Vines was willing to be a part of this.

Something about all of this felt vaguely familiar, though. Gavin didn't know why.

A power play. He was certain of it.

A sorcerer. Enchanters. The Captain. And the constables.

All of it was connected.

The enchanters attacked him using a strange sort of enchantment. He thought about what he'd seen within

Zella's home. The sculptures there had suddenly been able to stretch, turning into something more dangerous.

What if they were using sculptures like that?

If they did something similar now, he'd have to be careful. There might be a limit to what he could handle.

Gavin sprinted forward. The bracelet enchantment gave him speed that took the others off guard. He caught the first of the enchanters and swung the sword around. In the glowing light, he recognized one of them from Zella's home.

Gavin carved toward them and twisted the blade, slamming into the man with the hilt. He spun and kicked toward the other, driving his heel into their stomach, and then he flipped into the air and knocked down the last attacker.

All three of them were down.

"There were three enchanters."

"Three?" Gaspar asked.

"Yes. Three."

"What did you do?" Gaspar said.

"I didn't kill them, if that's what you're getting at."

He turned around and headed back toward the building. The sword continued to glow brightly, which worried him. He had no idea what the source of the glow was, but whatever power was out there was enough that it was calling to him.

Gavin spun around, and he searched into the darkness. A shadowed form stalked toward him. It certainly wasn't one of the enchanters. The shape of it reminded him of the strange wolf that had gradually grown when he'd been in Zella's home.

This one was larger. It had taken on its full form.

"Wish me luck," he said.

"What do you mean?" Gaspar asked.

"They have a strange enchantment out here. Do you remember that creature she called upon in her home?"

"I remember," Gaspar said.

"Well, there's at least one. I don't know if there are any others, but I wouldn't be terribly surprised if there were. I'd caution you to be careful."

Gavin darted toward the creature. The shadowed form of it started toward him, and he jumped. The speed enchantment seemed to augment that as well. The jump carried him high into the air, and he twisted and turned as he came down. He didn't have control over it the way he needed to.

He landed too far behind the creature, which reacted, but thankfully not as quickly as Gavin was able to. He surged forward, sweeping out with the sword. He didn't have to pause the way he did with the enchanters. Knowing that a creature like this wasn't real, he swept his blade and carved through it.

The blade met heavy resistance. Magical resistance.

Gavin danced back, the enchantment the only thing that saved him. The creature swiped at him with one of its claws. Had he not been enhanced, he might've been caught by it.

He jumped again, this time controlling it better

than he had the last time. When he landed, he slammed the sword down, driving it into the creature's back.

A howl split the night. For a moment, Gavin thought that the creature had been alive and that he'd killed it, but he realized that the howl came from somewhere near the wall. He raced toward it.

The enchantment carried him quickly, and he saw another shadowed figure that had a series of small figurines scattered around them.

Gavin leaned forward, holding onto the sword and bringing its light up.

"Kegan?"

Kegan reached for one of the figurines and tapped on it, and it started to elongate. Gavin drove forward with the sword and swept it down, crashing it into the figurine. It shattered. Before Kegan had the opportunity to do anything else, Gavin did the same with the others. He swept the blade through them, and all of the figurines shattered in front of him. With each one that broke, Kegan cried out. By the time Gavin was done, the boy was whimpering.

"I'm sorry," Gavin said, turning away. He raced back toward the building. "It's a distraction," he said into the enchantment.

"I gathered that," Gaspar said. His voice was terse and sounded strained.

"Where are you?"

"Look for the five enchanters."

"Five?" Gavin had a hard time keeping the incredulity from his voice.

"Do you think this is the first time I've gone against magic before?" Gaspar asked.

Gavin raced toward the magic. He couldn't see anything, but he could feel the resistance. As he brought the sword around in a sharp arc, the resistance guided him, and he raced into the darkness until he came across the five figures standing in front of Gaspar.

He fought well, but Gavin recognized why Gaspar was struggling. He was trying not to harm them, the same way Gavin had not wanted to harm them.

Gavin jumped into the air and landed behind the others. He sheathed his sword quickly and used his fighting techniques. It was far easier to do that than to risk accidentally killing someone. The only problem was that he wouldn't be able to carve through any magic.

In the case of fighting hand to hand, he had to navigate around the possibility of a magical attack. The only thing that he had going for him was the enchantment. The speed was far more beneficial than he ever would've expected. He'd always been quick when fighting, but this was something else. This was otherworldly and reminded him of the speed Davel had attacked him with.

Gavin darted forward and drove one foot down, catching one of the enchanters in the knee and forcing them to stumble forward. He twisted and swung his other foot around, catching another enchanter in the chest. Gavin worked through the line of enchanters, fists and feet swinging and spinning, and before he had a chance to even comprehend whether or not they were throwing magic at him, they were all down.

Gaspar worked quickly, binding each of them with a length of rope that he pulled out from his satchel.

"Is that going to hold them?" Gavin asked.

"I had Olivia enchant the rope."

"What will it do?"

"If it works, then it'll keep them from being able to break through it with magic."

Gavin looked at the five enchanted individuals lying on the ground, and then he guided Gaspar over to where he'd attacked the other three. Gaspar made short work of tying them up, and they headed to the back wall where he had knocked Kegan out. When Gaspar was done tying him, they looked up toward the fortress.

"There can't be that many enchanters remaining," Gaspar said.

"There were several dozen in Zella's home. That might have only been a part of it," Gavin said.

Gavin unsheathed the sword, and they stalked toward the building. When they neared the door, he hesitated. They didn't know what they were going to find on the other side of the door. Possibly even more powerful enchanters.

He looked over at Gaspar, who nodded at him.

"Keep an eye out," he whispered to Wrenlow.

"I don't see anything. You know, I could help—"

"Just keep watch. We can talk about training you more later."

He wasn't sure that was what he wanted, but it was what Wrenlow wanted. With enchantments, it might even make sense to work with Wrenlow a bit more.

"Do you mean it?"

"Will the two of you stop?" Gaspar snapped. "We've got more important issues at hand here. Unless you'd rather wait and do this later."

"We'll do it now," Gavin said, then pulled the door open. Something lunged at him.

He dropped to the side. Darkness blurred past him, and he swung upward with the sword, preparing for whatever was coming toward him. He had no idea what it was. Gaspar cried out, and Gavin rolled to his feet. He brought the sword around and carved through another enchantment. The sword shattered it, much like it had before.

The creature fell apart. Gavin kicked it, sending the fragments scattering off to the side.

"What was that?" Gaspar snapped.

"That's what I've dealt with a few times before. Kegan had been responsible for those, but..."

He knew who was responsible for these.

Mekal. Kegan's older brother would have been the one tied to the power here.

Gavin returned to the door and pulled it open. He dropped low and shouldered his way through, and he kicked at the nearest creature. The one that lunged toward him was enormous and nothing like the others. He managed to catch it on the underside of its belly as it jumped, but the creature was quick, and its claws raked across his arm.

Gavin cried out, pain surging in him. It forced him to call upon the core reserves of energy within him.

He hadn't even tried that yet. Perhaps that was a mistake. The core reserves gave him an additional advantage, and there was some sort of magic within what he could do. He could feel that power coursing through him, and he knew that he needed to use everything in his ability to be able to fight what was coming.

The massive wolf, if that was what it was, turned back toward him. He held onto the core energy within him and jumped again. His power, combined with the enchantment, carried him up and over. He flipped and landed on the creature's back.

Gavin stabbed the creature with the sword. The force of it jerked up his injured arm, and he cried out again, but he held on as tightly as he could. He wrapped his arms and legs around it and shoved the sword through it again. The creature shuddered. He continued to push power out through the sword until it exploded.

That was new. And definitely magic.

Gavin dropped to the ground and rolled off to the side. He glanced back at Gaspar, who stood near the door.

"Watch—"

Gavin didn't have the opportunity to finish.

Another creature dropped toward them from above.

He glanced up to see where it had come from, but he didn't find any sign of what was out there. He could only react.

By holding onto his core reserves, Gavin drove upward and again landed on top of the creature. He borrowed from that power, and he jammed the sword into the creature's side, blasting through it. He held on, jerking the sword around until the creature exploded.

Gavin turned toward Gaspar. "I don't know how many more of these I'm going to be able to take down."

"Then we need to find the one who's controlling them," Gaspar said.

Something lumbered toward them, the sound of its footsteps loud on the marble though he couldn't see it. The thudding sense that came from it was enormous and powerful, and Gavin shuddered at the sound. He swung the sword around, using the light coming off the blade—a considerable light, he realized—but didn't see anything.

That troubled him.

Holding onto the core reserves was depleting his strength quickly. There would come a time when he would run out of strength. For now, he had enough.

Gavin glanced over at Gaspar. "Stay behind me."

"I have every intention of staying behind you," Gaspar said. "If anyone's going to take the first attack, I figured it might as well be the one who's trained for it."

Gavin moved forward. They didn't move at full speed, reserving the power of the enchantment for now, but even as they stalked ahead, he could feel the trembling beneath him.

Darkness. Something about it was strange. It felt off, and it took Gavin a moment to realize what it was. What he saw was the entirety of the hall in front of them filled by the darkness.

He grabbed Gaspar, ignoring his protestations, and jumped. The high ceiling allowed him to jump higher than usual. He powered the jump with everything in him, all of the core energy that he had, and it carried them up. The lumbering shadows appeared in front of them.

Gavin landed on top of some sort of statue, but it was enormous. He tried to drive down on the statue with his sword, but the statue resisted him with its incredible power. As he tried to stab the blade again and again, there wasn't enough within him to overpower what was here.

He grabbed Gaspar again, and then they jumped.

"Hurry," Gavin said.

"You're not going to deal with that?"

"Be my guest."

They raced forward. Gavin swept the sword side to side, watching as the blade surged briefly with light and feeling for resistance. *There.* It was down a side hall. He pointed the blade in that direction, and the glow increased slightly. He ran toward that.

There was a shadow in the darkness. Rather than one of the strange creatures, he saw a person. As he darted forward, the light coming off the blade began to illuminate the figure. It was Mekal.

He looked up and threw something at Gavin. It started to enlarge as soon as it was in the air, and Gavin swung with his blade, sweeping the power through it. The figurine shattered.

He reached Mekal, and he brought the sword to his throat. "Call it off," he said.

"I can't," Mekal said.

"You can. Call it off. If you don't, this sword is going through your throat. I'd rather not do that if I don't have to, but if it comes down to you or me, the decision is easy."

"I felt what you did to Kegan."

"Your brother is alive outside."

"He'll live?"

"I wasn't going to kill him. Have you not been paying any attention when you've been around me?"

"You said you were an assassin."

"And I am."

Gavin turned and looked down the hallway, feeling the rumbling. If Mekal continued to hold onto his enchantment, this creature was going to storm toward them, and Gavin didn't think that he would be strong enough to resist it.

"There's only one person here I intend to kill tonight," Gavin said.

"Who?"

"Don't make it you."

The shadow filled the hall in front of them.

"You'd better hurry," Gaspar said.

"I'm not in charge of any of this," Gavin said.

"Then *he'd* better hurry."

Gavin cocked a brow at Mekal. "Well?"

"If I do this, what guarantee do I have that you aren't going to kill me?"

"None."

The creature continued to come toward them. It was faster than Gavin would've expected, and with the lumbering steps, everything shook underneath. He brought the sword up. He sliced slightly, bringing it only a hair's breadth through Mekal's throat.

"Now," Gavin said.

The creature stopped.

"Bring it back to the way it was."

"What do you mean?" Mekal asked.

"Make it small again."

"I can't," Mekal said.

"You can. You just won't."

"Please…"

"I'm not going to argue this with you. Either you shrink this damn thing, or I'm going to shrink you, and then I'm going to have to fight through it. Seeing as how I had little trouble with the other ones, I doubt I'm going have any trouble with this one." He was bluffing, but Mekal seemed to believe him. His eyes grew wide.

Mekal flicked his gaze toward Gavin. Power surged along the blade. It glowed brightly, and then the massive creature shrank down to little more than the size of Gavin's foot.

"Grab it," he said to Gaspar.

"What?"

"Grab it."

"What about him?"

"We might need him."

Gavin reached for the rope in Gaspar's pouch, and he quickly bound Mekal. He tied up his hands but left his legs unbound, then forced Mekal to march in front of him. "I will know if you're drawing upon power," Gavin said.

As they reached the stairs in the main part of the hall, Gavin shoved him again. "Where is she?"

"You don't understand what we've gone through. All of this is finally an opportunity for us to get to safety."

Gavin shook his head. "Not like this."

"You don't understand."

"I understand well enough. I understand that if you go through with this, the city is going to be plunged back into a war. You're too young to know what a magical war can do to a city."

"You aren't from Yoran," Mekal said.

"I don't need to be from Yoran to know just what will happen if a magical war breaks out here. I've seen it often enough to know what happens in cities when magic fights magic."

They headed up the stairs, and Gavin held onto the sword, using it to guide him. He could feel the pressure and the power that was out there, though he couldn't see anything.

He glanced over at Gaspar. "Be ready."

"For what?"

"I don't know. For anything."

When they reached the top of the stairs, the landing was coated in strange swirling shadows. Gavin held the blade down and saw that the shadows were green lines that covered everything.

The Mistress of Vines was here.

Gavin hesitated a moment, looking along the length of the hallway.

Was the Captain down there as well?

"What are you waiting for?" Gaspar asked.

"Because the moment we do this, she's going to be aware we're here. I have to be ready to draw her attention."

"Do you really fear her?"

"Don't you?" Gavin asked.

"Yes."

"Good. Me too."

He took a deep breath, and then he carved into the vines.

CHAPTER TWENTY-FIVE

The thick vines withdrew as soon as he cut through them with the sword. Something changed around him, as if the air constricted and some energy within it started to shift and shimmer.

Gavin looked down the hall. "Where is she?"

"I don't know," Mekal said. "My job was to ensure nobody else got in. She was concerned you might come after her."

"She knew I might come?"

"Yes," Mekal said.

"Interesting," Gavin said and glanced over to Gaspar. "You might need to stay back here."

"I'm not staying behind."

"This is magic. You don't have any way of fighting magic."

"I can do well enough," Gaspar said.

"If you say so," Gavin said.

He started forward, pushing Mekal in front of him. The boy resisted a little, but he was forced to keep going as Gavin shoved him with the sword. He didn't want to stab Mekal, but he also didn't want Mekal to resist him as he headed along the hall. The sword continued to glow, the blade getting brighter and brighter as he made his way through here.

At the end of the hall was another staircase. It was wider than the other, a grand staircase that led to another level of the fortress. The glow—and the resistance—came from that direction.

"Please," Mekal said. "Don't make me go up there."

Gavin shoved him. "You don't get much of a choice in this. You've been complicit in all of this."

"You don't understand."

"I understand well enough."

They started up the stairs, and Gaspar stayed behind him. Gavin glanced over his shoulder, checking to see what Gaspar might be doing. Gaspar should have known more about what was happening now. Still, he had left the constables. There was some aspect of what Gaspar had done and his willingness to leave the constables that left Gavin troubled.

At the top of the stairs, Gavin hesitated. A deep green energy swirled around in front of him. He carved through it again and forced Mekal to take a step. The vines swirling along the ground withdrew, but not all the way like they had at the top of the previous landing.

"Let me see the figurine," he said to Gaspar.

"Why?"

"Just let me see it."

Gaspar handed it over, and Gavin set it down.

"Activate it, and send it that way," he said to Mekal, motioning into the darkness.

"What are you going to do with it?"

"Seeing as how I'm not the one who controlled it, I'm not going to do anything with it. I'm asking you to use it. Send the figurine that way," Gavin snapped.

There came another surge of energy along the sword. Gradually, the figurine began to grow until it filled the room. Gavin remained ready to jab Mekal with the sword if he tried to turn the humanoid figurine toward them, but he didn't. He did as he was instructed, and the figurine started to walk—lumber, really—into the room.

Gavin held the sword forward, using the light to guide him. The vines swirled around the figurine. The creature was massive and continued to grow, occupying almost all of the space. The vines wrapped around and slowed the statue, but not so much that it was effective.

"Why did you do that?" Gaspar whispered.

"She needs to use her power to slow it," Gavin said.

"You don't think she can?"

"This golem is incredibly potent," Gavin said. "It's going to take her time to slow it down, and I don't really know how much time she'll have to continue to work at this."

Gavin followed the sculpture. Mekal stayed with him as they moved forward, and the lumbering sound of the stone dragging across the ground echoed. The creature moved slower with each step. The Mistress of Vines used power on it, but even with everything she was doing, she couldn't stop it completely.

"What happens when she gets through with that?" Gaspar whispered.

"Then we have to be ready," he said with a smile. "Don't worry. This is what I'm trained for." Mekal tried to pull away as they continued into the room, but Gavin held onto him tightly. "I don't think so," Gavin said. "Not if you want to get out of here alive."

"If you drag me in there, there's no way I'm going to get out of here alive."

"Not with an attitude like that. You just have to trust I know what I'm doing."

"You're an assassin. People die because of you."

"That's right," Gavin said.

The figure slowed. Vines wrapped all around it, constricting from head to toe. Gavin waited to see if there was anything more he could learn from what the Mistress of Vines was doing, but he couldn't tell anything more about the nature of her magic. He could feel the energy she was using, but nothing more than that.

He stopped.

The vines continued to squeeze, and the light along the sword surged, growing brighter for a moment but then fading again.

Something clicked for him then.

The power play.

He'd seen a manipulation of power like this before.

And had barely survived it.

"Do you remember Kevlin?" he whispered to Wrenlow through the enchantment.

"I do. You removed the Tanran from power."

"I was hired to assassinate the Tanran, but I failed," Gavin said.

"Why is that related?"

"Because I think I'm facing the Tanran now." The type of magic fit. Both were powerful. Both used strange fingers of power. He'd only seen her once, but could imagine her changing her appearance through magic.

It fit with what was going on.

Another maneuver for power.

What better place than somewhere magic had been exiled?

She wouldn't have anyone to oppose her. His presence here must have been a surprise.

Unless she'd wanted him here.

"Now," Gavin said, looking over at Gaspar.

They darted forward, and he carved through the vines.

Beyond the massive statue stood the Mistress of Vines. She had her attention turned to the statue, power streaking away from her.

"Tanran," he said.

She sneered at him. "You were easy to draw into this, Gavin Lorren. When I learned you were here, then offered this opportunity…"

She *had* come because of him.

Which made all of this partly his fault.

She laughed at him, waving her vines. "And you would use an enchantment against me?"

"It's not so much that I used it as it was that I had one of your people use it." He flashed a smile. "The threat of death makes a powerful motivator."

"They will suffer."

"Will they? Because I've been trying to understand just what it was you wanted to do by getting in here. If you wanted to overthrow the Captain, it would've been a straightforward thing to do, but that wasn't what you wanted anyway." It had taken him a bit to find understanding, but the more he considered everything the Mistress of Vines had been after, the more it started to come together for him. "You wanted his place. You wanted his position. You didn't want to simply overthrow him. You wanted to *be* him. Like in Kevlin."

He looked over and found the Captain lying on the ground, wrapped in vines. His eyes bulged, and he didn't move. The last time Gavin had seen the Captain, the man had looked vibrant, powerful, fully enchanted. Now he was thin and weak, the enchantments having been destroyed, whatever power he possessed sapped from him. Now the Mistress of Vines practically taunted him, and soon she would destroy him completely.

Gavin darted over and carved through the vines that were swirling around the Captain. He coughed, sucking in a ragged breath, but he didn't get up.

Gavin turned back toward the Mistress of Vines.

"Now, your other helpers might not know what you do, but I've seen it."

"You've seen nothing."

Gavin flashed a dark smile. "The Mistress of Vines. An interesting title. At the time, I didn't know what it was, or whether or not there was any connection between you, but now I see it."

"What is this?" Gaspar asked.

Gavin looked over. "I've been trying to figure out why *I* was involved. We have a little bit of history, you see. I'm the reason she lost power in the last place she ruled. If she were to gain power, I know exactly the kinds of things she would do this time."

"What?"

"Destruction. Violence." He glanced over at Mekal. "And she would kill them."

"If they helped her take power, what reason would she have in killing them?" Gaspar asked.

"Because they have substandard magic. At least, according to her."

"They *do* have substandard magic!" she roared. She turned toward Gavin, and the vines began to swirl away from her again, twisting outward and racing toward him.

Gavin swept at the vines with the sword and sliced through them. "Really? I think that you should be thrilled with anybody having any sort of magic, not calling anything substandard."

"You don't understand. You are—"

Gavin darted forward, driving with the sword.

He met resistance. He swung the blade as quickly as he could and tried to carve through the vines. He still wasn't quick enough.

She was fast. It wasn't even so much that she was fast as it was that her *magic* was fast. The Mistress of Vines brought the power around and flung it at him.

Gavin reacted on instinct, using everything in his power to endure it. He could feel the resistance within him, and he could feel that there was something else going on. Even as he worked, he struggled. He had to embrace the enchantment.

Olivia had given him the enchantment to help with his speed, and as Gavin drew upon it, he could feel energy flowing within them. He held onto that and added to it by pulling upon the core reserves within him. He had used quite a bit of strength trying to get into the fortress in the first place, and already he didn't know if he had enough strength to withstand this attack.

Without it, he wouldn't have been quick enough.

Gavin swept the sword around. It slashed through the vines. He carved through one after another, and each snaking attempt of the vines to reach him missed. Gaspar stood to the side. One of the vines started to slink toward him, and Gavin rolled, sweeping through it.

He glanced over at Gaspar. "Be careful. She's incredibly dangerous."

Gavin ran forward, still holding onto his core reserves, but there was not nearly as much power left. He could feel that fading.

He thought about what he needed to do to weather this attack. If only there was some way of replenishing his stores of the core reserves. The El'aras had some way of doing so, but he didn't.

Something wrapped around his ankles, dragging his feet out from under him. Gavin swiped at it with the blade and missed.

He got to his feet, and he tried again. The energy within him continued to fade. He stumbled and rolled on the ground, then slashed at the bindings that she'd wrapped around his ankles. He managed to get up to his knees, and he swung the sword again, trying to sweep through the power she used on him. She lashed at him with another series of vines, which held him. Gavin couldn't move his arms. He tried to jerk them free, but he couldn't.

"Here you thought you would displace me again?" she asked, moving toward him. "I made sure you were involved. Let us call this your complete payment for services rendered."

She constricted the vines around him, and they held tightly. Gavin jerked, trying to free his arms, but he wasn't able to get his arms to move. She had too much power, and she was holding onto him too firmly.

"You made a mistake, Gavin Lorren," she said with a smile. "I heard the rumors about you. Of course, in a place like Yoran, rumors about Gavin Lorren would be unusual. Then I saw you."

"What do you mean you saw me?"

"You were there the day they claimed the egg. They were supposed to hand it over to me then, but the constables intervened. I decided to find a way to ensure your involvement and negotiated a trade. A child for the egg." She grinned. "It was easy to maneuver it after that."

"You were responsible for what happened to Alex for revenge?"

"Seeing as how you always have a soft spot for doing the right thing…" She grinned at Gavin and shook her head. "Such a foolish notion. I would've figured that with your training, you would've viewed the world in a different way. But since you're the reason I'm here…"

The vines continued to squeeze around him, and Gavin thrashed against them. Reaching for his core reserves, he still couldn't call upon the strength he needed to get free. There wasn't anything left within him.

The Mistress of Vines stalked toward him. A tendril of power streaked from her hand and started to wrap around his neck. "Once you are removed, then the rest of them will be too. I will solidify my power here. It won't take long for me to remove even the constables."

"No," Gavin said, glancing to his partner for a moment.

"Do you really think you can stop me?"

Gavin tried to tap into the core reserves. All he needed was a little. Just to touch that power. Nothing more.

There wasn't much strength left. Some bubbled deep within him though.

Could it be enough?

"No," he said again.

"If you can't hold me, then who can?"

"He can," Gavin said.

The figurine moved forward. It slammed into the Mistress of Vines. She cried out, and Gavin was released enough to wiggle the sword. He carved through the vines holding him, and he scrambled back.

"Where is the powder you found at Cyran's?" he asked Gaspar.

"Why do you want that now?" Gaspar asked.

"Because I think it may be the only way we're going to be able to defeat her."

She wrapped her vines around the golem and started to tighten them. Mekal cried out, as she crushed the power from the creature. With a surge of energy, it shattered.

Gaspar reached into his pocket and handed the pouch over to Gavin. He dug into the pouch and hurriedly began to shake its contents loose.

Hopefully this will work!

Gavin darted toward the Mistress of Vines. She spun to face him, and the vines twisted and stretched toward him. They reached for his arm that held onto the sword. He struggled with them, but with his other arm, he shook the powder at her.

It created a cloud.

She coughed and then took in a deep breath. "What was that? Do you think your distraction will hold me?"

Gavin jerked on the vine, trying to free his sword arm, but he couldn't.

The powder hadn't worked. Here he'd thought it might have been poison that would eliminate magic, but that hadn't been it at all.

What had Cyran used on me?

Maybe it wasn't even the same thing. She turned toward him, and the vines started to squeeze again. This time she used a much thicker vine around his throat. As it constricted around him, Gavin coughed, trying to hold his breath.

The vine was too powerful, and it crushed his throat. Gaspar rushed toward her, but she swept at him with a surge of vines, and he was thrown off to the side where he collapsed.

She turned to Gavin. "I should keep you alive long enough to watch what I do to those you care about. Because if there's anything that I know about Gavin Lorren, it's that you do care. You've made that clear time and again, not only here, but where you and I first met."

The vines started to squeeze even tighter.

"Only, that would take away my enjoyment of removing you. It would disappoint me, letting you live—at least letting you live that long. Perhaps killing you like this is only fitting."

As the vines constricted even more, Gavin couldn't move. He couldn't breathe. The sword glowed with the power she held. He stared at it, praying that the powder—the poison he believed it to be—would work.

Then the light within the blade began to flicker.

The vines holding him started to loosen.

"What is this?" she roared.

Her power started to fade even more. The vines collapsed. Gavin jerked on his arm, pulling it free, and he swung the sword around, driving it into her belly.

Her eyes widened, and he leaned close. "This is you losing."

She stared at him. Another pair of vines tried to streak toward him, but then they shifted course and darted toward her, wrapping around her.

She wasn't strong enough to heal herself this time. She had done so once before, and Gavin hadn't known how to prevent it from happening. This time, he left the sword in her belly. The combination of the sword and the poison was too much.

The Mistress of Vines held his gaze as she died. Finally, he withdrew the blade. She fell to the ground, blood pooling out from her. Gavin watched, waiting for her to wrap power around her, but she didn't.

"Gavin?" Wrenlow's voice sounded in his ears.

"I'm still here."

"What's going on?"

"She's gone. I finally finished the Kevlin job. The Tanran is dead."

Wrenlow breathed out slowly. "Do you think they'll still pay?"

CHAPTER TWENTY-SIX

Gavin slowly got up, and he looked around the Captain's home. Now that the Mistress of Vines was gone, he could see the inside of the room where he stood. It was enormous, and another staircase at one end opened toward the top of the fortress. No doubt a way for the Captain to look over the city.

Gavin knelt down next to the Mistress of Vines and quickly searched her. He found several enchantments that she wore. Two of them were bracelets, similar to the one Olivia had given him. She had a necklace that he suspected was an enchantment as well. He peeled all of them off. He removed the rings from her fingers and then began to search through her pockets.

He found the jade egg.

It was warm, glowing with a pale green light, and perfectly smooth. It was about the same size as what

Davel had described, not that Gavin was altogether surprised by that. He stuffed it into his pocket.

A cough from the side of the room caught his attention and he turned to see Alex sitting there, her eyes wide.

"I'll help her," Gaspar said to him. "You check on the Captain."

Gavin looked to Alex. She didn't seem injured, just shocked. Maybe she hadn't known what the Mistress of Vines intended from her. "We need to get her out of this place as quickly as we can," he said to Gaspar.

"That's my plan," he said.

The Captain lay motionless, though he was still breathing, each breath coming with a steady gasping sound. Gavin made his way over to him and crouched next to him.

"Thank you for saving me," the Captain said.

"Remember what I did," Gavin said. "If I find you've harmed any other enchanters, buying them into your form of slavery, I will return." He pulled out the El'aras dagger and held it up to the Captain's face. "You owe me, and do not think I will take any pity on you the next time."

The Captain held his gaze and nodded.

Gavin pulled the dagger away and glanced down at the body of the Mistress of Vines. The poison was eating away at her, and she was fading, with little remaining of her.

"Come on," he said to Gaspar.

He lifted Alex, carrying her. "You haven't finished your job," Gaspar said.

Gavin nodded. "No, but I think I know what I need to do now."

"What about him?" Gaspar stared at the Captain. There was a hint of darkness in his eyes, and Gavin watched him for a moment. "You'll just leave him?"

"There's nothing I need to do to him." Gavin said. "Killing him creates a power void within the city, and who knows who's going to get involved at that point?"

"Even with everything you know that he's been doing?"

"What has he been doing all that differently than what anyone else would do? Holding those who have the ability to place enchantments. That's about it. I think he's going to be less inclined to do that moving forward."

"And if he doesn't?" Gaspar asked.

"I've made it clear that I'll return."

Gavin headed down the stairs slowly, watching for any movement out of the shadows. He wasn't convinced that the Captain had decided to leave them alone. He worried that there would still be a time when he would try to come at them, which was reason enough for Gavin to keep his eyes open. Gaspar watched quietly as well.

They reached the main level of the fortress and headed out. Mekal followed them, his hands still bound, and Gavin no longer feared he might work magic against them. He didn't know what Mekal might try, but now that he had heard the truth about the Mistress of Vines, Gavin didn't think that Mekal would attempt anything. Mekal looked at Alex with a question in his eyes, but she hadn't spoken.

"What about them?" Gaspar asked.

"Why don't you let Olivia and Desarra deal with them. Or Zella when you bring her daughter back to her."

Gaspar stopped, and Mekal hurried over toward where Kegan lay.

"You don't know what you're talking about with Desarra," Gaspar said.

"Probably not, but I have a bit of an idea." Gavin glanced into the distance. He couldn't see Desarra's home from here, but he had a general sense of where she was. "You fell for her. You didn't realize that her sister was an enchanter. When you found out, it changed things for you."

"Careful, boy."

"I've been trying to figure you out, Gaspar. I might not have the whole of it, but I suspect it has something to do with Olivia and when she was taken by the Captain. You knew what she was." The timing was right for that, at least right enough that Gavin thought he understood. "When you realized what the constables would do to her, you left. You needed money. She needed money."

"No."

Gavin smiled. "So you turned to thieving. Once you paid for her rescue, you couldn't return to the constables. And I suspect you didn't want to. Maybe I'm right. Maybe I'm wrong. Either way, like I said, the timing fits."

He waited for Gaspar to argue with him, but he didn't.

That didn't explain what Gaspar had been doing in the time since he'd left the constables. Those would be questions for another time.

"What about you?" Gaspar asked.

"I have to finish my other job."

"You can't give it back to them," Gaspar said.

"I don't know what I can do. I'm not so sure the enchanters need to have it either. Not after what they were willing to do."

"Their families suffered for it."

"They did, but…"

Gavin didn't know what to do or say, only that he felt as if the jade egg was too powerful to leave to those within the city. They'd already proven they didn't have the right mindset to handle power like that.

"Just work with them," Gavin said.

"Will I see you back at the Dragon?"

Gavin glanced over, and he stared for a moment. "I don't know."

He walked away, and when he reached the wall, he quickly jumped to the top of it. Gaspar still looked back at him, and Gavin didn't have anything he could even say.

"What do you want me to do?" Wrenlow asked, creeping along the wall toward him.

Gavin crouched in place a moment. "I want you to do what you want."

"What's that supposed to mean?"

"You don't have to be a fighter," Gavin said. "I never asked that of you."

"I know—"

"And some of the things we've faced are beyond even my ability."

"That's why you need me." Wrenlow shrugged. "You might not always see my value—"

"I know your value," Gavin said softly.

"But you need me. Others. You can't do this alone. You don't have to *be* alone." He held Gavin's gaze without flinching.

Gavin smiled. "You're right."

"Am I?"

He nodded. "Now get away from here before the constables show up and decide they need to pull you in for questioning."

"What are you going to do?"

Gavin smiled. "Deal with the constables."

He scaled down the wall, and once he was in the street, he worked his way around until he found a pair of constables on patrol.

Gavin headed straight toward them. "Call Davel Chan."

The two constables turned and advanced on him. "What did you just say?" one of them said.

The fight was quick. Gavin darted toward the first of the constables and drove his fist into his midsection. The man bent over slightly, and Gavin jammed his open palm into his forehead, knocking him back. The second one darted toward him, and Gavin swept his knife hand around, catching him on the side of the neck. Neither would be seriously injured. He crouched over the first man he'd knocked down.

"Call Davel Chan."

He waited, but not for long.

There had to be a dozen constables coming toward him. Gavin remained near the edge of the street, watching the coming patrol. He remained hidden and ignored the rest of the constables. It wasn't until he caught sight of where their leader was hiding that he stepped forward.

Gavin crept up to him and nodded.

"You really prefer to take a dangerous approach," Davel Chan said.

"I figure it's the only way to get a hold of you."

"You could do so without calling attention to yourself."

Gavin shrugged. "I figure you'll take care of things for me."

"What do you need now?"

"I've completed the job."

"You have the egg?"

Gavin nodded. "I have it."

"Here," Chan said, grabbing a pouch and tossing it at Gavin's feet.

Gavin lifted it and glanced briefly inside to check to make sure the gold crowns were there.

"This is where you're supposed to give it to me."

"It was destroyed," Gavin said.

"What?"

"That was what the others wanted. They destroyed the egg." He flashed a sad smile. "Unfortunately. I know how much you wanted the egg, but I couldn't preserve it."

Chan narrowed his gaze. "That wasn't the agreement."

"The agreement was that I recover the egg. Which I did. Then it was destroyed."

"You don't want to make an enemy of me."

"And you don't want to make an enemy of me. You see, I've been trying to figure out just what's been going on. You're the one who's been selling enchanters to the Captain. It had to be somebody who had the position and authority to make a bargain. If others in the city were to learn that, I think there would be an uproar. The constables were allowing enchanters to stay here?"

Davel Chan glared at him. Gavin kept one hand on the sword, waiting to see if it might glow. It didn't. With the enchantments he now possessed, some of which were borrowed from the Mistress of Vines, he wasn't nearly as concerned about his own safety as he had been when he'd faced Davel Chan before.

"You don't need to keep going after them," Gavin said.

"That's our responsibility."

"Perhaps it once had been, but no longer."

"Why?" Chan asked.

"The enchanters were your allies. It's time for you to start treating them that way."

"And if we don't?"

"Then you'll make an enemy of me." Gavin turned a dark eye at him. "I'm quite certain you don't want that."

"I thought you wanted money so you could leave the city."

"Perhaps I did earlier. Now I don't."

"I'll consider your suggestion," Chan said.

"That's not good enough."

"What you're asking is impossible."

"About as impossible as enchanters being enslaved by the Captain?" Gavin shook his head. "I think there are many things that are possible. You just have to have the right attitude about them."

Chan glowered at him. "It might be best if you leave the city."

"I'll consider it," Gavin said. "When all of this is stable." He had no idea how long that would take, but he felt as if he had to stay now. The enchanters needed his protection. For now. They didn't need an assassin, but there were other ways to use his skills. He had friends here now.

Wasn't that enough?

"Just consider?"

"I need to ensure you aren't going to continue what you've been doing. Once I'm satisfied with that, then you might find that I leave the city."

"I might find that."

"You might," Gavin said, shrugging. "Or you might find that I continue to eliminate your constables. I think we both know how that will go." He glanced back at the dozen or so constables behind him. "I could start now, if you would like."

"I don't think you'd find it as easy as you believe."

"Are you sure? I'm certain I could change the dynamics in the city in a much different way. It wouldn't be the first time I've done something like that."

"No," Chan said.

"Then you leave the enchanters alone."

A hint of tension in his arms left Gavin thinking he might attack, but then he relaxed. "Fine. They are not to practice openly."

"Have they been?"

Chan stared at him, and the blank expression gave Gavin the answer that he needed.

"Now I'm going to go, and I don't expect to be followed. If I am, you'll find yourself down several constables. Oh," Gavin said, pausing as he backed down the street, "you will leave the Roasted Dragon alone."

"And if I don't?"

"The consequences will be the same."

Chan continued to glare at him, and Gavin only shrugged, heading away.

Gavin was tired and needed to sleep, and he had to find a place where he could do so safely. Until he knew what Chan might do, the Dragon wasn't going to be safe for him. Given what he'd done to the other enchanters and what he'd done with Gaspar, Desarra's home wouldn't be safe for him either.

His feet guided him to Cyran's home. By the time he

snuck inside and went down the trapdoor to the lair, he was exhausted. He used a hint of the core energy to pull the door open, and then he sealed it closed behind him. Once inside, he sank to the ground, resting just inside of the door and pulled out the egg to look at it.

All of this for the egg.

He'd been in the city too long. Longer than he had intended. Longer than he'd ever been in one place since leaving Tristan's training. Now he didn't know if he could leave yet. The enchanters needed him.

Here he had come to the city for work, looking for jobs that might have a level of danger but that would permit him a level of freedom. Instead, he found himself caught up in something different. Worse.

I might be the breaker of chains, but what chains are they?

Gavin couldn't help but feel that the chains he'd broken inside of Yoran were around the entirety of the city. He had no idea if he had freed the people, or if he had unleashed something worse.

The next book in The Chain Breaker series: The Fates of Yoran.

When the Fates attack Yoran, the Chain Breaker must fight back.

After establishing an uneasy truce with the constables, Gavin has settled in Yoran to offer protection to his friends and the remaining magical element in the city.

When a job reveals a dangerous new threat in the city, Gavin must take action. This time the target isn't Gavin, but the city itself. Magic was banished a generation ago, but the Fates have returned. They bring a dark magic Gavin has never seen before—and might be helpless to control.

It will take more than an assassin to stop the Fates.

It will take magic the Chain Breaker barely understands and can't control.

SERIES BY D.K. HOLMBERG

The Dragonwalkers Series

The Dragonwalker

The Dragon Misfits

Elemental Warrior Series:

Elemental Academy

The Elemental Warrior

The Cloud Warrior Saga

The Endless War

The Dark Ability Series

The Shadow Accords

The Collector Chronicles

The Dark Ability

The Sighted Assassin

The Elder Stones Saga

The Lost Prophecy Series

The Teralin Sword

The Lost Prophecy

The Volatar Saga Series

The Volatar Saga

The Book of Maladies Series

The Book of Maladies

The Lost Garden Series

The Lost Garden

Printed in Great Britain
by Amazon